LAUNCH

LAUNCH

Neal Davis Anderson

EDITIONS

Cover design by Doowah Design.
Photo of Neal Davis Anderson by Jennifer Macbeth.

This book was printed on Ancient Forest Friendly paper.
Printed and bound in Canada by Hignell Book Printing Inc.

We acknowledge the support of the Canada Council for the Arts and the Manitoba Arts Council for our publishing program.

Library and Archives Canada Cataloguing in Publication

Title: Launch / Neal Davis Anderson.
Names: Anderson, Neal Davis, 1964- author.
Identifiers: Canadiana (print) 20240461169
| Canadiana (ebook) 20240461177
| ISBN 9781773241517 (softcover)
| ISBN 9781773241524 (EPUB)
Subjects: LCGFT: Novels.
Classification: LCC PS8555.H525 L38 2024 | DDC C813/.54—dc23

Signature Editions
P.O. Box 206, RPO Corydon, Winnipeg, Manitoba, R3M 3S7
www.signature-editions.com

for JMA

1

He could make a complex thing simple, so he'd have made a fine teacher, they said, though he'd as soon turn a plain thing bewildering from overwork, so they banged on about rabbit holes and Rube Goldberg. He'd make a face that claimed he saw the fun in it and that night he made the face because they had him dead to rights and nothing was simpler than your birthday. Still, who really knew sometimes whether he was perceiving a thing or event or interaction in its essence or doing the other thing when a thousand ideas and sensations blew up and whipped him around like a kite in a squall, and telling sturdy discernment from nonsense was beyond him, given the general hallucinant vividness. It would scare him stiff when an alarm felt old, like an echo but sharper, so he blamed it on the Judge and that whole Armageddon-greedy generation and supposed he'd come to this mental convoluting honestly back then as the best means available to a peculiar thirteen-year-old. It was his row to hoe now, sure as the sky.

It was his birthday, just before cake, and it ought to have been fine—just the four of them, devoted wife, Alice, son Addy, and Addy's girlfriend, Rosemary, and what could be better?—and he'd managed well enough until Rosemary said a thing that should have been lovely but landed like news the world was finally ending and stole his breath, much as Kennedy's had when he announced the missiles in Cuba the night of his thirteenth birthday. That pretty boy's address to the nation had laid full waste to Theo's 1962 birthday dinner, but Rosemary's words landed harsher because her soul was good and, unlike Kennedy, she was no sabre-rattler and hadn't been provoking the other side for years, but mostly because of their inevitability.

"You have perfect lives," was all she said, but they fell inescapably and horribly, the second shoe he at once understood he'd been expecting all these years. It was too much for the evening, after such a day. He tried to get a breath, subtly, not to make a scene, told himself things were different with Kennedy gone and Khrushchev and other cold warriors dead or on their way, and the Earth was still hanging on and Rosemary had meant nothing bad and there was no such thing as accidental invocation.

"What do you want to hear?" Addy was saying on his way to the stereo, so evidently the last record had finished. There was only the clatter of the windows from the wind. The rattling was another intrusion, the wind blowing for three days, bringing more dead leaves into the garden, and Hubba-Bubba wrappers and Old Dutch bags, though Moose hadn't stirred on his sill and that was a consolation.

"Earth to Theo," Addy said.

So first to mind was *Space Oddity*, though it amplified the alarm somehow. Second was Berlioz's *Great Mass for the Dead*, but you don't play a requiem on a birthday. Britten's *War Requiem. Requiem æternam dona ei, Domine.*

"Crosby, Stills," he said. It seemed safe.

He needed to take charge, so he stood, though too quickly, given the dizziness, and it was as though an echo of Rosemary's words grew fingers and yanked a strand of yarn at the waist of his sweater hard enough to unravel the bottom row and spin him around to unbind the second and the third, accelerate up through the belly and chest, the centrifugal force throwing his hair out wide.

"Jesus!" he said and braced against the table. He was suddenly as chilly as if there was nothing left of his old sweater but its silver-grey crew collar around his neck like a saggy woggle, the rest a mess of yarn on the hardwood.

"Okay there, old fella?" Addy said.

Theo tried to orient to the sound of his boy's voice, the sense of his palms laid flat, Moose asleep on the sill, Graham Nash, singing about the cozy room and evening sunshine. But also the wind buffeting the dining room windows. He guessed he'd best sit.

"Birthdays, huh?" Addy said. Smart-ass. Then Alice called and he turned the music down. Rosemary pushed her glasses up and hit the dining room lights. Theo saw the candlelight before Alice rounded the corner with the cake.

Alice started singing because she insisted every year. The others joined in. He reckoned, given Addy's expression, that his attempt at smiling had come off crooked or creepy. Rosemary had the voice of an angel.

Alice set the thing down before him, and hadn't she gone with the full forty in red, and a blue one in the middle for luck? They held the last note. He envied Moose, sleeping through it on his sill, oblivious to birthdays and time.

"Well now," he said and sucked what spit there was in his mouth. He began to draw a breath.

Something happened then, or, rather, penetrated the room: a great danger, the leading edge of an emergency. He straightened and looked, but there was only Alice, Addy, and Rosemary, Moose by his window, a chocolate zucchini cake with candles.

Part of him had uncoupled, seemed to be floating over the kitchen doorway, so he watched them set the plate down, saw how his face reflected the dreadful light. His lungs were full but only hovered, and he heard the window rattle but knew the peril was more than a south wind. The pitch of the room had dropped lower, sounds had slowed and retreated, except his heart, which had the roll of a kettledrum, and some little gasps as he drew in more air. From above, he made out a twitch or tremor at the junction of his shoulders and neck, and the vibration of fingers, as though readying themselves.

Whatever it was had an awful familiarity: it was fixed and brittle, as old and awful as the Judge in suit pants and undershirt, shaving at his mirror, while Verna fried eggs down the way, the old man rubbing Royal Crown into his black hair, reaching for his comb like a gun, and the scrape scrape as she buttered toast. He caught the heavy mix of pomade and butter.

Which is when he wondered if it was a heart attack, and found relief in that because it accounted more reasonably for the bashing in his ribcage than whatever Cold War scars he might be carrying, and this being a cardiac event would mean Rosemary's words weren't the nausea's proximate cause, and would remake the pomade and butter as his life flashing through him.

"Theo?" he heard from his place by the ceiling near the kitchen wall. It was Alice saying his name, her hand on his shoulder.

"Blow out the air, Theo," Addy said and demonstrated blowing.

Which also made sense—that breath holding would speed the heart—and, for Christ's sake, who died blowing out birthday candles?

Moose was on his feet, back arched. Glaring at the cake, hissing.

Moose made the threat unmistakable. It sent all of Theo's focus to the blue candle in the middle, the one for good luck, and its flame moving so easily, cooly on its wick, while the forty others stood as straight as forty pieces of blown glass. The blue candle's flame stretched and forked its tip like a snake's tongue, reached forward with its top half like it was bowing, then stood straight again, sides moving in and out, while the smoke stream ran upward smoothly and confidently, the slimmest jet stream, then broke apart like Challenger after it exploded.

The explosion made Theo spring up and back, considered warning the others but recognized the best option was attack. So he dropped his palms down firmly, leaned in, blew powerfully, downing flames by the dozen, though the one on the blue candle pushed back before it yielded, leaving only the red at the tip of its wick, which did go dark like the others, but disturbingly, like a slow, lacertilian wink that promised there was more to come.

He was reaching out to snuff it when he glimpsed, at the far edge of his vision, something scurry from the dining room to the kitchen, so he spun but saw nothing because of the flash blindness, and he heard Alice call him again and Rosemary tell Addy to leave Moose because he was going to scratch, and Moose dropping down and bugging out.

Alice was asking what was wrong. She sounded alarmed. Her hand on his wrist.

He wanted to ask whether they'd seen it but the words wouldn't come. His lungs were empty. Alice seemed to be taking his pulse. Her fingertips were stained from peeling beets, which meant his vision was reassembling.

"My god," she said. "That's, what, 204 beats! Theo, sit down. Addy, get some aspirin!"

"I'm fine," Theo managed to say, though his legs were sandbags and sitting was a relief. Rosemary said he ought to lie down. He heard Addy say *ambulance*, which meant he was back with the aspirin. His chest felt crushed. Something had pierced the socket behind his right eye. He chewed aspirin.

He wanted to say everything was fine, that it had been like the instant before the car crash when you see the impact coming, except that things had turned out fine, but he doubted he'd get it out, so he tasted the aspirin and marvelled at the immensity of the dislocation, how it tore you out of your warm, familiar ground and threw you up into the sky, the soil coming away from your roots as you ascend, and at how you could not predict which scraps of your life would flash through your mind. Then, as he sipped water, Addy told Rosemary this was the look of age angst and that was a comfort.

2

Alice told him Addy and Rosemary had gone to their party. "I already told you that," she called as she drew his bath, and no doubt she had, but he'd been orbiting since cake and contact with ground control had been patchy. He lay on the bed naming things. Crown, window stile, muntin. Curtain and bracket. Water running into tub.

This part of a birthday could be manageable. He'd soak a while and then she'd massage him back and front, crown to feet—align his soul, she'd say, free the stagnant energy, words that would be Addy's cue to say, *Too woo-woo by two*, if he was within earshot, which he evidently wasn't. Alice's terminology hung onto its slippery slope but, just then, her pseudoscience endeared her, like the way she gave *athlete* three syllables and made a knife of her hand to slice the tension right off of him, and bury a fist under his ribs. The evening of his birthday was a single event—bathe, align the stagnant opposites, do the wild thing for a while, and rest in the arms of Morpheus until morning. It always worked and it would work this year and screw the blue candle and sense of someone watching.

He'd fix the window tomorrow, and the plaster where he'd sent the chair flying backwards. He hoped he hadn't upset Rosemary when he lost his shit. Alice and Addy had taken it in stride and steered him to the living room like a grandfather, propped him up with cake. He'd tasted it and said, "Delicious," though the sweetness turned his stomach. Alice had started back up about counselling, which she believed was always good, like Vitamin C; he shut up, partly because he didn't need one of her looks but mostly because time was playing tricks again, so it felt for all the world like it was simultaneously 1989 and 1962, and he was at once next to Alice on the sofa and standing in the men's lounge at Busch's Garden the night of his thirteenth birthday, the Judge declared him ready to stand among the men and their whiskies and cigarettes and cigars, and Omar was about to reach up to switch on the little TV so Kennedy could announce the end of the world.

His heart was going hell for leather when another gust of wind shook the windows and he'd had enough of the rattling. He'd stood a bit spasmodically, like a tin man who needed oil, didn't care their eyes would follow, because he'd had enough of the wind and because moving was better than sitting. Then he was at the window, pushing upward on the slider frame. When it didn't budge, he got down lower and drove upward hard.

"The latch," Alice called, but too late.

Addy was on his way over, saying, "Whoa, big fella."

He'd bent the latch and pulled the screws halfway out of the wood. He made a show of assessing the damage, though he was as much assessing his foolishness, which was as deep as the ugliest sea, so he turned and thanked them for everything, said he was calling it a night. At the periphery, he saw the corner of a napkin wave like a little white flag and thought he heard a chuckle, hoped it was someone passing by out front, though it sounded closer.

Ever since, he'd been everywhere at once. He'd been forty and then a kid, a father at his dining room table, then, as vividly, a boy with his parents, and everywhere a different regret or dread.

There was Addy and his Professor Dillard—All hail Dillard—this time her obscene claim that the slimmest government intervention in the economy was a one-way road to authoritarianism. The boy's description of Dillard's shiny glasses and big hair always brought Dame Edna to mind. For the little it was worth, he'd mentioned that neoliberalism made society into a sack of individuals, ignored solidarity and guaranteed ecological disaster, but these days Addy was all privatization, deregulation and Dame Edna Dillard. If there was a God, this would all turn out to be an awkward phase.

Then he was back to his thirteenth birthday, fighting with the Judge the whole way home and upsetting his mother. It started reasonably enough, Theo asking what did you expect when we had missiles in Turkey aimed at the Soviets and, when the Judge called the Reds deceitful, asking, What about the Bay of Pigs, right after Kennedy promised to lay off Cuba, and how honest was that, or the lies about civil defence and there being the slightest chance of surviving the next war, and why would the Cubans believe the President when so many Americans didn't? So far, the Judge had been talking through Verna, as though his wish had come true and Theo wasn't there, saying *impudent* and *know-it-all* in his disgusted way and wondering who ever talked to their father like that, until Theo called Kennedy *your guy* and the Judge turned his head and raged, even spat as he said in times like these John Kennedy had damned well better be *everyone's* president, young man. Verna did her best, said, "Now both of you." Theo had said Kennedy might be the last president, and the Judge asked whether he had that idiot Sid Nolan to thank for this nonsense. Theo had said, more or less, that the Judge was the real idiot, mainly because silence would have been worse with the Judge's lip curled like that, and the Judge raised a fist and shifted right to strike backward. Verna's face stopped him and he forced the hand back to the wheel, but Theo half-wished he'd followed through because it would have ratified things, made explicit what had been tacit for so long, that the enmity was mutual and the Judge would have traded him for most any other kid.

He'd felt outside of himself the night of his thirteenth birthday too, as though he was hovering up by the roof liner of the Judge's hideous Continental. Then, when they pulled into the driveway and it was time for him to get out of the vast, ugly car to open the garage door, he had an overwhelming sense that the Judge was going to hit the gas and run him down.

Alice turned off the tap and called him, thank God, because he was stuck on his thirteenth birthday and how he'd gone inside before his parents and pulled the candles out of his cake—all fourteen, with the one for the year to come, which was a laugh when the missiles had pushed the odds of there being another year so long.

He lowered himself into the water and told her it was fine because it would be when it cooled a few degrees. Alice bid him breathe the steam, to let the heat enter his spirit and give him joy and, who knew, he might end up singing. It was a lot. She kissed his head, went out and back downstairs to her Cyndi Lauper.

Now the only light was the candle at the corner of the tub. She'd added a cup of fine French clay and a handful of dried chamomile. He breathed the sweet scent, lay back until his ears were below the surface, followed the incense stream upward until it forked.

Which brought back the blue candle and the Challenger explosion and sat him up straight. He snuffed the incense and dried his hands to roll a smoke.

"Girls Just Want to Have Fun" was finishing, which left two more tracks and then, odds on, she'd play Ferron, though tonight, that seemed like a small thing, and he told himself that, objectively speaking, it had been a terrific autumn day. He'd spent it with his three favourite people: Alice, who was far too good for him, Addy, who was bright and curious and had a good heart, and Rosemary, and the Indiana Jones movie might have been fun if he hadn't driven himself around the bend before they got there. He was the luckiest man in the world but for this dislocation: his distress through the matinée was symptom and not cause, and the interminable southeast wind and Rosemary saying their life was perfect, which she intended as another gift, for Christ's sake. The cigarette was helping. Alice's candle was nearly manageable. He butted the smoke and lay back. He opened the hot tap with his foot. With any luck, some heat would let him stay forty and in 1989. Let it scald.

But no, his thoughts spun back around, returned him to the start of everything, which seemed uncalled for on the day he turned forty when the last thing he needed was another reminder of eternality, or another exclamation point, which he noted is an upside-down birthday candle. The fact a stick of wax with a wick shot through and an unlikeable little flame could reel him back to an inner ring St. Louis suburb and that lane and that bungalow the Judge always called *his*, like it wasn't Verna's too, proved all over that time was a circle as dizzy as a Tilt-A-Whirl and all of the wishing in the world wouldn't make it a river running one way.

It was both shocking and monotonous to be so unstuck: one moment forty, six feet tall, bearded, twenty-three months from mortgage freedom and the next a slip of a thing in grade school among Nephilim because the best his parents and principal could think of was skip him like a stone in the direction of some academic peers, even though they'd be peers in no other dimension. His brain was inconvenient that way, not to mention toe-curling in Ike's spaniel America, where no one liked an outlier, and what did they expect a kid like him to do but manage his daily dread by pointing out the gravest of Mr. Arbore's blunders at the board, because it tidied the chaos, though, much as the giants despised their teacher, they loathed a pipsqueak know-it-all more and Mr. Arbore took correction like paper cuts, so speaking up exacerbated the stunting and the loneliness. How could they have been surprised when he leaned harder into solitary pursuits for safety's sake or that he'd try to tame his daily dread by reading everything and puzzling things out or that the more he read, the more he twigged the perils of the late fifties and World War III and Armageddon?

Was it his fault he saw through their fibs about civil defence and recognized the fraud in their drills, which amounted to kid-sized barbiturate hits to dull fears that should have been abject, though, here too, saying so in his fun-sized voice nudged him still farther from the others, not to mention gave Mr. Arbore a fresh glimpse of his ineptitude? Of course, Mr. Arbore retaliated and told his parents, so he got to relive things at supper but with the Judge interrogating instead and Verna witnessing in place of the Halberstadt twins. The Judge's glare was harrowing as he demanded the insolence at school cease. Verna, well-meaning but conflict-averse and button-lipped, tilted her head as though it was perplexing.

Nine out of ten days he'd have switched places with any of those sweet, docile normals, traded his curiosity for their lamb-like unconcern about the dangers. What good was there in knowing when he and they were heading for the same incineration or radiation sickness? How much better to play ball at recess than to watch from the first-base line and know how swiftly the smallest difference could turn deadly and how willing those warlike old men were to kill their young?

Ahh, there they were: the opening bars of "Almost Kissed." If Addy were home, he'd remind Alice that there was more music in the world than Ferron and Cyndi Lauper and *Graceland* and Leonard Cohen. He'd say it like he was telling her a secret.

He sat up and the air felt good on his shoulders. He dried his hands to roll another smoke, told himself things would be better next year, that he'd get some Valium or some such, blow out the damned candles like a normal person, make a wish or not, not wreck the plaster or window hardware. He simply would not worry because maybe worrying was the whole problem. He'd see past the catastrophe in things and agree when Alice called the toughest times with Addy the unfurling of his personality. She hadn't liked the piercings or stick-and-poke tattoos, or his look when he shaved his head, but hadn't made a fuss. Those things hadn't bothered Theo, or the boy playing The Viletones *Screaming Fist* before school or forgetting how to close a door without slamming it; what bothered him was the sullenness and the slow drift from embarrassment about all they stood for toward contempt. In twelfth grade, he took to looking at university business programs, began talking about progress through purchase and claiming nothing happened until someone sold something, and said *taxpayers* instead of *people*, as though living had an admission fee, and all the while denied it was hostility. He still went to punk shows, smoked the odd joint and didn't eat much meat, but now he was buying shares in mutual funds invested in gold mines and tobacco and McDonnell Douglas and General Electric because apparently, nothing happened until someone sold a deck of Du Mauriers or a rocket launcher or a nuclear trigger.

Alice would focus on the positives—he was doing well in school, he'd never been suspended, much less arrested and, if his foot could ride heavy on the gas, he'd never had an accident. She said other parents liked him at least as much as their own kids.

Still, the tension was a mystery and sometimes seemed to come less from either of them than from some vandal just out of view. He could knock on the kid's door with an innocuous agenda, determined to keep it light, and things would still go to shit. He'd get hung up on tone and Addy would ask what was so bad about the grid anyway.

Alice told him not to take it personally, but then Addy never aimed his indignation squarely at her. She claimed he was *finding his way*, like she knew the first thing about being lost. He rolled his eyes when she claimed they were too much alike or said the rancour was so much sand in an oyster and it would be beautiful in the fullness of time, but the times she referred to them as *Strahl Men*, he'd had to leave the room because that invoked the Judge and the way that particular generational interplay had come to a head twenty years ago, ten days before his final university exams, in a second-degree assault with one of the good steak knives, which was a Class C felony, so forced his quick departure, and permanently, because his years of absence from the state apparently lengthened the statute of limitations. The *Strahl Men* turned his and Addy's ingrained antagonism into a knock-on effect of his own lousy upbringing.

Theo might say he didn't recognize the kid anymore, wonder whether he had a single hero or knew what made a soul good but if he should vent to her a little, as though she was his spouse or something, likely as not she'd say in one of the four of five ways she had that he needed to be extra careful given what he'd been through and the trick was not to pass on the ugliness, and that would be the worst of all because it meant that, after twenty years, she didn't know the first thing about him.

Things had been better since Rosemary came along. These days, if Addy wanted to see his girlfriend, he might have to roll up his starched sleeves and churn the compost or pick some summer squash, not that it stopped him from calling the triple lot Funny Farms™ or claiming he somehow knew better than Theo how to space bean seeds in a trench. The gods of Olympus could not have dreamed up a more sparkling reward for a kid who'd sneered for years at his parents than turning his eye toward Rosemary.

At dinner, when talk turned to Saturna, she could not have been more fascinated, and she'd wanted to hear the whole five-year plan. Alice had obliged, covered rehabilitating the old cabin that looked out over the water to Boundary Pass and the San Juan Islands, putting up a shack to make cheese and digging a cave into the hillside to age it, fencing the pasture for the sheep.

Addy said there was nothing better than being out on the channel and spotting an orca pod. He promised Rosemary they'd go next summer no matter what.

Of course, they'd build a sauna, Alice said, and grow a holly hedge maze for the grandchildren. "No pressure," she'd said, and Rosemary laughed.

Their Saturna plans were undoubtedly fine and, any other day, he'd have contributed, maybe mentioned the butterflies and how he'd spotted a pair of red-and-black Edith's Checkerspots (*Euphydryas editha taylori Edwards*) two summers ago, say the gnarly cedars on Saturna were like no other, and the stands of fir and salt air, whir and zip of hummingbirds, glimpsing kingfishers and oystercatchers, terns, guillemots. An eagle wheeling high over Mount Warburton Pike. Cheese-making had been Alice's idea and he'd thought of the cave and now, years on, it was as clear as eyes: their little flock of Polled Dorsets in the hollow, grazing on tender grasses and flowers and herbs, their milk the colour of ivory, and they'd set the curd in the cave with two thousand species of mould to build flavours of mushroom, mint, smoked paprika. Any other day, talking about Saturna would have made a bent day straight, been a balm, so what on earth had possessed him to say that the sheep would eat the violets, which would be a bummer for butterflies like *Zerene Fritillary*?

His pessimism didn't bother Addy, who said the blackberries were as big as your thumb and the vines sagged under the weight of them all.

Which took Theo back too suddenly, far too vividly, to Addy at seven or eight, picking blackberries between the cabin and woodshed, examining each one and eating it with the most profound focus and, when he'd had enough, squashing some in his bowl and drawing blue-red warrior lines onto his face and small chest and belly, then dropped screaming from a tree in front of Alice. The memory hit hard and sat there like the saddest thing in the world. It was stupid.

Addy said the only hitch in their whole plan was Theo's irrational fear of the world underwater.

"You're really doing this?" Theo said, though he didn't mind the distraction. He tried to be a sport, addressed Rosemary. "It's called thalassophobia," he said, "and it's a real thing, and the ferries are a nightmare. Though it's not so irrational when you think about what lives down there. You take your Zombie Worms and Giant Isopods, and the goddamned Stonefish, which kill you just like that. There are monsters that pluck ships right off the surface."

"You know he swam competitively in school, right?" Alice said,

"In pools," he said. "With lines on the bottom, and in Missouri, which is as far from the ocean as Winnipeg."

"Plus he's an aviophobe," Addy said.

"Aren't you supposed to be nice to me on my special day?"

"You'd never get the guy on a plane."

The bath and nicotine were helping. Theo took one last drag of the cigarette and his head swam. Maybe Alice was right and things would turn out with Addy and him. The Judge had been shit as a father but he'd been better. It wasn't magic. You didn't take anything for granted but things were starting to look up.

"Oh?" a voice said with full, rich bathroom reverb and persistence.

Theo bolted upright, eyes scrambling. The water splashed out the back of the tub, then rushed back, wave cresting in front halfway up the candle, nearly dousing the flame. The adrenalin was a deluge, pressed through him. His fingertips throbbed. There'd be water all over the bathroom floor.

The room was quiet now but for the rushing in his ears and pounding heart. Had he dozed off and dreamed it? He searched the possibilities, but there was only the same overpowering, unholy inevitability he'd felt in the birthday candle. The dread surrounded him and forced his breath higher, wanted to close his throat.

The flame brightened, as though taking a breath, and Theo's fear dropped low and made him want the toilet. He knew he'd never make it, so he clenched himself tightly.

"You know it's not sustainable, don't you?" the voice said from the candle flame. Low, self-satisfied, the faintest drawl, melting pot Missouri vowels, nothing longer than John Wayne's. It reflected and enriched itself over the tiles, mirror, and porcelain of the little room.

"Don't think what's sustainable?" he said, to say something, but it came out thin.

"Now don't do *that*," it said and set a terrible, familiar weight below his diaphragm. It was at once impersonal and intimate—*déjà vecu, déjà senti*—and he recalled the blue *luck* candle bending 90° toward him.

The flame expanded again and said, "Theodore, we'd best talk," with a familiarity that penetrated and doubled the pressure at the bottom of his gut. He wanted to cover himself but there was only the washcloth, and he thought his sphincter could give way if he moved.

"How about take a breath."

"Who are you?" Theo said.

"Don't do that either."

"Do what? he said. Pushing back lessened the abdominal pressure.

"Play dumb."

"Who are you?"

"Well, obviously I've got a message."

"*What* message?"

"What do you think?"

"What, that it's nearly over? Is that it? Because it's not. There's still time… Take David Suzuki…"

"Oh my."

He'd committed, had to keep going. "He says we've got ten years to turn things around," he said but he'd uncoupled again and was hovering at the ceiling. He watched the flame take its breaths, heard the voice claim things had already tipped, and mention the vast microplastic ocean gyres, ruptured plaques and clotted flow, and inevitable infarctions, a billion cows grazing where the rainforest used to be, farting like Trojans, and on and on, claiming Theo knew better than anyone that things were only palliative now, and the mightiest efforts of politicians or protesters amounted to denial and bargaining. The busyness was so much terminal confusion and restlessness because systems really were shutting down, and those in the know had an ear out for the final moan and rattle.

From his place near the ceiling, he looked down at his long body rucked into its tub but heard a preadolescent voice deny a truth he'd known his whole life. He said things weren't that bad, though he'd been sounding alarms and watching the Doomsday Clock since he was a kid in Ladue. He asserted what scraps of optimism came to mind, because he'd done his share of protesting and he'd spread the good word, practised what he preached. He'd found meaning and beauty in things other people threw away, re-envisioned and re-invented their cast-offs and, on his best days, almost felt he was closing in on the heart of things, verging on some small rapprochement with creation. His friend Gracie said he was *shifting the paradigm*, though you just knew all it took was some asshole getting excited and punching the codes.

It must have gone like that for a while, back and forth, the candle telling him to fuck the paradigm shift and get serious, pronouncing in a chain-smoker huskiness, and Theo exposed there, too naked, chasing his breath, wondering where the strength of his voice had gone, needing to evacuate his lower parts.

He could feel the bathwater again, so guessed he'd recoupled. The water had cooled and it occurred to him this other had only the unreliable sway of a bully, an authority less earned than declared, and he recalled the ridiculousness. He whispered, "Fuck it," leaned forward, blew out the candle. For a moment, he felt something approaching confidence.

The darkness was a relief. He felt settled for the first time since morning, he put his hands on the sides of the tub and the metal chill on his palms felt fine.

He was hoisting himself up when the flame hissed and relit, like a joke candle made with magnesium. The thing took one of its breaths and said, "Obviously there's work to do."

Theo hovered in that disappointment, half in the water and half out.

"I work," he said.

"You know what I mean."

"What do I know?"

"Theodore."

"What?"

"Well, you're gonna build a fucking ark."

It came as a relief because it was stupid and he should have seen it a mile away. He saw pairs of zebras, pigeons, and tigers waiting to board the *Alice Edith*, all thirty-one dry-docked feet of her, each pair unaware of how cramped they'd be below decks with Alice and him, and Addy and Rosemary, Moose and some comely stray, and the Rubbermaid bins full of spare parts on the teak floor. The 1963 Bertram needed engine beds and bilge pumps, wiring bow to stern.

"Not a boat. Obviously. The water's so nasty the fish don't want to piss in it."

"So what, some sort of spacecraft?"

"Hallelujah."

"Like *Salvage 1*?" He'd watched that short-lived show with Addy: a junkyard man played by Andy Griffith determined to go to the moon to salvage the remains of Apollo missions. He built the ship from a Texaco tanker and cement mixer. Addy was nine or ten, and still believed people could do anything.

"You're not taking this seriously."

"I'm talking to a candle." He blew out the flame again.

It relit. It said, "I hope we're not going to have a problem," and the familiarity was alarming again.

"Who am I to build a spaceship?"

"You're all there is, for one thing." The voice paused, then said, "Don't tell Alice."

"I'll do what I want."

"Just not yet."

"Who are you?"

"You know."

"Stop saying I know things when I don't." His eyes ached from staring; now they stung as some tears pushed forward.

"Name's Ford," it said, almost as a sigh, and at last the flame went out. The wick tip glowed orange a few moments and went dark too.

He'd heard Alice padding up the stairs, singing Heather Bishop's "Waltz Me Around," but it still startled him when she knocked.

3

The bathroom was dark as Stygian blue-black, the impossible colour that leaves you blind, and the bathwater was cold so his butt sat in the fine French clay like a rock in the mud of an awful, monster-stocked salt channel. Alice was saying something about prunes, and he turned toward her voice it, wanted to call back, Here I am, or, even just, Prunes, but the chill was calamitous and speech was beyond him. He blinked and the movement of his eyelids was a ripping. He reckoned, Dry eyes, listened for Alice but only heard his heart. The sudden draw toward the strip of light at the bottom of the door was desperate.

His muscles engaged in their hundreds simultaneously but inelegantly and without leadership, boosted him mostly upward from the water, though his right hand slipped and the force of the uncompensated left side resembled violence, pitched him up and right with a measure of bathwater and as he passed the vertex, there was a whoosh of light as Alice opened the door at long last. His cheek reached the toilet seat as his right palm crash-landed on the tile; the deceleration shot through the straight arm, reduced the facial impact but aggrieved the shoulder. He recognized the mixed blessing.

"Oh my God!" Alice said. "Are you all right?"

Her nearness was a solace, even seeing her from the vantage point of the toilet seat, though the light was still intense. He saw no alternative to deferring an answer to her question, there being several points to assess before he could get to that: the effect of palm to hard tile between tub and toilet, the shoulder, the cheek, a rib or two that had come down hard on the side of the tub. The perplexing sole of one foot—whether the left or the right was unclear—pressed against some far-off surface, the light bleaching the photopigments. He thought of Grandma Maggie warning him not to stare at the sun and he'd warned Addy, though of course the poor kid had been baffled because Theo had said solar retinopathy.

"Down here," he did say.

"Wait, I'll help you."

"Where's Addy?" he said because it felt like the most pressing thing.

She tried to hoist his right shoulder and he cried out, then apologized because she meant well.

"Please just tell me where Addy is."

"With Rosemary," she said as though it was obvious. "Can you get up? Are you saying you need Addy? Do you mean you need more help?"

He hated to hear her worry. "I'm perfectly fine," he said. "I just need a minute."

So she got the towel and waited.

When he was upright at last, she began the drying. He said he could do it, but made no move to take over, and focused on the light switch to distract himself from the pain. She claimed his blue lips and weird speech meant hypothermia. She guessed he'd fallen asleep. She did not turn him but moved to his side in a gingerly way.

Once behind him, she stopped and said, "Whoops," the way she used to when Addy was a baby and his diaper was full. She reached for the washcloth.

Which meant he'd pooped after all. There was another wave in his belly.

"Just clay," she said.

He lay between flannel sheets and under every blanket in the cedar chest. Now and then, his teeth still chattered, but the weight of the quilts was a comfort, prevented him from floating away.

He kept tabs on the room and on the moment: bedside table, highboy, mirror, shadows, scarf over the shade softening the light.

The house's creaks and groans. The maple out the window moving in the wind. Alice had put new incense in the holder but he'd asked her not to light it.

"It feels like winter," he said, though she was drying the bathroom floor and couldn't hear.

When she slipped in beside him at last, her skin was cool. She ran a hand over him, more examination than caress. When she pressed his side, he resisted flinching as best he could.

"Did you hear us?" he asked her.

"Who?"

"The voice… from the candle."

Her hand stopped. "Oh?" she said.

"It said the world was on its last legs and I had to build an ark."

She got up onto an elbow.

"You really were asleep."

"Not a boat like Noah. More of a spacecraft lifeboat."

"God, the day you've had."

"You think it was a dream?"

"You were in there so long. I should have checked."

He said he'd never had a dream like that, with his eyes open and drying out. He described the flame enlarging before it spoke, as though inhaling, saying the Earth was dying, and ordering him not to tell her.

"What are we going to do about you and birthdays?"

"Ford."

"What?"

"He called himself Ford."

"Like a pickup truck?"

"It had to be a dream, right?"

"A bad dream."

"Definitely," he said, "but vivid and with my eyes wide open, right? That can happen, right?"

"A tubmare," she said.

It got better after that. Alice worked from the base of his spine, up the long muscles to his shoulders on either side, then back down, over and over, her silent, miraculous hands delivering him from his tension, taking the knots and hurling them over the horizon, over the moon. He lay with his head to one side, opened his eyes to take in the sight of her, and it was like returning from a journey. "Perfect," he said, though hearing it startled him. The word still had power.

Then, as she worked his legs, she said she wondered whether Noah's wife massaged him on his birthday.

It made him smile. He said middle age for an Old Testament patriarch would have been around four hundred, and that Noah had to be crotchety, so an *old* four hundred. His stagnant energy sure could have used some freeing.

She pressed her fists into his hamstrings.

He said, "How she put up with that self-righteous crank all those centuries. The way he must have gone on about folks failing the Lord, and don't get him started on those Temple know-it-alls with their heads up their asses. How she put up with his friends, including El Shaddai Himself dropping by for coffee most mornings to kvetch about the state of things, saying one of these days. That poor woman: talk about your nightmares."

"Okay, hush." Still a smile in her voice, but she'd had enough.

She had him roll over. He said Genesis would have been different if Mrs. Noah'd had hands like hers.

After a while, she said, "You don't really think the world is ending, do you?"

"I guess not. No, of course not."

She'd been working his ribcage, avoiding the area where the bruise was going to form. She said, "Theo?"

"Mmm?"

"The spirit's name was *Ford*?"

He opened his eyes. He'd heard the smile and needed to see it, and what a fine thing to have her mock this shitty day. This woman, Alice Edith, more stunning at forty-one than she'd been at twenty-one, whip-smart, sensible, and decent, and she got the joke, because what was Ford but the maker of exploding Pintos or a bumbling President who pardoned his mass-murdering predecessor. Or *his Fordship*, Mustapha Mond, World Controller in *Brave New World*, or a modelling agency, or a theatre, or a shallow place to cross a river? Sure as shit, Ford was *not* one of the names of God.

"Why not Datsun?" she said.

"Dr. Studebaker, most high and humourless," he said, though he couldn't help but wonder whether he'd pay for it later somehow. They could not have been closer. He was caressing her too.

The next thing was a wave, crashing down: he said, "You think Addy's okay, right?"

She said, "Theo, Addy is fine. He's a great kid. Theo, *everything's okay.*"

"Okay," he said. "Good."

"And so we're clear: If you build it, I won't come."

"Good," he said.

"Life is good."

"Promise me you won't make me celebrate my birthday next year."

"Can I get you a card?"

"Maybe not even that."

"Bake you a cake?" she said.

Her mentioning cake sparked a craving that persisted beyond the love-making, so he rolled out of bed and stalked naked down to the kitchen, where he stood on the cool marmoleum eating a wide wedge of it, and looked out at the yard, almost like he had on that loneliest of nights in October 1962, when no one went to bed expecting to see morning. He had to look away.

He licked the icing from his fingers. He cut another slice to share with Alice.

4

He woke before the alarm went off, sweating, jaw aching, flattened by the dreams running him over like a line of boxcars, hoppers, coil cars, and well-wagons. He knew he wouldn't sleep again with the earliest bird song, the wind worrying Alice's chimes, and Moose on the bedside table, eyes like red dot sights ready to take the shot.

He rose quietly so as not to disturb Alice. His ankles hurt more than most mornings as he pulled on his jeans, and so did his ribs and shin from the rough landing last night. He closed the door softly and tied his hair back as he descended the stairs, careful not to trip over Moose.

Alice would sleep another couple of hours. She had a busy week: clients nearly due or on their way, following others who'd given birth, and two days in some kind of workshop—Reiki or some such. She'd worried about leaving him with so much garden work, but he didn't mind, with these poignant fall days still warm and busy with meadowlark songs, and longspur and swallow, the machine-gun report and return of squirrels in the elms and on power lines. If the wind would let up, the days would be wonderful.

When he sliced bread, the scent hit hard, raised another memory—the smell of warm loaves in a paper sack leaving KUB Bakery in winter. It occurred to him his dreams had been nostalgic, and he set the knife down firmly enough that Moose looked up.

He made the coffee strong, drank it with oatmeal and toast and last year's crabapple compote, and leafed through the book Addy had given him. A translation of the ninth-century *Persian Book of Ingenious Devices.* Somehow the kid had remembered Theo mentioning once, months before, that he'd been carried away by it in the Engineering library at WashU, practically heard dulcimers and ney and tar and tanbur. On the orders of the Caliph of Baghdad, the three brothers, the Banū Mūsà bin Shākir had scoured the Earth in search of ancient Chinese, Indian, Greek and Persian texts, described and drawn them along with their own inventions. *The Persian Book* had influenced the Muslim world for centuries, made its way to Europe and the Renaissance, and to Leonardo. Somehow Addy had found a listing in a magazine, had it sent by air from some hole-in-the-wall London shop. The boy knew how to give a gift.

Moose had finished his breakfast and watched from the sill as Theo sipped his coffee and focused as best as he could on the Mūsà Brothers' drawings: a player piano with interchangeable cylinders, a programmable flute, a gas mask and an early crankshaft, a water boiler with hot and cold taps. *We wished to make a fountain in which the water rises above a datum in a lead pipe*, the Brothers wrote. *If God, may he be exalted, wishes.*

Still, echoes of the nonsense yesterday kept sounding, so when Moose began pacing, he closed the book and jotted a note to thank Alice for blowing his mind in bed. As he carried his dishes to the sink, his eye caught a piece of tape on the archway left from the decorations. Above the record of Addy's height through the years, the lines and dates in their writing at first and then, higher, in Addy's small hand. He'd have plucked off the tape, but for another ripple of something, so he hurried into his boots and jacket, snatched up Addy's book and went outside.

The wind filled his ears. The pre-dawn light was strange. There was a stillness in the lee of the sauna and a whiff of cedar. Moose padded by the workshop door and Theo could see that things were undeniably good, that they were nearly perfect, if you excused the word.

"*We wish to make a fire in the stove,*" he murmured like a Mūsà Brother twelve hundred years ago, "*if God, may he be exalted, wishes it, to drive out the chill, and we wish to brew another pot of coffee because our sleep was such shit.*"

He filled the firebox and lit it, put on the coffee, then stood and watched the flames grow, listened to the drip, and wondered why it felt for all the world like something unwanted and unwelcome really had landed. Any other morning, he'd feel a pull toward the shop as he walked the path from the house and the work would sweep him up like a current as he stepped through the door. The invention would take him over: his hands would have a deftness, the problems solved themselves. Yesterday, he'd hardly turned on the light and seen the lamp base on the bench when he remembered a Soviet-made Maelzel metronome crammed somewhere up on one of the shelves. He'd climbed up and found it before he lit the stove and in no time he'd turned the metronome into a switch for the base he'd built from some pistons and a camshaft and flywheel, was plugging the cord into the outlet and watching the bulb switch on and off in its bottle-green shade in time with the slow tick and tock as the pendulum swung 44 bpm. He'd felt that flow and barely flinched when his birthday came to mind, and he'd felt fine until he slid the metronome weight to the bottom and the light became a strobe. Whether it was the flashing that broke the spell or Alice calling him in for a birthday lunch was a toss-up.

This morning though, he watched Moose, already dozing in his bed above the stove, and noticed he couldn't bring himself to turn toward the steel cogwheel leaning against the counter because suddenly that was alarming too after six months of happy living with the thing, mulling the possibilities since April when he stumbled over it in a scrap pile and knew that somehow it would become the centrepiece of this lamp base and light switch series and rolled the rusty three-foot diameter thing into the shop. As he built the bridge-arm floor lamp of welded fireplace tools that switched on and off with the barometric pressure, and the chandelier of knotted galvanized pipe whose bulbs stayed lit as long as a single candle flame did, he'd run a hand over it every time he passed and grown to love it. Now that he was nearly done with the metronome camshaft light, eighth in the series, the time had come to turn it into a solar system because he'd envisioned a main light source at the hub with steel planets and woven wire moons orbiting on an ether of gears and coloured lenses, maybe a bell crank lever turning an array of spur and sprocket gears, bevel, mitre and helical gears to open and close the simple circuit with a mechanical complexity Rube Goldberg, may he be exalted, would have admired.

These nerves were lunacy, because an otherworldly entity, vivid as it might be within a stress dream or acid trip, did not exist like a 300-pound steel wheel. The characters of myths who explained great floods, fires or famine, birth and death, or who gave warnings about desecrating nature, meaningful as they may be, did not decamp their myths and had no being beyond their stories. Any burglar could intrude and steal your shit, a tornado really could descend from a summer sky, and no heart attack asked permission, but a voice barking pessimistic shit from a candle flame simply was not real, and it was time to get the damned day going.

He poured coffee and told himself the worst thing to do with an episode of flow flaccidity was let it bend you out of shape. See it for what it was: as simple a thing as more or less hating your birthday since your thirteenth happened to mark the start of the most dangerous week in human history, and a bit of lingering anxiety after twenty or so hours of adrenal overload should be no surprise, and you didn't need to bring luck into it or fate. None of it needed a supernatural explanation.

He took a mouthful of hot coffee and used the pain to propel himself around to face the wheel, but the light fell on it somehow sickeningly, turned its rust into the sores of a flesh-eating disease, which, as ridiculous as that was, spun him back around.

There were bound to be days like this, and you had to roll with it. Today, you do busy work and get back on track that way. You do brainless, useful things, like sort through the accumulated crap on those high shelves at long last, or machine screw threads into the body of this next vacuum cleaner rocket. Or, if sticking around the shop seems likely to make you crazier, get outside and moving, dig the damned beets or get out on the Roadmaster and poke through some Autobins. Scavenging always sharpened his eyes and got him out of his head.

The big doors swinging open was Moose's cue to move from his bed to his perch on the buggy. Theo kicked the stand and gave a nod to Gustave Hermite on the wall, Gustave being the name he'd given the Parisian *chiffonnier*, circa 1900, in third-hand clothes, shabby, shiny-brimmed hat angled far back, looking warily at the camera, his handcart piled high with patched burlap bags full of treasures. Gustave was stooped, bone-weary, his boots worn enough his soles would have read the cobblestone dips and bumps. Theo had hung the photo above his scavenging bike and buggy in a found twisted glass frame by Barovier & Toso Murano as an honour and a redress. He rolled the rig past his old pickup and into the lane. He always rode instead of driving, to be close to the ground and to keep from burning gasoline, only drove the pickup when he had to, and of course, the thing had a load of cast iron radiators and other metal junk he hadn't taken to the scrapper.

It was nearly eight and so far, the sun was staying its upward course despite the gusts. A blackbird fought her way west. Across the lane, Harvey Borsok moved joylessly out toward his crappy yellow Datsun and pretended not to see him. The wind lifted his comb-over like a pie pan. Theo called out, "Harvey! Good morning!" because the dour bastard needed badgering. Borsok gave a nod. Theo had never called him *Dr. Borsok*, though the guy had actually introduced himself that way years ago. Theo pedalled west, so Borsok turned the nasty B-210 east, his radio no doubt tuned to CJOB and its mean-spirited, small-c shit.

The going was harder on McGregor, beyond the shelter of the lane. The south wind felt somehow old, seemed to come from far away or long ago, almost insisted, but Moose faced it bravely, eyes narrowed, fur parted. The sight of him in the mirror, braced up, head bobbing with the bumps, was a comfort, and the fine morning light and warm air, and only a bit of traffic. He passed the cluttered window of the hardware store with its bowed-out brick wall. He saw the Esso guy help a customer with the air hose and he could almost smell the grease from the open service bay. He passed a hand-written sign that read, *Readings by Ruth & Merlin - Cash or Visa*.

The corkscrew barber pole startled another memory loose: driving with the Judge, kneeling on the passenger seat so he could put his elbow out the window, the old man holding the wheel easily, pointing and saying, "If the pole's spinning, Rudy's cutting," and not meaning to be a wise apple when he pointed out that another way you knew Rudy was cutting was because you could see him through the big window, then feeling like he should say sorry because the

Judge had pressed his lips together. He'd sat down properly on his bum so the Judge wouldn't have to tell him.

He'd planned to ride a few more blocks but, weakened by nostalgia, the next gust of wind connected like a straight arm and he swerved left into the lane between Cathedral and Bannerman.

He dismounted at the bottom of the lane and Moose got down to explore. He was glad to start working, felt sure that an hour or two of scavenging would still his monkey mind, and didn't even mind that some idiot had poured gallons of grape mash over everything in the first bin. Two decades of picking had taught him patience. He felt his eyes settling into the hunt, waking to the suggestions of contour and colour as he shifted top layers of trash to reveal lower ones. There was an electric motor in the third bin, the usable base of a brass floor lamp beside the fourth, and beneath a layer of carpet underlayment, a bag of jigsaw puzzles and box games—*Operation, Stock Ticker, Monopoly*—and a stack of vintage hotel memorabilia—room layouts and menus from The Macdonald in Edmonton, things to do in Saskatoon during a stay at the Bessborough—a booklet, *Dining Car Menu for the Little Folk*, with black and orange illustrations of happy Caucasian children and cheerful verse. *The chairs are right, for they're just your height / The bibs are of pink or blue... From model farms along the way / Come daily fresh supplies / Of vegetables, eggs and cream / For puddings, cakes and pies.* There was a carton of VHS movies by the next bin and someone's collection of fancy glass bottles.

As he rolled the bottles in bubble wrap and stowed them in the Roadmaster's panniers, a middle-aged woman a few doors down in rubber boots and floral housedress tossed a black bag into a bin and shot him an ugly look. Her bangs were Scotch-taped to her forehead. Theo waved but she turned away and no doubt would be giving him the stink-eye from her window as he passed. This was business as usual: certain people disapproving of his vocation, perversely bonded with their trash, convinced they should be left alone to waste the Earth's resources since they'd paid for the privilege, appalled that someone would interfere.

He looked for Moose, saw him shuffling in his raccoon way—the short, wide face and bandit's mask, ears rounded from frostbite, locomotion more platigrade than digigrade. Moose was at home here and it did feel good practising the back lane basics he'd written about ten years before, after interpreting the discovery of two dozen mostly unused primary school scribblers as a sign he ought to set down in longhand the Good News of scavenging for the benefit of humankind. He'd filled the notebooks then typed it up double-spaced: his guidebook for anyone who wanted to be *Part of the Solution*. Alice had said the sooner it was published, the better, though, in fairness, she'd always had a soft spot for a manifesto. None of the fifteen or so publishers he'd sent it to since seemed to agree that it was exactly what the times were calling for, and who could blame them when they read the bombastic condemnation of consumer culture supposedly in its dying days and when he'd made himself sound like a grubby urban prophet. He didn't mind the how-to sections or the parts about reimagining everyday artifacts but, six weeks ago, he'd decided that the next time the four-pound thing came back in its self-addressed package, he'd put it away in a drawer. Deciding had been a relief and he noticed now that his first mistake had been seeing the sack of notebooks as some sort of sign.

Someone had set a cardboard box on a base of empty paint cans beside another Autobin. There was a TEAC cassette deck and a ColecoVision with games—Donkey Kong, Lady Bug, Zaxxon. As he loaded them, he spotted the Scotch tape lady glaring through her kitchen curtains and smiled again. It was a good bet she hated the Autobins as much as any of the others who'd ranted on the call-in shows when the city began plunking down one beige steel bin for every four or five lots through a thousand back lanes to make collection easier and cut municipal costs. That old guard saw the bins as a slide further left, as though garbage was private property and such forced mingling got between a taxpayer and their personal salvation, like welfare and the Pope. Theo didn't like the bins either, but because they did nothing to encourage reuse or recycling and, because they anonymized disposal, probably assuaged some of the healthy shame that could still come with flagrant waste. True, getting rid of individual trash cans made scavenging slightly safer because the kind of property rights extremist willing to use threats or violence to ensure their cast-off plant pots or bicycle wheels found their way into the garbage truck stood on shakier ground.

Only two blocks in and the buggy was getting full. The run was turning into something special. He'd already become more selective, left some good things where they lay. Just before Powers Street, he found a box of orange-spined Penguins and a Marantz turntable that only needed a drive belt. He loaded them and decided to call it a morning.

He rode east toward the river, thought he'd take a break in St. John's Park or the Cathedral cemetery, roll a smoke, have some coffee, give Moose a treat, see how they felt after that. Moose seemed content. He sat in his place and watched the scenery like a senior on a bus tour.

Nearly at Main Street, he needed to pull in behind a three-storey walk-up, where a building super seemed to have cleared out an abandoned suite. Back when he spent more time in the back lanes, he might leave a renter's pile alone when he sensed misfortune or sadness or unravelling: removals after a suicide, or when a child's things had been left—board books, stuffed toys, small clothes—in a way that suggested her mother had needed to get her away in a hurry. This pile felt content and well-loved, and there were some fine things. A small hardwood nightstand, a cedar blanket box with a crazy quilt, more VHS movies but better titles, and a six-inch pile of jazz LPs—Chico Hamilton, Shorty Rogers, Gerry Mulligan with Chet, Stan Getz, Miles, and Eric Dolphy *Out to Lunch!* A Duratec Singer sewing machine, a blue metal trunk full of tinned food—sardines, and oysters, unopened bottles of vanilla, Québec maple syrup, pineapple slices, bing cherries. A carved wooden box stuffed with old postcards—military, railway, hold-to-the-light ones.

He loaded as much as he could and had to wonder what the chances were of finding so much in so short a time. It was enough to spark thoughts of a guiding hand or of stars having aligned—after all, what were the chances?—but you can't have it both ways. he thought, and imputing events to good luck made no more sense than imputing them to bad. Things were what they were and didn't need to be more. It was enough that the hour had improved his outlook.

He rode toward home and thought of the barber pole. He and Alice had done so much better with Addy than his parents had ever done with him, not that it was a high bar. For one thing, they'd let Addy have a say in how he dressed and wore his hair and, when he was five or six and he declared he wanted his hair short, Theo had taken him to the closest barber. He'd had his doubts when the barber's eyebrows rose, and he'd braced for a remark about father and son hippies, but the barber had only gestured toward the chairs and promised he wouldn't be long. Addy had been too excited to sit, and took everything in through the hotbox haze of cigarette smoke: the banter, the bottles and brushes and their reflections in the wide mirror, the towels and clippers, every clever saying framed on the wall, the big leather chairs with their levers. When Addy looked through a stack of magazines and found a *Playboy*, his eyes had gone wide. "Oops," the barber said and got Addy up on the booster next. He'd fitted the cape, lit a fresh Sportsman, sheared off most of Addy's fine hair, and said, "Well, what do you know: there was a boy under there," and Theo said, "Looking good!" because it was true. How thrilled Addy had been running his fingers up the sides and back of his scalp, looking like he belonged in 1954 instead of 1974.

Suddenly the thought of sitting in the park with a smoke and coffee from his thermos and with his meandering thoughts was too much. Better to head home and harvest beets, cook for Fourth Monday. He turned onto Main and the wind pushed him along faster than he could pedal, got under the buggy and jostled the load. He needed to get off the wide thoroughfare and back onto side streets, so he signalled left, made his way across all four lanes, and began the turn onto Bannerman. He could see the old men in the AquaMagic looking up at the TV. There was Alfie in front of the 7-Eleven payphone, on his Harley, leaning back on his elbows, looking at the sky through his dark glasses. A couple of his guys were coming out of the store. Alfie lived a couple of blocks north. He was a big guy, looked mean in his leathers and scruff. He always had a pager or two and made his calls on payphones. As Theo passed by, Alfie greeted him with an easy wave of the pointer finger. Theo nodded in return and wondered why the old men on their plastic chairs in the laundromat, holding Styrofoam cups and staring at the screen over the washers seemed so damned sad.

A cardboard carton in the lane caught his eye. It peeked out between the dumpster and the fence and somehow he needed to turn in.

Brass and steel contents spilled out one side: spur gears, assorted sprockets, a rack and pinion, worm gear shafts, a couple of planetary gears, a dime bag full of tiny watch gears, faces, hands, cogs, and bezels. Someone had evidently dropped the box when they found the dumpster padlocked, blowing out one side of the cardboard and smashing the glass jar of used grease inside. It was a brilliant find, maybe enough to build the cogwheel lamp base. He looked for something to hold the mess and his eyes went across Bannerman to the little lot and a clear plastic bag of shredded paper among some black bags and old metal shelving.

He tried to remember any luckier single day of scavenging through the years. He walked across to the lot behind what he thought had been a government office of some kind but was being turned into a daycare.

He was crouching by the box of grease-covered gears and sprockets when a front-loader garbage truck pulled into the lane, brakes shrill as it stopped a few yards away.

Theo gestured, Just a moment, and began pushing the box away from the dumpster. He heard the forks lowering, and then the air horn. He glared back, mouthed, Seriously? and saw the scowling, round-faced driver swear. He shook his head and went back to shifting the broken box, but slowed to half-speed now. He ignored the next horn blast.

He undid the bag of paper as the driver slammed the forks into the dumpster slots. Moose's ears were back.

The 7-Eleven dumpster rose above the truck and threw a shadow.

Theo thought he'd make a nest in the shredded paper and let the paper absorb some of the grease.

The driver shook the dumpster and debris floated down. The bin descended quickly, landed hard enough to shake houses down the block. Moose finally ditched the buggy.

"Bum!" the driver shouted as he backed out.

Any other day, Theo would have flipped the bird but something was more pressing. He'd been about to take a first handful of gears and sprockets when it registered, half-seen, a quarter or eighth recognized. It raised an alarm. His eyes resisted returning to the paper strips and the row of five or seven strips that had landed together on top and maintained some of their adjacency. The better part of a round-cornered N, and an A, most of another A.

The truck driver revved the diesel again for luck.

NASA.

Theo knew suddenly and completely that the clear plastic bag sitting open and just touching his right knee contained disassembled drawings from the National Aeronautics and Space Administration and that, notwithstanding his assumptions from the cramped confines of his slim perspective, fetching the thing from behind a small brick building with limestone trim at least a thousand miles from any NASA facility had been the point of the morning, its real purpose and intention and no accident.

Predestined, was the first word to mind, and then, *Ford*, the name of a pickup truck and a clumsy president, and then he had to wonder whether there was even such a thing as an accident or whether some other will had been at play all along, leading him here, step by step, filling his buggy and panniers as inexplicably full as the nets of the Jesus's fishermen friends, and then what sense there was in wondering when the day was always going to fall down around him this way?

The remains of breakfast forced their way up and out of him, splashed the bottom of the bag.

He closed it with the twist-tie, then felt an urgency to leave, so lifted, as carefully as he could, the exploded carton and its contents, felt its bottom give way over the Roadmaster's front basket. He snatched up a few pieces from the asphalt, kicked the stand and called Moose, set off to the south at first, away from home, plastic bag perched in front. He felt as pursued as a wheel man with the loot as he pedalled desperately down streets and back lanes, through sidewalk accesses and over narrow paths, as though he could stay ahead of whoever or whatever, downwind of the hounds. He rode a tortuous ninety-minute path and, a block from home, remembered what Grandma Maggie used to say about miracles, that only a fool goes and questions one because it was a clue about what Heaven looks like.

He stood in the lane behind the shop. His legs shook like he had the flu. Moose was down and stretching. He swung one of the big doors wide, set the bag of paper down, rolled the bike and buggy inside, but wasn't ready to be inside himself, so stayed behind the door to smoke. The match lit like it had double sulphur.

Moose hissed. He stood, back arched, fur standing, and scrambled around the corner.

The match burned his fingers.

"Careful," the voice said.

Theo's eyes went to the cherry of his cigarette.

"After a while, randomness doesn't do the trick, does it?" Ford said.

He could not have formed words. He pulled hard on the cigarette once and flicked the butt into the lane. The wind returned it to the gravel between his boots.

"You've got a lot of work to do," Ford said. "Plan the work, work the plan."

Theo raised his foot.

"That won't help."

He crushed it anyway, ground it side to side, though there were so many other flames—the fire in the stove, Alice's candles…

"Pilot light on the stove," Ford said. "Even the sun…"

The thing heard his thoughts…

"For pity's sake, there doesn't need to be a flame. The end of a cigarette isn't really a flame now, is it? Some heat just helps the focus and, goodness knows, anything to help you focus."

Theo glanced across the lane. A relief Denise Borsok wasn't at the window watching him argue with himself.

Ford snorted and said, "And the sooner you stop telling Alice everything the better."

Theo needed to get away. He emptied his mind and acted, best he could, without thought. Hurled the puke-scented plastic bag toward the front of the shop, past the bins of camshafts and crankshafts, shelves of old magazines and books, past the steel cogwheel, all the way to his drafting table so it sent a coffee cup flying. It hit the garbage collection map he'd kept up because Addy had coloured it when he was little, long before things turned awkward. He cleared his mind as he latched the big doors and turned toward the front. He pushed away the thoughts of escape and hiding.

"Will you sit down?" Ford said.

"Fine," he said and visualized the green chair. His head was hot. He'd read a story somewhere about spies reassembling shredded papers. Maybe World War II.

"Where there's a will, there's a way," Ford said.

He made the mental image of drawing a fistful of shredded spacecraft drawings from the bag but then, two steps from the table, faked left and went right, burst through the side door.

"Oh, Theodore," he heard Ford say, but slammed the door so hard it shook the shop.

5

He had mixed feelings about this Fourth Monday. Fourth Monday Supper (Because You Have to Eat on Mondays) had met most months for two and a half years, and was a potluck more or less, vegetarian, give or take. Alice, Gracie, and Meg had started it after someone said Monday meal prep was a drag after the weekend. Tonight, he doubted he'd be good company.

He and Alice walked the twenty minutes to Denis and Kael's. His face felt cool and naked, ticklish in the wind because he'd shaved off his beard. He caught her glancing at him as they walked and twice she'd reached over and run her fingertips over his cheek, and why not, when she'd never known him without a beard? Her initial expression had been a mixture of shock and puzzlement, though she caught herself and apologized, managed to say he looked *just fine*, but with a clenched little nod and unaware of her eyes. She did not say he looked *handsome* or *better* because she did not tell lies and his proportions were peculiar in a way that could have been sweet in a middle teen who still had a chance to grow out of them.

Looking like a different person had been the point, stupid as that was. He'd had the impulse toward the end of an afternoon spent working furiously in the garden and kitchen in the hope it would occupy him fully, steel him against more nostalgia and hearing the awful voice again. He dug up both long rows of beets and, when he thought of Addy's barber, made himself focus on the sound of the milk bottles he'd buried to their necks around the garden, singing in the wind like monks, though they'd been no more help with the jays and blackbirds than any of the scarecrows. The wind stole all but traces of the pumpkin vine scent, and tomato stalk, chamomile. He removed most of the greens, layered the beets into crates with peat, and carried them down to the cold room. Then he'd played the stereo loud as he made the tarte and the soup: put the pumpkin in to roast, chilled the pastry and made the custard, sang if he knew the words, fetched stock from the freezer, sautéed onions and thyme, added the pumpkin and thawed stock and let it simmer while he washed the dishes, polished the counters, swept and mopped the floor, then he blended the soup smooth, added the cream and Gruyère. He'd showered and was polishing the mirror when he found himself pulling out the scissors and putting a new blade in Addy's razor.

"Think about this," he'd said aloud because the thought of disguising himself was ridiculous and no self-respecting ghost or spirit or whatever would be fooled, but the shaving had been urgent and in ten minutes he'd stood looking at himself, horrified, aware he'd made a huge mistake, the bits of toilet paper he'd used on the nicks resembling so many miniature Japanese flags. Where the hell was his chin? He looked like a hawksbill turtle.

Kael and Denis's red brick bungalow was tucked into a bend on the river side of Scotia Street. Its polished west-facing windows reflected the sunset. The neat Virginia Creeper had gone burgundy. There were a few gold leaves sprinkled over the lawn like rose petals over pressed sheets.

Kael opened the door. "Come in, Alice," he said, "and introduce me to your friend."

"Smart-ass," Theo said and handed him the tarte pan. Denis waved from the front room. He was by the fireplace, talking with a man Theo couldn't place. The man petted one of the cats and called it gorgeous. Theo heard Denis say that Birmans had been bred by Burmese High Priests, known for their white paws.

"You didn't know Burmese priests had white paws, did you?" Kael said and led him to the kitchen. "He likes those beasts more than he likes me. If we ever run out of kibbles, he'll turn me into pellets. Come get yourself a beer."

Friends called out greetings or waved and he nodded back. Meg ran her fingers over his cheeks and chin as he passed.

Kael wanted to know how Theo's lamps were coming and complained about his current piece, a commission, a triptych, oil on plywood, chiaroscuro still-lifes with pigeons. He'd decided he hated the whole thing, though he always detested a piece when it was 95% done.

They were back out in the dining room. A water drop fell onto the hardwood from Theo's bottle. Kael swiped it with his sock.

"Smooth," Theo said.

Alice was in the sunroom with sad, earnest Elena Wolczkiewicz—*Ms W* to her high school English students. Elena wasn't a teacher, but an *Edge-U-cayy-torr*, and she pronounced the U like she was going to whistle, and now she was training to be a *therr-a-pisst* too. She listened to Alice with excessive raptness, listened *actively*, as she'd been taught in her course. Her neediness broke your heart. She hadn't gotten over her husband, Marlon, who'd dumped her five years ago for a younger and, presumably, less intense woman. Elena had worked her devastation into a slim volume of incomprehensible verse she'd called *The Spaces Within Bone*, which had fortunately never been reviewed so the unintentional suggestion of osteoporosis remained unspoken. Elena meant well.

It was a beautiful home. The pale green leather and mahogany, antique rugs on bleached hardwood, Denis's two Birmans brushed plump, posed on either side of the fire. Number Six and Number Seven, after *The Prisoner*; they might have been taxidermied for all they moved, unlike Moose, who'd been known to dive from a height to snatch food from a guest's hand. Theo wished he'd worn better jeans. He had his doubts about the green shirt. He felt small and on edge, the way he used to trailing his parents into the Governor's mansion when Warren Hearnes was there, on notice to mind his manners. He felt out of place, like he mightn't really be a part of it.

Doc McVay stood with Louise Bach, one of Elena's teacher friends, and Llew Pope. Theo liked Louise and always worried that her students called her *Ms Bach with the Walk* because of her gait. Louise laughed at something Doc said. Llew smiled but wasn't convincing. Apparently Llew had brought another girlfriend. He'd dated a long, briskly-moving line of women since his divorce, and none of the endings had been pretty. He'd once been a devout

Marxist-Leninist and worked to make the Revolution, but now he was a muckety-muck with the UCCO, the federal prison guards' union. He wasn't an easy person. Doc said something else funny, but shifted as though his itchy-looking sweater was actually very itchy. Elena called to Llew from the sunroom, but said, *Llewellyn.* Ms W had a thing about diminutives, didn't find them intense enough. She insisted on *Arthur* for Art. Theo had asked her not to call him *Theodore.*

Nalani arrived with her new man, Ben, and grinned like a schoolgirl as she introduced him. Kael said it was good to put a face and carnal presence to the stories.

"Nalani, you didn't," Ben said, eyes wide, then blinking, his free hand going up to his floppy hair. He said, "You did not mention the support hose? Nalani?" It made her laugh. "Oh God, not the peanut butter…"

Nalani's joy was contagious. She said, "Ben, this is Theo, the one who pretends he's not an artist."

"Right you are," Kael said. "And I'm Kael, the one who pretends he *is* an artist."

Ben's handshake was doughy, the hand of a cherub. His cheeks were either pink from being outside or always that way. Theo swiped the dishtowel from Kael's shoulder and took Ben's casserole dish. He caught the scent of baby powder on Ben, like a toddler out of the tub.

He carried the dish to the kitchen, through the lacework of friends and acquaintances, but realized too late that he was on course to collide with Wally Plouf, evidently between conversations and looking for a buzz to kill.

"Coming through," Theo said, as though the casserole was scorching him through the towel because Wally would talk and talk without saying anything. He was a social worker of some kind, and worked with ex-convicts, as if adjusting to life outside wasn't hard enough. He wondered why Alice's two best friends had married such idiots.

"Theo," Wally Plouf said, inconsiderately, given the intensity of the fake heat, "I hardly recognized you without…," but the sound registered doppler-like.

45

He needed to see Gracie and Meg, though it meant putting up with Lloyd, since Lloyd stuck to Gracie like a lamprey to its shark at these things. Lloyd was uncomfortable wearing anything but a suit and tie. Tonight, it was a pair of carefully ironed brown cords and a tight orange turtleneck.

Gracie had to kiss both of Theo's cheeks.

"Don't you look like a million bucks?" Lloyd said as he went with one of the two-hander shakes he'd learned in Carnegie.

"Nice turtleneck," Theo said.

Meg ran her fingertips over his face and said he was a different man without a beard. He heard *different man* and wanted to confess that shaving had been a feeble attempt at disguise. Maybe if Lloyd wasn't there. He said it had seemed like a good idea at the time, but already couldn't wait for it to grow back.

"It'll take getting used to," Gracie said. "Not that there's anything wrong with your face."

"*Veritas omnia vincit,*" he said.

Gracie loved it when he spoke Latin.

Lloyd said he liked the new clean-cut *sort of thing*. He made his bug-eyes face, as though widening his eyes and turning down the corners of his mouth made him likeable.

And there it was: the first sort of thing. If it was a drinking game, they'd be shitfaced in half an hour. He tried to feel his feet on the hardwood, hoped that would slow the images that kept surprising him: candle flames and paper strips, a cartoon rocket blasting off, Pretty Boy JFK announcing the end of the world on TV. He wondered whether the adrenalin bursts were making him wince.

Lloyd guessed birthday wishes were in order. Who said *in order* anymore?

"Lloyd," Gracie said and nudged him with her foot. She wore no-nonsense woollen socks.

"Big Four-O," Lloyd said, eyes wide behind his big glasses.

"Just another day," Theo said. Lloyd had cast a powerful spell on Gracie their first year in university and she'd been nuts about him ever since, called him brilliant and generous and gentle and a terrific father. Eighteen years on, her immunity to his stupid faces and the *interjectio* that riddled his speech hadn't waned. He imagined putting his hands around Lloyd's orange roll neck and squeezing, but Gracie's preposterous love forbade murder. You're not exactly perfect either, Alice would say and, No, you can't punch his lights out if he calls you Teddy.

He wanted a smoke.

Thank heavens Meg changed the subject. She said that Llew's new girlfriend, Marnie, seemed fabulous. Theo looked at the woman standing where Louise Bach had been. Llew had his arm around her and she was saying something to Doc McVay. Meg said Marnie was a fragrance chemist, which meant she worked with aromas for lotions and perfumes.

"Easy on the eyes, that's for sure," Lloyd said, which was true but didn't need saying. She was in her early thirties, had long, dark, permed hair, wore a stylish long white jacket, maybe linen, smaller shoulder pads. Plum-coloured stretch pants, leather boots with buckles.

"Where does Llew finds these women?" Gracie said.

"A real head-turner," Lloyd said.

"As you've said, dearest."

Lloyd did his Marty Feldman face. Theo couldn't watch.

Doc McVay seemed intrigued by Llew's date. He leaned in to catch her every word. Marnie was the latest in a line and it was best not to get used to any of them because some switch inevitably flipped in Llew around month four. As though he took a phone call with a post-hypnotic command, and suddenly some small fact or feature about his latest beloved would hold staggering meaning and transform her from interesting and decent into sinister or tedious. He'd be devastated for the week it took to meet the next woman and swear up and down she was the one. He'd broken a lot of hearts and, at his best, even Llew could see how profoundly messed up it was.

"Anyway, Teddy," Lloyd said, so there it was, ka-pow and lights out.

"Theo."

"Time to get going on your midlife crisis," he said and giggled like a girl. "I turn forty in May: I'm thinking maybe a red Miata or a twenty-eight-year-old sort of thing."

"A twenty-eight-year-old *what*?" Gracie said. "Like, a pony?"

"Or a bungalow?" This was Meg. "A practical twenty-eight-year-old bungalow. Charleswood? St. James?"

"I was thinking more of a blonde," Lloyd said.

"A blonde pony?"

"A blonde pony with a visual impairment," Theo said. "No offence, Gracie."

"None taken."

Lloyd lapped it up, like he was the life of the party and not a death force. That Gracie still hadn't smothered him in his sleep was final proof that love was blind like a blonde pony. Now Lloyd called Gracie G- and wrapped an orange shoestring arm around her, said she was the only bombshell for him. He went in for a lamprey smooch and Theo had to look away.

Gracie wondered why the hell they weren't eating yet. She told Lloyd to go light a fire under Denis. His leaving was a relief.

Meg said she was glad Theo had come.

Gracie said she'd worried too, after yesterday.

"Seriously? Is there nothing she doesn't tell you two?" He glared at Alice but she was deep in it with Elena.

"She thought you were having a heart attack when she brought out the cake," Meg said.

"Just something about birthdays…," he said.

"Then falling asleep in the bath…"

Hearing it wasn't bad.

Gracie said, "And God telling you to build an ark? God, Theo: you and birthdays. It's so messed up."

"She makes me sound like a head case," he said though hearing it all aloud was helping, putting it into perspective, because candle flames don't give orders and, if there was such a thing as a god or angel, it wouldn't tap a guy from Winnipeg to build the ship, and NASA drawings didn't turn up in clear garbage bags behind office buildings.

The relief that came from saying a thing aloud could still surprise him. Alice had taught him about that twenty years ago, and he'd been astonished to find that yakking through the accumulated agony of a year on the run since he'd fled home felt like having the venom sucked out of a bite. How much less would it take to dispatch the bleakness of the past twenty-four hours? Gracie and Meg were close enough to touch, Alice was at his seven o'clock, four or five steps away, Kael was right there, and Art. They were his people. Everything could be fine.

His eyes were stinging, so he stood straighter. "Actually not God," he said, and didn't even mind the little waver in his voice. "It called itself Ford."

It was a detail Alice must not have passed on.

"Ford?" Gracie said.

"Like Wally's Festiva?" Meg said.

"Like Wally's Festiva, or a banana-yellow Pinto," he said. "And another thing: it didn't tell me to build an ark: it told me to build a *fucking* ark."

"Whoa, Jehovah," Meg said. "What is with the F-bombs?"

Gracie leaned in and wrapped him up. He held on tight.

He said, "Okay, I went a little *non compos mentis* there."

"Cockamamie, baby."

He was getting out from under this thing.

He whispered so they both heard, "Please don't tell Elena."

He'd turned a corner. Now, if he wasn't quite himself, whoever he was could almost enjoy the evening and if he wasn't the life of the party, at least he wasn't a downer. He felt good in his green shirt again.

They were sitting with Ben and Nalani. He ate potato and black-eyed pea cakes, Meg's bang bang chicken skewers, and a couple of cashew ravioli. Nalani was working on a cup of his pumpkin soup and some spanakopita. They were grilling Ben and he was being a good sport. He'd joined the UofM faculty that summer, having come from some Vermont college to be closer to his family in Biggar, Saskatchewan—*New York is big, but this is Biggar.* He said it had been inevitable he'd pursue Asian Studies: his family was Finnish on both sides, sure, but he'd known the family who ran the Cantonese-Canadian restaurant in town so was a shoo-in for a student exchange in Shenzhen when he was seventeen. He seemed to have forgotten to iron one shirt sleeve.

Ben went to get more wine. Alice gave Nalani a thumbs up.

"You like him?" Nalani asked, grinning again. "He was nervous about meeting everyone."

"He has a terrific bum," Alice said.

A berry-red tint rose on Nalani's cheeks. It was sweet.

Bum was the right word. *Ass* or *butt* would not have fit the guy.

"So, you're *Benjamin*," they all heard Elena say.

"Yes, well, Benedikt, with a K," Ben said. "You must be Elena."

Lloyd sat next to Doc and Llew, and Llew's new girlfriend, Marnie. He started right in. He said, "The only thing wrong with these vegetarian nights is the lack of meat."

"Animals are our friends," Theo said. "I've always thought it best not to eat my friends."

"You have friends who are chickens?"

"You wouldn't eat Llew, would you?" Theo said, then looked at his plate so he wouldn't have to see whatever face Lloyd was making.

Lloyd said, "Don't get me wrong: the vittles are terrific, but a good burger…"

"Try not to think of animals as objects," Doc said. "Think of them as other nations." Doc was no more strict a vegetarian than Theo was, but the Dalai Lama himself would feel compelled to tussle with Lloyd Freaking Whitaker.

"Interesting, Doc," Theo said. "So, if I understand you correctly, the differences between humans and cows are a bit like the differences between Canada and Sweden."

"That's right, Theo, and who wants to eat a Swede?"

Marnie covered her mouth as she laughed.

Llew didn't seem to like his date's response to Doc. The frown was subtle.

Wally Plouf had taken prisoners by the dining room table. They listened politely as he spoke a long series of words. It was cheerful enough but pointless, all of the clauses, subclauses, and word fillers left him sounding brain-damaged. Two of the three smiled and slipped free; the third, a man called Isaac, took the full weight, tried to sort out what Wally was trying to say. He'd learn.

Denis was coming around with wine and Theo held up his glass. He complimented Denis on the new living room paint.

"It's called Murmuring Peach," Denis said. Lloyd tried to interrupt but Denis pushed on, which was good, since Lloyd's mouth was full.

"We were putting it up," Denis said. I was doing the cutting and Kael was rolling. The CD finished so it was quiet and suddenly Kael was shouting, "Damn you, Peach, *stop that murmuring*! It killed."

Lloyd said, apropos of nothing, "I guess those scientists in Utah haven't saved the world with their cold fusion box after all." No one was interested, so of course he pressed on, called *the cold fusion thing* a hoax, claimed that all the *top scientists* had debunked it. He guessed it had been some kind of publicity grab.

Theo didn't bite, though cold fusion was an interest and, since the spring, he'd been reading everything he could find about Pons and Fleischmann's work. There seemed to be no theoretical explanation for nuclear fusion taking place at room temperature. It called laws of physics into question.

"Have you heard this one?" Lloyd said. "A cold fusion reactor will be incredibly cheap to build, there will be no radiation or pollution, and it'll solve the world's energy problems. The Saudis can kiss our keisters. The only trick is finding the *Unobtainium* it needs to run." As he said the word, he did the stupid eyes. Marnie's mouth had the shape of a smile but her eyes didn't match. Her wineglass reflected the firelight. Theo noticed that all of the glassware gleamed.

"Uh oh," Theo said, "Sounds like someone's been reading *Time* again."

"What? Yeah, did you..."

"Lloyd, we've talked about this. *Time* is not a good magazine. It doesn't do nuance at the best of times, but it really dumbed this one down. The science is really interesting, but also the David and Goliath showdown between two electrochemists and the whole hot fusion establishment, from MIT and Cal-Tech to the Pentagon and CIA."

"What does the CIA have to do with anything?"

Theo said, "Marnie, did I hear right that you're a chemist?"

"Yeah, though a sessional at the UofW at the moment."

Doc said, "What do you mean, just a sessional? You have a Ph.D."

"You must know my friend Gerry Fittig," Theo said.

"Of course. He's a legend around there."

"Gerry's one of my oldest pals. Anyway, you actually know something about this, unlike my friend here with his C in Grade 9 Science. What do you think about it?"

"Cold fusion? I'm not sure. Martin Fleischmann and Stanley Pons are world-class scientists, so you have to take it seriously, but no one's had much luck replicating the findings. Say more about David and Goliath."

"Okay, except it's harder with you listening because I can't just make shit up the way I would if I was only talking to Lloyd, say." He waited a moment, but Lloyd missed his chance. Theo said, "The amazing thing is the urgency of the attacks by the physicists. If cold fusion was really nothing, they'd just ignore it, but for some reason they're going at it hard, you know? Trying to squash Pons and Fleischmann like a couple of bugs. I'm not saying that *all* twentieth-century physicists are born evil—some of them were probably all right as kids."

Marnie said there had been a lot of chemistry-bashing by the physicists. She said lunchtime in the faculty club could be like the Spartans meeting the Los Brovos.

Lloyd still wanted to know what the CIA had to do with anything. He asked whether Theo was making up some new conspiracy theory.

"Follow the grant money and you find pretty quickly that certain research institutions are in deep with the nuclear power industry, which means they're bought and paid for by the Pentagon. Official Science gets a boner for anything nuclear."

"A *nuclear* boner?" Denis said. "Am I flushed? I feel flushed."

"An *official* nuclear boner," Marnie said.

Lloyd said, "Those guys, Fleischmann and Pons, they called a press conference to say they'd solved the world's energy problems, but then it turned out they'd made rookie mistakes or fudged the data."

"Lloyd, Lloyd, Lloyd. Say you're a hot fusion physicist from Georgia Tech…"

"A *smoking hot* fusion physicist," Marnie said.

"I'm going to faint," Denis said.

"It's March, 1989. Your lab's got four million bucks' worth of tubes and magnets and you're driving a new Audi, you know, and a couple of *chemists* come along claiming there's a cheap, safe nuclear process that your kid could bang together in the garage. You're going to worry about your funding."

He gave Marnie a wink that Lloyd couldn't see. She smiled, seemed to get it.

"You and your buddies from MIT and Cal-Tech get busy making cold fusion as professionally toxic as phrenology. You get on the phone with the White House and get Bush to put you all on a *Blue*

Ribbon Panel, you know, to get to the bottom of it. You repeat the experiments and you find a lot of heat, but you call it *artifact* and leave it out of the papers. In the press release, you focus on the lack of neutrons, and when *Time* comes to see you, you wear your nicest monogrammed lab coat and some half-specs like Brian Mulroney and you repeat the word *debunk* over and over. Voilà, cold fusion is the *Ishtar* of the scientific world."

Marnie said she'd liked *Ishtar*. Llew said he had too, but he was trying too hard. Of course, Lloyd hadn't seen it but he'd heard it was awful.

Monday Nighters moved through the kitchen for the mains. Drawn there by the food-filled island, they orbited once or twice, then followed a tangent out to the dining room or living room or sunroom. Roasted cauliflower curry, tomato cakes with smoked feta, Brussels sprout tacos, and cauliflower baked with Gruyère, Gracie's Dragonfly Dumplings with soy-ginger dressing. Theo filled his plate full.

Benedikt Heikenen was fitting in fine. He'd brought something called *Mápó dòufu*, which he said translated as *grandmother with a pockmarked face*. He'd learned to make it from an authentic *Ma* in Meishan, Dongpo District, Sichuan Province. He said, "Chili oil, Sichuan peppercorns, heaven-facing pepper, fire-breathing dragons, so it's got both conventional *heat* and the *mala*—numbing—spice of Sichuan cuisine. Authentic *Mápó dòufu* will really make you sweat, but I've toned this down a little."

Theo had found his feet. The evening was turning out fine and it wasn't even devastating to have Lloyd follow him back to the living room, no doubt hoping to spar about cold fusion or Free Trade. Lloyd sat in his ironed turtleneck, overfilled his mouth, and made creepy pleasure sounds. He set his fork down, listened to Marnie and watched the tension develop between Llew and Doc.

Marnie was saying, "If I was a boy, they'd have called me Beaker. I owned Science Fair, I bought textbooks with birthday money. You know the type."

"Ha. Love it," Llew said.

"I was awkward as hell, mind you."

"I doubt that," Doc said.

Llew and Doc sat on either side, each trying to be more engaged than the other.

"In junior high, I noticed that perfumery and chemistry were related... I should have mentioned that perfume was a very early passion."

"No, no, I got that," said Doc.

"My brother got to have a darkroom in the basement, so I made my parents let me set up a perfumery lab."

"That's great," Llew said.

Good thing Alice wasn't there because she'd have found a way of saying Theo had been that kind of kid too. She'd have meant it as a good thing because, though she'd tried, she'd never really understood.

He did his best to ignore Lloyd's eating. He heard Gracie ask Ben about the demonstrations in China. They were behind him in the sunroom. Ben said he'd met some of the student leaders. Wu'er Kaixi. Feng Congde. And Chai Ling, one of the hunger strikers. "Wonderful people," he said.

At the big dining table, Elena asked Meg who made the chard and saffron tart. She had to have the recipe.

Denis was complaining that Kael had stayed home for Pride again that summer. Three years in a row. Denis wondered how Kael, the fearless visual artist, could be less outspoken than his actuary husband.

"I don't need a march to feel proud," Kael said. "And there's gardening. Annuals don't deadhead themselves."

"The one day of the year the community..."

"The *community*? Oh, Denis."

"Forget it."

"It's so dysfunctional. The sub-communities and sub-sub-communities, so much friction. I swear I'll go to Pride when the lesbians and sodomites learn to get along."

"I hate it when you use that word."

"Caucuses and factions and camps and splinter groups and cliques."

"I think lesbians prefer *clique*," Alice said, rhyming it with *brick*.

"Nice!" Kael said.

"... needless to say, a lot of moving parts," Wally droned. "At the end of the day, though it could be said there's more they need to know about the matter..."

"As you've said, Marguerite..."

"... get an evening to ourselves and we're walking in Assiniboine Park and notice we have nothing to talk about but the kids and the house..."

"... the crumbling Soviet Block." This was Lloyd, no doubt about to assert that history had always been moving toward a global, free market. Bets on whether he'd say *inexorably* but it was a sure thing he'd use *democracy, freedom,* and *capitalism* as synonyms. On another night, Theo might bite and go back and forth with him until Alice or Gracie stepped in, and then he'd kick himself because none of it meant a thing to Lloyd and it was only argument for argument's sake.

"...when Bush signed off on the launch, he was literally playing Russian roulette."

"... Paul Parquet and coumarin in 1894 with his Fougère Royal was *a lot* more interesting than *MacBeth*, and I was in the basement in East Kildonan exploring vetiver molecules and musk and amber and florals, training my nose... I spent a winter learning about ambergris, which is very complex—woody, incense-like, maybe musk, tobacco, and, allegedly smelled like the ocean, though I'd never been out of Manitoba."

Doc chuckled and Llew's eyes said, Man, what the fuck? She's with me.

"I got back into scent in grad school in London. *Chromatographic and spectroscopic studies of a group of essential oils from Artemisia sieberi.* This must be so boring."

"No no, it's fascinating," Doc said.

"The students had read the signs: the beginnings of a market economy, more people willing to question the leadership, all of the calls for press freedom, and the government's responses had been uneven for sure. Of course it turned out the Regime was perfectly willing to take the most unspeakable road to shut the students down. It was much more afraid of democracy than a bit of international outrage..."

"...because scent was language. A form of communication."

" I'll tell you what!" Wally Plouf said, though he never would.

"... kick out foreign journalists, fire CCT anchors who displayed the slightest sadness on air, round up any more student leaders they could find..."

"It is what it is," Wally said. "It is what it is."

"... okay, sometimes I hide in the laundry room for a long time, you know? Does that make me a bad parent?"

"The hardliners were set in their old ways. Of course, they sent in the PLA. What a waste of beautiful young *lives*." Ben's voice cracked when he said lives. "Young soldiers' lives ruined too. But democracy is inevitable..."

"Imagine the annual general meeting of the so-called *Gay Community*."

"No one's interested, Kael."

"They'd have to alternate the presidency between the lesbians and gays, though who knows whether the parties would hold together, given all the factions—the boys and bears and mother superiors, such a mishmash, and the only thing in common being the abomination of lying with mankind as with womankind."

"Maybe go around with wine?"

"Across the aisle, you've got the whole kitty of lesbians, activists in front and, you've got to admit, better spoken. Lots of shirts buttoned to the top, and femmes, and chapstick lesbians..."

"And the bisexuals?" Alice said.

"Expect treachery from the bisexuals. And the *curious*, of course, like foreign students, when you don't know whether they'll stick around once they finish their degrees. And the uranians and the onanists. And the celibates with their principles, though they *never do anything*."

"The voyeurs with official observer status," Alice said.

"Go Alice! Oh, and the middle-aged gap-toothed realtors..."

"Wow, you are *such* an asshole."

"Okay, that might have been over the line."

"A much much stronger resemblance to her mother..."

"Empowering them to think outside the box."

"...back from Berlin when my brother got sick, decided to stay. Teach a bit, do my thing. I own some patents and a couple of them earn a bit, which helps..." Theo imagined Marnie in a pressed white lab coat, facing a wall of small, labelled bottles, notebook and pencil at her elbow. Taking down a particular bottle, unstoppering it, breathing it in, putting a drop onto a slip of heavy paper. Setting the bottle neatly back in its place, smiling as she reached for another.

Wally Plouf passed by and the scent of Barbicide and talc in his wake caught Theo like a crisp left jab. He saw the freshly clipped horseshoe of hair on Wally's head, its sharply defined edges, and could have sworn he was a kid back at Rudy's waiting his turn for a trim, the stink of cold coffee in Styrofoam cups, the hale fellow barbershop banter, one ugly take after another on the news of the world. Those old men, willing to burn the whole planet for the sake of their dominoes. The dislocation took his balance.

"They called mass protests in hundreds of cities *a counter-revolutionary riot*," he heard Ben say.

"My God," Gracie said. "All of those mothers losing their only child."

Which sent him flying like a cartoon punch, launched him into black and white outer space toward the moon and, even as he sailed up and away from the thin comfort he'd felt among his people, he knew he should never have dropped his guard because the worst things can appear from nowhere if you do—Kennedy's chiselled mug on the little TV set, Nikita Khrushchev beating the table with his shoe and vowing to bury everyone—and it's only in retrospect that you see it coming from miles away: this time the snappy jab of Wally's hair the shape of an institutional toilet seat setting up the knockout blow of losing your child because nothing could be worse than that.

He began to sense the room again but felt the same real and durable threat he'd been feeling since his birthday. He thought he might be sick again, and the image of barfing took him back to the shredded paper and NASA.

The main thing was avoiding another flat spin. He needed to do something. Find the present moment. Slap himself to raise a bit of colour, try to get one proper breath.

Someone described being little, only four or five, in the passenger's seat, sitting on their feet with a *Popular Science* draped over his knees. Looking at his mother, who was a nervous driver, and chasing the courage to say what needed saying.

Llew and Marnie and Doc seemed to be looking his way and he felt Lloyd's eyes from the left, but it still took time to ascertain that he was the one speaking and a bit longer to sort what he was going on about. He and his mother on their way to have Dr. Everett look at his ears again because they kept popping and he still wasn't allowed to swim. His mother's hands at ten and two, three buttons on each beige glove, her back straight, chin raised to see over the wheel. The front seat a stripy grey.

He'd decided he wanted to be a scientist and make inventions in a laboratory and wear a white coat over his clothes, though it meant not being a lawyer like his daddy or Grandpa Case, and maybe not working at the court at all. For days he'd kept his silence but knew he had to risk it, see how it landed with his mother before he told the Judge.

"I said, 'If I grow up, I want to be a scientist instead of a lawyer like Dad.' She was backlit so I couldn't quite see her face but she said, 'Theodore, what a thing!' the same way she did when my Uncle Gill visited and cussed. It wasn't the *Reach for the Stars* response I'd hoped for."

"You said, '*If* I grow up?'" Marnie asked.

"Yeah, and didn't think twice about that part. We were in St. Louis, Missouri, basically the middle of the United States. It was '53 or '54. The question wasn't whether there'd be a nuclear war but when."

"You poor thing," Marnie said.

Either the music went louder or the last few people had gone quiet.

"Cold War tales," he said and felt himself smile. "Eight million stories…naked city, right?" he said, because their attention was awful.

"It wasn't as bad up here," Doc said.

"That's good," he said then praised the Dragonfly Dumplings. He retraced the conversations—hardliners, Tiananmen Square, a rotating presidency, Marnie in her lab coat with her bottles and notebook, Wally spinning his tires.

Just this once, Lloyd speaking up was a blessing. The king of conventional wisdom beaking about the Iron Curtain and Communism's days being numbered. It helped right the tilting, restored the buzz of the room, as though the others were doing their best to drown Lloyd out.

"With the old East German leader out..." Lloyd said.

"Honecker," Theo said.

"Yes, and the country flat broke..."

Lloyd would preach about the Mighty and Glorious Judgment coming down on Communism.

He turned and saw Alice at the dining room table, looking at him with a combination of perplexity and sympathy that said, I didn't know that, though how could she when the memory had wandered out from the depths of its secluded cerebral fold for the first time in thirty-five years just then and, agreed, the whole thing was a head-scratcher because he never said the first word about growing up and it had suddenly taken the floor. People understood he hadn't had an easy time *down in Missouri*, which was an unknown land to them, not that he'd ever given details. Gracie and Meg and a few others had heard the name Judge and knew his mother had been better, but a woman of her time and disinclined to speak up, but there'd been no call for specifics. Alice knew more than anyone about the early, chronic dread and sense of having grown up far too early. Her face guaranteed they'd circle back.

He got up to go for a smoke, alone because Gracie was with Ben, learning about the low rate of organ donation among North American Chinese because harvesting organs disrespected a departed ancestor. As he fetched his jacket, he heard Ben say he'd only learned to honour his parents after a decade away from them and on the other side of the world.

The fresh air and the darkness under a waning crescent moon were a relief. Lighting the smoke was fine—no voice and no sensation beyond ones that fit the evening and the riverfront yard, the wind and the trees, scraps of laughter from inside.

There was plenty Alice had never heard, and he guessed she'd learned there was no point in asking past some limit. She knew the basics: that he'd finished high school at fifteen, been too young to go away, so gone to WashU as a commuter, crushed his Engineering courses but been more lost than ever until senior year when he finally met Rivers and the others. That he hadn't said a word to his parents about his new life, kept things separate and safe, hung with his friends, smoked some weed, tuned into campus politics, went to lectures and read books none of the Engineering advisors would have recognized, but let his parents believe he was the same book-smart, socially abortive kid he'd always been. He'd told Alice about his double life: cultivating the face he showed them, guarding his legend like a spy, propping it up with documents and the right amount of detail.

He'd told her about suppertime in the Strahl home: how the Judge would have had a snort or three reading the paper, then get rolling as Verna filled his plate, then tuck in and smack his lips and go on about his ugly day, occasionally interrogate them if their attention seemed thin. This prosecutor would be a good man and just doing his job but the defence was a sad sack or shyster and, listening to him, the defendants wouldn't be human, but only larcenists and arsonists, burglars, murderers, dope fiends, ne'er-do-wells, no-goodniks, and weak of character, embarrassments to their mothers. On the bench, as there at the supper table, the Judge was Sherlock Holmes and King Solomon combined.

Theo made his way across Denis and Kael's lawn down toward the river. He had definitely told Alice that, by first grade, he'd guessed that much of what his father did from eight to five was make life difficult for nonconformists and outsiders, and anyone with the gall to be poor or black or both, and men he said were light in the loafers. He seemed to deal with bad people too, but the clues about his prejudices were not subtle. The Judge fancied himself fair and wise, but he was a cudgel, and supper at the Strahls allowed the most alarming glimpses of him. Theo had told Alice that, by middle school, he'd taken the measure of the man and understood that somewhere along the way the Judge had lost the line between his job as a circuit court judge and himself, forgotten that counsel and witnesses and the people in the gallery wore their Sunday clothes and minded their manners, stood until told to sit and spoke in their turn out of respect for the rule of law but not for him personally, and that every other formality and deference was an offering to the institution and not his 190-pound bag of hot air and bones and meat and blood. The Judge's error was obvious, he'd told Alice, in the way everything had turned personal. A witness arriving five minutes late offended him, Judge Judge Bogges Strahl, and he was himself the institution without which there would be chaos through the land and he himself embodied an awesome purity and incorruptibility.

At supper, when he should have been a husband and a father in the stylish casual wear Verna laid out, he maintained his soulless rectitude but also displayed a murderous side, not only in the way he slashed a lamb chop but in the glee he could never conceal when he talked about pronouncing a sentence. Theo had told Alice that it could not have been clearer if the Judge had worn his robes to the table and kept a gavel by his plate, but how many shades of apeshit would he have gone if Theo had ever said?

He stood with the scrappy willows and cottonwoods of the channel shelf, watched the light on the water as he finished the smoke. It seemed almost trustworthy.

In a while, he buried the butt end and started back. He wondered how long until Alice was ready to leave.

He was at the patio step when Elena Wolczkiewicz came outside. "Theodore," she said.

"Hi Elena."

She wanted to know whether he'd heard from the latest publisher. She considered herself an old hand in publishing because of her bone poems, which had sold 150 copies in three years. By now, Elena probably cared more about *Living out of Your Back Lane* than he did.

He said the manuscript was somewhere in Vermont, but that he'd decided to turn the page, as it were.

She made a tragic face, made her eyes brim with intensity through her little glasses. He wondered whether they practised making faces in therapy school.

"No, it's a good thing," he said. "It's a matter of taking the hint, that the world might not want a how-to book about back lane scavenging."

She still didn't speak, but tilted her head farther to the fervid side and stared. She'd always been intense, but therapy school had made her unbearable, which was a shame because she had a good heart. He wondered whether he should break it to her that her active listening face made her seem weird.

"Maybe I'll go back to it sometime. Parts of it are cringy…"

She touched his arm and asked, "How *are* you, Theodore?"

"I'm good. You? How's teaching?" He felt his lip quiver.

"Your birthday," she said. "You know…"

"Oh, that." God, but Alice blabbed. Alice telling Gracie and Meg was one thing, but Elena? His ankles hurt and he wanted to sit. He glimpsed Doc McVay and Llew's date, Marnie, through the window. Just the two of them in the kitchen, standing close. Things weren't looking good for Llew.

Elena's silence verged on menacing.

"I just lose my shit when I have a birthday," he said. "For whatever reason. Then you put a zero at the end—forty, right?"

Didn't she murmur and give the smallest nod? Fuck her therapy school.

He said, "Which is batshit because life is good. Family, friends, work I like, a roof that doesn't leak, food to eat, and all my teeth." He'd had enough of Elena. He hated giving in and filling her silence. He said, "I guess a birthday's going to raise doubts."

Elena's eyes said, Go on, or, Tell me more. It occurred to him that he'd be gutted if all his lemon tarte wasn't gone. Which was stupid. Like this interaction, and her face's claim of unconditional acceptance.

"Well, it's not like planetary survival is an odds-on favourite, Elena. Even just the 70,000 warheads…"

"*If I grow up,*" she said, meaningfully, pleased with the call-back.

"Oh that." He'd have gone inside but for a new morbid fascination about how awkward she really could become, or maybe the manipulative silence was doing its magic. He said, "I don't know why I remembered that but really, Elena, this century! How we made it through the Cold War, then eight years of Reagan and now Bush, and the lid's blown off Eastern Europe and you can't keep track of the revolutions. Gorbachev's days are numbered and it's anyone's guess who'll end up with the nukes."

She actually squinted harder, as though squeezing out maximum empathy. Someone had to tell her.

"If you're not thinking about the nukes, you're not paying attention, though nowadays, I think Armageddon's more likely to be a slow breakdown of everything. As in, Spaceship Earth hasn't been to the shop for a long long time: she's burning oil, her tranny clunks, her brakes are shot. You smell exhaust in the cabin. The passengers are at one another's throats."

"Sounds like you feel pretty hopeless," she said.

He felt his jaw clench. How could she not know she was a parody? He said, "Not sure I'd use that word..."

Elena said, "Theodore, is there someplace you feel the hopelessness in your body?" She scanned her own body with open palms.

"Jesus, Elena, are you doing therapy on me right now?"

It stopped her. When she stood up straight, he realized how far she'd been leaning in.

"Seriously, what actual difference does it make if I decide my terror and rage about existential global threats feel more like they're in my elbow or my left ankle? We're talking about actual events. Actual calamitous, human-produced climate change because we've chopped down all the trees and irrigated deserts and pumped unimaginable quantities of carbon dioxide and methane and VOCs into the air and pushed the Keeling Curve up and up. The heat waves are real, and the droughts and the extra hurricanes, and the polar ice really is melting. A billion fish nets and Barbie doll heads have disintegrated into a plastic cloud that's choking life on the seafloor, a dozen species have gone extinct as we've been chatting here. We're all growing melanomas because of the holes we've blown in the ozone layer."

He stared at her, but she didn't say anything. She seemed to be at a loss, as though trying to remember what you were supposed to do when you had no idea what to say: wave your arms and make noise to look big, or play dead, turn tail and run like hell?

He said, "Is it my imagination or is everyone except me in some kind of therapy? This is a serious question, and I really don't mean to be harsh or to make you answer for your whole people, but isn't there a danger in people going to therapy distressed because things are distressing—the natural world falling apart, the rich getting richer, CEOs and coke-fuelled hedge fund assholes and industrialists in top hats getting away with everything, or whatever else, but an actual event—going to counselling and emerging fifty minutes later, $80 lighter and convinced that when you boiled it down, the perturbation was just unresolved anger at Mom and Dad or some *chi* imbalance. I mean, don't we defuse the terror and rage at our peril? It's amazing anything ever gets done."

Something seemed to shift in her face. Now she looked more like a human being than a robot empath, and she was more endearing for all of that.

"Look, no offence to you personally, Elena."

"No, it's fair."

"Not all of it…"

"I crossed a line," she said. "I wanted to help but I had no business getting into body mapping. I'm really sorry."

"Don't worry about it, Elena."

"You just looked like you'd been knocked sideways. Maybe it was just seeing you without your beard."

"No, knocked sideways sounds about right."

"Maybe I can redeem myself. Do you mind if I tell you about a thing that's helped me?"

"Okay."

"You don't mind?"

He shook his head. He'd never liked Elena as much as he did now.

"I go to a forest."

"Okay."

"It doesn't have to be a forest, but out of doors, and I sit on the ground, lay my palms down flat and close my eyes. After a while, it's like I feel the Earth's strength and patience. I feel very small but in a reassuring way, like I'm a drop in an ocean and that's enough."

"I like it," he said and meant it. He imagined going down to the riverbank, sitting on the fallen leaves among the saplings. Elena talked and it was fine, even when she brought up the Gaia Principle and said *text* when *book* would have worked. For the first time, he wished she would go on a little longer.

6

Finishing the chocolate cake had been unwise, his nerves being what they were, because when he closed his eyes, the thoughts and inklings had twisted and wound like snakes in a nest. He'd stared at the edge of the blind, waiting for sleep to come, mostly convinced that Ford was a figment and his only mission was to read about stress management before his next birthday, though each time he closed his eyes, another round of match light voices and shredded paper began, and six years to go 365 million miles and the severest expectations. The Doomsday Clock approaching midnight, the Mūsà Brothers called to prayer. He tried listing Jupiter's moons—Io, Europa, Ganymede, Callisto, etc.

Around 2:30, he decided the lack of elbow room was all the proof he needed. He'd been thinking about the *Noah's Ark* Little Golden Book Grandma Maggie had given him: how delighted he'd been with the orderliness of the animals lined up waiting to board— pink armadillos, brown kangaroos, tigers the colour of mandarin oranges—and Noah at the top of the rise, ticking a hippo off of his list, but how quickly the questions and doubts had formed. That you couldn't fit two of every kind of animal into a boat even if it were as big as Ladue, plus all the food, when the Lord hadn't said how long they'd be floating. Plus carnivores needed meat, which meant taking extra chickens for the foxes, etc. and never mind mutual predators and the dangers of boarding termites on a gopherwood vessel. Even at four, he'd blamed Disney, because giraffes didn't gallop on the spot and mallards didn't hover like helicopters, and Noah didn't have paper, since Moses was later and he'd had to use stone for the Commandments. Now, thirty-six years later, at 2:30 a.m., elbow room seemed like proof enough of the preposterousness, not that there'd been any mention of his taking aardvarks or bears. The Apollo 11 Command Module had been six metres square, barely big enough for three adult humans willing to sit still the whole voyage. Even Columbia's crew module had the square footage of the two upstairs bedrooms, so not what you'd call roomy for a long journey.

He woke terrified again and again. Once, he'd been thirteen again, in his pyjamas at his bedroom window, watching the confetti points of light on the pool and wondering whether, when the bombs came, there'd be an instant when he'd see the water boil. Then it was the Challenger explosion—its single exhaust plume rising in the sky, the orange and yellow explosion, and the breach of the plume at 145 degrees. Then it was Galileo exploding after lift-off and Plutonium 238 falling like a Scotch mist over Florida. This one sat him up straight. The sheet was soaked, his cheeks and neck itched. He went to drink cold water and fetch a bath towel to lie on, thought how good it was nothing woke Alice these days because she'd want to hear it all. She called dreams *portals to the soul*.

The final time, he closed his eyes, satisfied, more or less, that Ford and the whole spaceship lifeboat thing was nothing but the product of an anxious mind and that someday he'd look back on them as rock bottom of something. He drifted off thinking about the flybys of Venus and Earth that served as a gravitational slingshot to propel Galileo out toward Jupiter, and how those fly-bys were called shepherd's slings.

But there was no peace because this time he dreamed he was watching Addy sleep the way he had when he was a baby and toddler, though in the dream he was grown up and lying beside Rosemary in her apartment. The steady rise and fall of his chest was reassuring until Addy cried out from his own nightmare, sat up terrified, heart running wild, and Rosemary was saying, It's just another dream, as though the walls and ceiling weren't out to smother him.

It was 4:13 a.m. Theo got up and found his clothes, commanded the sorrow to subside but far too alive to the fact that any night of the week, you could be minding your own business and the ground could give way under you, or a meteor could knock the waning crescent moon out of orbit and off toward Neptune.

It would be a decision: he would decide to get back on track, back to work on the lamps and switches, tap holes into the Electrolux canister for the Barbarella ship, deal with the buggy full of finds. He'd do anything so long as it was work, until the afternoon when Rosemary was coming to help in the garden, which meant Addy was too. Things could be fine again.

He tossed the bag of paper into the Autobin, didn't give a shit about recycling. That was a choice too. He let the lid fall hard.

He waited for the coffee. A *Popular Mechanics* from 1961 on the counter lay open to stories about feeding ground apricot pits to jet engines and a fifteen-foot-long wire, detached from Explorer VIII, orbiting the Earth like a vast garrote. He closed the magazine. Maybe don't read about spacecraft for a while. Another decision. The coffee dripped. The wind harrassed the shop.

As he reached for his cup, the spines of Mrs. Kern's diaries caught his eye, and he knew at once that he'd spend the morning on the pop-ups. He took down the diaries. So much decisiveness.

He sat by the stove sipping coffee and browsing pages he'd flagged a year or more ago. Mrs. Kern had written two seasons into each volume—Spring and Summer, 1972, June to November 1975—filled both sides of the pages with a cursive he guessed had been flawless once. The unsteadiness had its own beauty. *July, 1975,* she wrote. *The jays have nipped off the marigold blossoms again. Poor beggars need them to treat the mites, but it's vexing*, and he imagined these two pages opening and the pop-up of birds' wings, legs, and heads contorted from itching, a storm of yellow blossoms, the decapitated rows.

The first thoughts of engineering structures into old books had been years earlier, when he found a single volume of a 1961 Colliers encyclopedia set—*15, PAL to PRI*—and begun sketching and building prototypes to illustrate articles on *Pessomancy* and *Pigeon Photography*. He'd always liked the way pop-up pages swelled two dimensions into three, then tucked neatly away again. He thought of pop-ups right away the day he spotted the soft leather covers and gilded edges of Mrs. Kern's diaries, like a short stack of King James Bibles. It had been ugly finding them like that, in a metal trash can discarded with filters full of coffee grounds and tins from Libby's beans, and taking them had been urgent. Back in the shop, he'd sat reading, dismayed that anyone could throw out the memoirs of a great-aunt or grandmother once she'd gone to her reward, and the thought of illuminating passages with pop-up structures felt like reparation. He would engineer them to open up and close back down, standing on turntables maybe, opening and closing as though breathing.

Theo got more coffee. It sounded like children were squealing in the lane, but he knew it was only the wind. He refused to open the back door to confirm.

October 14, 1976 and the Millers had driven Mrs. Kern to a funeral at B'nai Abraham. She'd needed a boost up to the seat of Earl's pickup. It was embarrassing, but she managed some little joke. He saw Jacob's ladder rising to the towering bench seat of a Dodge. She'd put up two dozen jars of crabapples, and he imagined the tree unfolding from the crease, branches sagging under the weight of the ripe jars.

Any element could be a pop-up—Mrs. Kern's nephew fishing from a rowboat, a bed of sword lilies, teacups and pinwheel sandwiches—and you wondered what *could not* unfold from flat, because even shadows could. You could make a new world.

He needed to choose. The impatience was an intrusion, but Moose hadn't stirred, which was a blessing. He stopped to roll a smoke. He knew the first few drags would focus him.

"Pick one," he said. He said it aloud to hear something other than the wind. One image was as good as the next.

This one: July 8, 1972. Mrs. Kern wrote that the dogwood under her window would need severe pruning come fall, and he liked the drama of nature pressing and the violence that *severe* brought to mind. He sketched her tidy home and the wild, wolfish dogwood in front, many-headed, lunging and snarling, yellow eyes and bared teeth, and Mrs. Kern in the window in her housedress. He considered the structure, ways of raising the house and its monster as the page opened, how to make Mrs. Kern's arms and her loppers rise last. Sure enough, working settled the butterflies. Sketching, cutting, folding, and gluing toward a prototype felt as comfortable as an old sweatshirt. Nalani would say the fact he'd already thought of turntables proved the audience was no afterthought.

Not that he'd give her the point because it was a dance they did: she would call him an *artist* and he'd say he was a journeyman, a rehabilitator of trash. He'd say garbage is a lack of imagination. She'd refer to the things he made as *works*, and he'd call them piecework. She'd say *oeuvre* to get a rise out of him, allege parallels with Russian Futurism or Dada or De Stijl, and he'd say he was an oddball who plucked bits of metal and paper and plastic from the waste stream and reorganized them a little.

He really did still wonder about all the fuss—it wasn't like he'd invented gunpowder—but who was he to argue if strangers wanted to pay enough money for the things he made that he'd needed to have someone do his taxes? It wasn't like he'd have stopped making things if people didn't take them off his hands; he couldn't have stopped if he tried, and why would he when life was never so uncomplicated as when his hands and imagination synced? He told Nalani he only had the slightest grip on his life when he was knocking some strange thing together and, before she came along, getting rid of things was trickier because Alice didn't want any more in the house, the shop was filling up and, happy as he was to give them away, the thought he might be foisting something on a friend or a neighbour, like a macrame giraffe your kid made at craft camp, was horrifying, so he'd minded the line between generosity and infliction. These days, the reception things got was more hushed than it used to be at the flea market and they were much less likely to end up back in the trash.

What changes there'd been since the first time Nalani had come to the house in 1984. Over dinner, they'd talked about her move to the UofW to teach Art History and how bad the winter would really be, and about Alice's midwifery practice. Gracie told them about a bill she was working on. Addy recited lyrics from *Hollywood Diary* and Nalani knocked his socks off when she said she'd seen Siouxsie Sioux in Manchester, though the predictable pall had fallen over the poor kid when talk went to what Theo did. It turned out she'd been wondering about the *assemblage* in the front room—the wide, glistening eyes of a paint-by-number fawn looking out from the creamy satin lining of a 1940s American Tourister hat case—and how much she'd liked it, and Gracie said she had to see the shop.

He'd shown her around, aimed a trouble light at pieces as they went, noticed how she faced each piece squarely, legs straight, head up, hands clasped behind her back. Another *assemblage* so-called, this one made from a medicine cabinet he'd found at the demolition site, its paint worn through or chipped, shelves holding plastic toys and cutouts from a Cold War *Popular Mechanics*, an exposé of Aeroflot, instructions for building a jetpack out of stovepipe, ads laying out the proper aims of a sixties man. He admitted he'd puzzled over the elements of another box, *Real Men Canoeing*, added, deleted, reorganized, started over three or four times, and she'd seemed to hold her breath before the box with the velvet and ribbons, combs and pins that he called *Bubbles* as veneration of a girl from the beginning of the century, whose headstone he liked to read in the cathedral graveyard. She hadn't wanted to move the switch of an early lamp, but almost squealed when the tiny motion caused every other gear to move and the bulb to come on, and they'd laughed.

Back inside, Alice and Gracie were three sheets to the wind and they'd all heard the ludicrous words Nalani used—*multimedia* and *avant-garde, assemblage* and *kinetic art*—and her claims it was beautiful that every element had been rescued and given new meaning. Her accent made *marvellous* sound like *mah-vellous.*

"I've been telling him for years but he won't listen." That was Gracie.

"Look, just say you liked the nut loaf," Theo said.

"Take a compliment," Gracie said.

Later that week, Nalani came back with a professor she said knew more about contemporary art than anyone. The woman had passed him in high black boots, short-cropped sunflower yellow hair, a tailored man's suit and double-Windsor, bold eye makeup and bright lipstick, like Annie Lennox in Berlin. He'd stood smoking by the big doors while Nalani showed her around and he heard them say the most ridiculous things—Constructivist versus Neo-Dada, Fluxist, maybe Flautist, the assemblages darker than Cornell's, more possessive. Annie Lennox said that, with students, it came off camp or twee, that it wasn't easy making nostalgia as respectable as lust or hatred, that it can't be longing for a place or person, or for some particular time—not, say, a longing for the innocence and optimism of the Space Age—it has to be about time passing and unattainability, and Nalani said, More like longing after longing?

"Yes, just so," Annie Lennox said. "Looking through a window at an old man who's propped up his dead wife in her chair at the table…"

It had been such bullshit. What old man and what dead wife?

"It's good," Annie Lennox said as she left, but spoke more slowly than she had to Nalani. Her eyes would have made a toddler cry.

Later, he'd told Nalani that if he'd had the gene for nostalgia, which he didn't, he definitely would not be nostalgic for the Space Age, and he'd never thought of science as innocent. He said the first time he read about Fritz Haber, he was a little kid: he'd read about Haber winning a Nobel for synthesizing ammonia to make fertilizer, but going on to weaponize chlorine for use at Ypres and Vimy Ridge, then at Auschwitz, where the Nazis used it to murder members of Haber's extended family. "Believe me," he told Nalani, "that dashed any possibility I'd ever think of science or technology as golden things. Never mind Oppenheimer. Technology is only innocent in Disney, and Disney's propaganda."

There was a first little show in the Exchange. A half-dozen boxes, a couple of rockets, the light switch. A pair of worn-out 501s with circuit boards stitched into the denim, some wires visible, an odometer riveted to the little pocket. At the opening, he thanked Nalani and thanked the gallery for the nice party, but said all he'd ever done was have a bit of fun redirecting an inconsequential bit of the waste stream, and didn't know the first thing about Retrofuturism or Kraftwerk, though to each his own. The *Free Press* ran a photo. Two pieces sold. There were shows in Edmonton, and Toronto and Saskatoon, mentions of his work in magazines Nalani said were important.

Somehow it had gotten to be noon, but he'd built a first model and a kind of drama did reveal itself when he opened the page to ninety degrees and a six-headed dogwood beast unfolded and towered above the little house and above her fence, which, in a later version, would rise up too with her perennials and annuals. The sequence had been tricky, but as the page opened wider, he'd gotten Mrs. Kern to rise in her window with the loppers, ready to execute the severest pruning. The construction collapsed mostly flat again when the pages closed. He made notes about adjustments, opened it all again. It pleased him.

It was time to go inside but he found he couldn't look away. Now the opening and closing had become somehow irresistible: the metamorphosis from flat, dense, and suffocating to bright and roomy enough to sustain life held him in thrall. He opened and closed the thing, made more notes, wondered what kind of idiot looked at a paper pop-up and felt an edge of dread?

The wind gusted twice, like the in and out of a great sigh. Then three short sounds, for all the world like, "tsk-tsk-tsk," and even as he told himself the sound was nothing but the workshop shifting, the dread rose higher.

Moose was up and arched and bristling.

He dropped the pop-up prototype like there were 110 volts running through it.

Moose was on the floor yowling, and out of the shop. Theo could feel Ford too, somewhere nearby.

He thought, *Elbow room,* and understood at once that he could take as many decisions as he liked—to get back on track, to work the way he used to and sleep through the night, decide things would be right again—he could be as determined as he liked, as firm as any hand, but something else could still be in charge. In other words, he'd been led here like a lamb and the point of the morning had been elbow room, because of course a craft could launch small and expand like a pop-up book out past the Earth's sphere of influence. Its flat surfaces could unfurl to create all kinds of square footage for whatever journey.

He let Moose out through the big doors and of course, the city truck pulled into the lane from the east just then, stopped to deal with the first bin along the way. If he was going to fetch the bag of shredded paper, he had to do it now. He walked that way and it occurred to him that, if he'd really meant to get rid of it—really decided—he'd have burned the strips in the stove by the fistful. It made him shake his head.

7

There was Addy, standing like mob muscle, back against the kitchen counter, glaring at the scruffy, wired-looking guy sitting across from Alice. Rosemary stood beside Addy, tempering the hostility. The man closed his notebook. His pen left an impression in the side of a nicotine-stained finger. His nails needed trimming. The kitchen smelled like cigarettes, though Alice would never have let him light up inside.

The briefest astonishment crossed Rosemary's face when she turned, so Theo regretted shaving all over again.

Alice introduced them: Barney Dogan from the *Province*.

"Well," Theo said.

"*Well* is right," Addy said.

Dogan's smell was a Pigpen cloud as he left. He lit a new smoke on the front step.

"He's doing a column on midwifery," Alice told Theo.

"This is *insane*," Addy said.

"You were rude."

"Mom, it's Barney Fogan."

"He seemed sincere."

"He's going to mock you to shit."

"You don't know that." She opened the window wider.

"Mother, sometimes you're so simple."

"Addy," Rosemary said. "Jeez."

Theo was glad to listen. It distracted him from the thought of space vehicles unfurling beyond the Kármán line. He watched Barney Dogan and his cigarette get into some nondescript, late-

73

model thing parked between Alice's sensible Corolla and Addy's funny orange 1973 Alfa Romeo Montréal. The Corolla needed a transmission.

"And we'll never get the stink out of here," Addy said.

He and Rosemary headed out to the garden. Alice said she'd be right out. She'd made a potato chowder. She said, "And I suppose you agree with Addy."

Theo ladled soup.

"Go on, say it," she said.

"Well, Gracie's going to have a stroke," he said. He didn't ask what she'd been thinking talking to the guy—Addy had clearly done that—or mention any of the shit Dogan had written about Gracie since she'd become Education Shadow Minister, or remind her that the guy's reason for being seemed to be focusing the rage of right-wing Winnipeg like a convex lens fixing the sun. There wasn't a cheap shot the clown hadn't taken, no straw man he hadn't propped up and pummelled, from ivory tower eggheads to the Québécois and the beautiful people of Parliament Hill, welfare queens so-called, and convicts living large in country club jails. Tree-huggers of course, and hairy, man-hating feminists. Gracie called him an arsonist and guessed he got a boner watching his fires. She called him Barney Fogan, short for Barney Ducking Fogan.

"Just prepare for the worst," he said. "I have plywood for the windows if his column draws the hordes."

"You and Addy, you think the worst of people," she said and went outside to supervise.

He turned on the radio, ate soup and rye bread, looked through Addy's *Free Press* in the hope it would keep him from thinking about pop-up books and the end of the world. More about the San Francisco quake and how the Nimitz Freeway wouldn't have collapsed if someone had bothered to do a bit of maintenance. Bush was scolding Ortega for bullying the Contras. If Bush didn't belong in an orange jumpsuit, no one did.

Speaking of orange, it had to be the godawful shade of it that had dropped the asking price for the Alfa Romeo out front enough for a part-time waiter to afford it. Any other colour would have doubled the ask. A year on, the car's profile had grown on him—its uncertainty about whether it was a Lamborghini or a Pinto or a

Gremlin—and the space-age gills on its flanks, funky headlamp eyelids, novelty oversized steering wheel, but the thing was thirsty, so people had more or less given them away since the fuel crisis. Addy had bought the quirky thing with his heart instead of his head. He cleaned the bowl with a crust and read about explosions at the Phillips plant in Pasadena, Texas. Scores dead, hundreds injured. The plant made high-density polyethylene. It had taken ten hours to bring the fire under control.

The Phillips story seized him: the vivid red and orange of the first explosion, a rocking so violent it registered on the Richter scale, water from firefighters' hoses turning chemicals to poison gas. The images played through him like movie jump cuts—flames and black smoke, people running, sirens, a crumple of body bags.

God but how this dread hung on. It lingered like the stink of Barney Fogan. He needed to get outside with the others. That was suddenly urgent, and so was smoking cessation. He was quitting once and for all. Those things he could be in charge of.

That afternoon, they pulled the parsnips and the rest of the carrots— Scarlet Nantes, Cosmic Purples, Solar Yellows—and he knew the vegetables were real, and these people. He knew he was now an ex-smoker and he'd endure the cravings, and he'd work in this garden with Alice, Addy, and Rosemary, and remind himself that if he was put on Earth to do anything it was to work the soil and build his machines and boxes and be a tiny part of the solution. The fire in Texas and the São Paulo landslide were as real as rock or rain, and the slaughter of kids by grownups in Tiananmen Square, but what could you do beyond bear witness?

You're a bright enough guy, he thought, you're creative and you've got a certain flair, but you cannot dream rockets into being, and this garden is alive and dwells with you from planting and thinning through watering, weeding, and taking the first smooth-podded snap beans, tender lettuce, firm red radishes. It is in you as you sneak new potatoes from hills when the flowers finish, harvest cabbage early on a cloudy day for best flavour and least wilting. You pickle cucumbers as soon as they leave their fragrant vines, take cantaloupes when the skin feels like netting, melons when the vine withers and the fruit knocks hollow, you pick peppers for roasting, tomatoes for sauce and sandwiches, you dry, blanch, store and freeze, choose seeds for trading or sowing next year, while Alice harvests her herbs and medicines. All of this was real and worthwhile, he fit inside of it and belonged, and Rosemary was the real deal: that spring, she'd helped with planting, then thinned shoots, weeded during the heat of August before heading off to wait tables until three a.m. Her interest in the differences between common horseradish and Bohemian had nothing to do with ingratiation. How different she was from the others—none of the raccoon-eye makeup or arty airs, none of the prickly sarcasm. She was smart and curious, she laughed easily and beautifully, and they'd thanked their stars Addy'd had the sense to fall so hard.

8

Next morning, first thing, he headed west toward the newspaper boxes on McGregor. He needed a *Free Press* for an update on the Pasadena explosions and a *Province* in case Dogan had written about Alice. The sun wouldn't be up for hours. When he turned south, the wind swallowed the clatter of the buggy. He'd have left it but Moose had insisted on coming.

By bedtime the night before, Alice had been properly rattled about talking to Dogan. Gracie predicted an old-time witch-burning, said Dogan would have her on a broom. She recommended Alice go visit her dad for a while. Theo said maybe it wouldn't be so bad.

He bought a *Free Press* first, stood under the streetlight and did his best to keep hold of the broadsheet pages. He found it on page two, and read like a drowning man sucking air. The Phillips plant was still burning: they'd let the fires burn themselves out because water made things worse. Searchers picked through rubble but held little hope for the twenty-two missing employees. Families waited in knots in a parking lot. A man called Fermin Lieja came back for his car. He'd been installing insulation in the plant when the sirens sounded and he'd fled toward the channel with others and they'd caught boats across. Witnesses said the explosions were like atomic bombs: they'd broken windows three miles away, hurled concrete blocks as far. An investigation was underway, but a faulty seal on a chemical reactor was the suspect.

A gust of wind tried to send him up McGregor. Fighting helped with the nausea.

Four sailors had been rescued after 118 days in an overturned trimaran. A monster wave in a 60-knot gale had flipped the *Rose-Noëlle* on June 4, three days off of New Zealand's South Island, and made land on September 30. The story asked whether the *Rose-Noëlle* was the world's greatest survival story or its greatest hoax? Twenty people, mostly children, were missing after a landslide hit a São Paulo favela. Developers had been excavating at the crest of the hill above and the mud that fell onto Nova Republica would fill 5,000 trucks. The story said Nova Republica was a dot in the middle of the Morumbi district, which had the biggest concentration of millionaires in São Paulo.

He was halfway home before he remembered the *Province*. He went back, slipped the thing into a pannier. He made the workshop at 5:15, too early to start the rototiller. He rolled the Roadmaster inside and closed the doors. He lit the stove, put on coffee.

He found the page for *Common-Sense Patrol* and saw Alice's photo. It captured her hands in motion as she spoke. The header read, *The Motherhood Pie*. He could almost smell Barney Dogan's cigarette stink on the newsprint.

Ever hear of a *motherhood* story? It's something near and dear that everybody agrees on. Goes with apple pie. Well, buckle up, because this story is actually *about* motherhood, and what you read will shock you.

For thousands of years, when the birth pangs started, someone ran to fetch the midwife. It was a no-brainer. Midwives had the know-how.

But for decades, fat cat Manitoba doctors have elbowed midwives out of the baby business!

Longtime Winnipeg midwife Alice Towne says the problem is that MDs have been taught to think of pregnancy as an illness and labour as a medical emergency. "Which is hooey most of the time," she says. "Pregnancy and childbirth are a normal part of life."

"Most deliveries aren't complicated," Towne says. "And what most women want—or *would* want, if they knew their options—is a skilled attendant who listens and leaves her in the driver's seat."

Towne says, "Of course a few moms need help from an obstetrician"—that's a doctor who specializes in pregnancy and childbirth—"and some babies need to be born in hospital. A midwife brings in the obstetrician when there are problems and, if things work how they're supposed to, she works alongside the obstetrician in hospital."

Sound like common sense?

Doctors claim they're protecting moms and babies from *quacks*. But listening to Alice Towne, you start to think the quacking might be coming from the hospital, and other places doctors gather, like the golf course, the Mercedes showroom, the annual tiara show at Birks they take their wives to.

Towne doesn't like the pails of pills the docs dole out to moms or the tanks of laughing gas, or how they give out epidurals like realtors giving calendars. She worries about the effects on Junior. She's no fan of reaching for forceps to yank an offspring out by the brainpan if things are moving slowly. She thinks the increase in chemicals and sharp instruments to induce labour results from impatience.

Got a dinner reservation, Doc? Quack, quack.

Want to know who's getting fat from all the round bellies? Follow your hard-earned money and you end up at Dr. Rich's eight-bedroom "cottage" near Kenora—miles and miles from Alice Towne's front door.

Q&A Time:

Q: What percentage of pregnancies end with a normal vaginal delivery? (Grow up, guys—it's the name of a body part possessed by half the human race!) A: 50%.

Q: Percentage of hospital maternity patients who are healthy young gals, demanding pickles and ice cream, bodies and hormones changed alarmingly but, remember, *normally*? A: 65%.

Q: Percentage of all health system dollars spent on pregnancy and childbirth that goes to healthy little ladies and their beautiful bouncing babies? A: 38% (But I thought hospitals were for sick people.)

Q: Amount Dr. R. Rich bills medicare to glove up and catch a baby? A: $1,500—and a $200 bonus for anything tricky.

Q: Number of babies born in the province every year? A: 15,000, give or take.

Q: Annual income of an obstetrician? A: His weight in gold if he's portly, plus a government bonus every year he doesn't move to Minnesota.

Q: Alice Towne's professional income last year? A: $12,500, plus some casseroles and jars of jam from ladies who couldn't pay. (Tax Man, don't you dare!) Towne would make more if the Province ever funded midwives, but she ain't holding her breath.

Q: Is Dr. Rich hooked on high-tech? Does he push drugs like some tattooed guy by the 7-Eleven? Have pregnancy and delivery become a racket? A: I hear the ring of common sense.

My proposal for the Health Minister: break up the doctors' monopoly. Think of the millions vacuum extracted each year from this socialized health system—Dr. Rich's slice of course, but don't forget the nurses and orderlies, cleaners and clerks, the cost of converting good food into whatever they serve in hospitals, plus the drugs and drips, forceps rentals, etc., then spare a thought for Alice Towne, working every hour God sends, but wealthy only in spirit and casseroles. Mr. Minister, bring in Dr. Rich for the tricky cases, but give midwives their half of the Motherhood Pie.

Call it the birth of common sense.

The storm had not landed, despite all predictions, and if Alice said, I told you so, who could blame her? He left Dogan's column open on the table.

It gave him a lift on the path back to the shop, and then there were the earthy autumn scents and even the light, as though dawn was making an early break. Later, he'd till in the manure and plant next year's garlic—Elephant, Red Korean, Basque Turban, and Chesnok Red—then layer compost and dried leaves over top, cover the strawberries and asparagus and rhubarb, and the perennials in the butterfly garden. Tuck the garden in for winter, warm as it still was, but it was too early to start the tiller and he needed caffeine.

After eighteen hours, he was desperate for a smoke and his thoughts rattled like loose change as he watched the coffee come through. He wasn't ready to get back to his switches and lamps or the vacuum rockets, and he could not consider Mrs. Kern's pop-ups. He poured a cup and sat down with the Mūsàs in the hope they'd inspire him, take him out of himself, distract him from the blood relationship of coffee and cigarettes.

The brothers had invented a self-trimming lantern and a hurricane lamp, which wasn't half bad for the ninth century. They'd been a power duo in their day. His thoughts went to those other two, Stanley Pons and Martin Fleischmann, in Salt Lake that spring, offering a sneak peek at their unassuming cold fusion set-up to the scientifically semi-literate reporters, who, whether impressed by the crisp white lab coats or just not knowing any better, implied or declared that these two had *solved* nuclear power, found a way to harness the atom without the meltdown danger or the spent fuel rods that need storing for a hundred thousand years half a mile deep in granite. The journalists mentioned that *fusion* was the process the sun used to unlock energy but, beyond that, it had been easier to make cold fusion out as a technological revolution that would open a wonderous new age than dig a layer deeper. Few seemed aware that fusion research had a history as deep as fission research or that the Los Alamos boys had done the math on cocktail napkins in the 1940s and found that a 50-50 deuterium-tritium mix might begin fusing at 100 million degrees, which meant no earthly vessel could contain the blessed event, and they were pig-ignorant about fast pinches, kink instability and cloud chambers, or Sceptre or Tokamak or Heliotron or *Perhapsatron*, and didn't seem to know that, after the Brits cranked ZETA up to five million degrees, the Americans rolled in with their over-developed frontal cortices and competitive little souls and, for reasons of their own, lied and said the British work was full of holes and turned fusion research poison for the next thirty years. The reporters all said Pons and Fleischmann were talking about fusion at room temperature and not thermonuclear fusion at all, but most didn't twig to the fact that fusing deuterium-tritium at room temperature was as likely as setting wet grass ablaze with the heat of your breath.

God, but hadn't Theo's buddy Gerry Fittig ranted about it over pints? Gerry had come north during the war and they'd been drinking beer together ever since. He had a Ph.D. in Chemistry and said that if nuclear fusion was actually taking place in Pons and Fleischmann's lab, the gamma radiation would have been lethal and would have killed most of the grad students replicating their experiment since.

"But the grad students just will not die, all right, Theo?" he said. "Not to mention there should have been a shit ton of helium, not that they even checked for that," Gerry said. "Calling a press conference before they'd published a paper was outrageous." He was offended on behalf of his whole field.

Theo had said it was too bad, because if cold fusion worked, it could mean the end of the Hydrocarbon Age and the planet might have a chance.

"And if I had a twelve-inch dick, I'd teach it to play the piano," Gerry said. He called it all a clown show.

It could be fun winding Gerry up. Theo said maybe they'd invented some kind of catalyst.

"Oh Christ, the secret sauce," Gerry said. "The goddamned Unobtainium. Give me a break."

Theo put wood into the stove. He could build an assemblage, play with the idea of making energy the way the sun did but in your kitchen by the dishwasher. Call it *A Kid's First Cold Fusion Set* after the century's fantasy that scientific and technological advances would make life easy and limitless and handle all the consequences, or do something with balloons because of the helium. *The Mystery of the Surviving Grad Students. Twelve-Inch Dicks.*

Pons and Fleischmann's cell was simple enough: electrolysis of heavy water on a palladium electrode. Electricity split heavy water into deuterium and oxygen, the deuterium atoms crowded the palladium like undergraduates on a little dance floor, bumping, grinding, finally coupling and releasing vast, satisfied energy and tritium.

He wished he hadn't flushed his tobacco so made himself remember Barney Dogan's cigarette stench. He decided that fetching materials to build a model would be easier than sitting and craving. He had a catalytic converter that some blockhead had destroyed trying to steal from a late-model truck and the honeycomb inside had palladium, rhodium, cadmium, and gold. There was the quart-sized jar of seawater that Addy had taken from Echo Bay and guarded like the bones of Jesus the whole drive back to Manitoba, and sea water was supposed to be swimming with deuterium. He collected jumper cables and a car battery, his torch and tank, gloves, goggles, and a beaten-up aluminum ice chest from the 1950s with *Grapette Grape Soda, Imitation Grape Flavour* in raised letters.

He started with the catalytic converter: cut away the heat shield and stainless body, then excised a pencil-shaped piece of the honeycomb, attached a bulldog clip to one end and fixed it to one side of Addy's seawater jar. He clipped another bulldog to a broken chain he'd been told was platinum, set the jar into the water bath and hooked it up to the battery.

The bubbles formed, sure enough, as tiny as the ones in champagne.

Okay, and now what? He turned to get more coffee. As he filled his cup, he glimpsed the end of a cigarette peeking out from behind the coffee maker. His hand trembled as he snatched the thing up. It was brittle and hard. It would be bitter and harsh. It would fry his throat if he ever smoked it.

It was his first big test as a non-smoker. He set it on the bench, drank his coffee and watched his homely replica of the cell that had caused all the fuss. It wasn't much to look at, probably wouldn't place in an elementary school science fair, but there might be an assemblage. Maybe a Rube Goldberg machine on a cold fusion theme. Maybe denial was the original sin of homo sapiens: ignoring the fact they've good and truly screwed the planet and themselves through their greed and short-sightedness, then latching on to a proposal as unlikely as stumbling over a colony of sonnet-writing bunnies in the woods. Call it *Unicorn Shitting Rainbows*.

It wasn't every day he felt this down on the human species, and if scorn like this didn't demand he spark what was guaranteed to be the raunchiest, most violent cigarette ever smoked, nothing ever would, so he grabbed the thing and dug the lighter out of his pocket.

He smoked needfully, palliatively and holy shit how it burned, but he pulled the smoke deeply, drew its ugliness down into every secret alveolus for transfer to a billion fresh capillaries. The drug took him over, dimmed the edges of his vision. He braced himself against the bench, fingertips tingling.

He disgusted himself: the weakness of giving in to the craving, the thought of starting a project from a seat of contempt, letting a bit of stupid worry run him so that he wasted hours on shit like this when it was nearly nine and he should be in the garden.

"Fuck!" he said, and the plosive force of the F shot launched what was left of the cigarette into the Gem jar between the electrodes. It gave a tiny hiss, then floated on the seawater.

He wanted to kick something but didn't. He left the shop quickly, closed the door hard, felt the cool air on his skin and the glorious autumn sun, swore that would be his goodbye smoke and he'd start carrying pumpkin seeds, and he'd chew gum. He'd snap a rubber band on his wrist.

He'd taken three or four steps toward the house when he heard the oddest sound behind him, a blend of whoosh and thump. It stopped him and spun him around.

The door handle was hot. He turned it and a blast of heat hit like a wide palm to the face. Addy's Gem jar was scorched now, the Grapette cooler and the rubber from the jumper cables all melted, and the copper clamps misshapen. The torch and tank looked all right but the wax figures, paper and wood of Saviour Scientist were unrecognizable.

He felt Ford in the flame and, as he went for the fire extinguisher, he began to say, "What have you done?" but stopped when he heard his ridiculous, high-pitched voice.

"There's your helium, I guess," Ford said. "And to think that in these health-crazed days, the secret sauce would be burned tobacco…"

He aimed for the base of the flame.

"I mean, the key to cold freaking fusion," Ford said as the retardant hit; then, having evidently moved, "What more do you need?"

"I don't know: what say you build the damned thing yourself? Or get corporeal and give me a hand? Show yourself?"

Ford did not make fun of the chipmunk voice. He sounded serious, as he said, Oh, you're not ready for that.

9

He walked east. He walked from his hips, the way he'd learned at a St. Benedict's retreat the day the so-called Master decided he walked from his head. The guy had already said some irritating things—about some of the past lives he recalled and the infiniteness of human potential—but he'd kept his thoughts to himself because Alice was enjoying herself. Then the joke had been on him because, sure enough, the more he focused on the swing of his hips and the touch and go of his soles on the ground, the better he'd felt.

It had been a week, and today the only agenda item was a breather. Stay out of the workshop, go for coffee somewhere and take a book, walk with his hips, stay away from back lanes, look at the leaves, watch for cracks. Get his shit together and settle the fuck down, or face Alice's valerian and chamomile teas, tinctures of lavender and linden, California poppy and catnip, and she'd insist on rubbing his back with oils, even though lying on his belly would be uncomfortable because of the bananas and quinoa and spirulina. She only ever wanted to help.

Yesterday, he'd worked compost furiously into the ground, but his head had worked harder puzzling the elements, seeking connections and, as he turned the soil with his spade, his mind had ended up like a detective's crazy wall pinned with too many cards— *NASA drawings*, paper engineering, *cold fusion*, whatever Ford was, and, at the top, *End of the world?*—red yarn in knots between the elements. Burned tobacco had nothing to do with anything but maybe the rhodium mixed with the palladium in the honeycomb?

He dug, he'd soaked his shirt though, the sweat ran into his eyes, he couldn't find the edges of things and the butterflies in his belly beat like a band.

Which was when Addy and Rosemary came outside, Addy asked what the hole was for, and he realized he'd been digging in place and gone down a good metre. He'd held up a hand as if catching his breath, but he was only coming up with an answer. To admit he'd been that lost in thought seemed somehow risky, so he'd said, between breaths, that garlic liked some shade so he thought he'd put in a maple tree. The kids tagged along to the nursery and they bought a red maple thirteen feet tall, root ball the size of a Toyota, that needed a forklift to load on the trailer. It was an adventure. Alice hadn't heard of shading garlic. As he passed the maple this morning, he couldn't believe what he'd done.

By the time he reached the cathedral, the sky had lightened enough he could read some of the stones, though he'd spent enough time in the graveyard through the years he knew many of them by heart. He strolled the plots and brought what discipline he could to his thoughts, noticed the press of the earth on his soles, reread the lives chiselled into granite, slate, or marble, or ran a hand over them. *Our Olive*, with weeping willows. Ivy for faith and oak for strength, ouroboros for eternity, clasped hands promising reunion, a lamb, a shattered urn or broken sword, alpha and omega. Grander structures for a colonel or bishop, gabled, arched, pedimented, carved with doves, evergreens, and hourglasses. He tended his breath, cool as he inhaled, warm as it left him. He heard the trash-talking crows and, after a while, some of the urgency had gone.

Here was Bubbles, whose life hadn't spanned the first decade of the century. He imagined her playing on a front lawn, laughing, as her two older parents watched nervously from the stoop. A single lily beside her name, and the words, *Lord take our dearest for cherishing*, though Theo suspected they'd have liked to go on, *But, Lord, had You nothing better to do?*

He could count on this graveyard to allow a glimpse of eternity: a kind of peace always came from seeing through the sorrows and the stonemasons' claims to permanence, when, no sooner was the finest stone laid than the rain and wind got busy rounding corners, remember that stone was set on smoothness and played a long game, and that, season by season, this ground heaved and tilted, and walked itself east toward the river.

The wind gusted and unsettled the butterflies, and heaven knew why he'd remember the Judge buying the plot in Ladue so he wouldn't end up back in Ozark. His mood set the weather for everyone. God knew, he wasn't happy and, sure, he'd seen some things, survived the Bulge, his leg being only the most obvious scar. Verna said she didn't care where she was buried and maybe she really didn't.

He was at the Aleshire family plot when he remembered Elena's clumsy therapeutic inquiry into his Cold War scars the night he accidentally told everyone that his childhood self had said, *If I grow up.* At least he hadn't yabbered about the week of the Cuban Crisis when he stood in his pyjamas at his bedroom window expecting the flashes and Armageddon, stayed there for what must have been hours wondering how his parents, next room over, could possibly be sleeping.

Poor Elena. Though he ought to try the thing about sitting and feeling the earth: he'd had his doubts about walking from his hips and that was worthwhile. What if a few minutes of sitting and feeling the ground improved things another five percent? You'll see, Elena had said and, what the hell, maybe it wouldn't hurt to picture the planet as something better than an ovalish rock hurtling through the void. Maybe he'd catch some edge of the inexhaustible patience blah blah and strength blah blah.

As he got down on the ground and read Margaret Aleshire, née Sutherland, b. March 27, 1859, Renfrew County, Ontario, he doubted anyone's patience was inexhaustible. There was Margaret, second wife of Harold, thirty years older than her, planted for all eternity on his starboard side, and, even now, cordoned off from the rest of his life—the first Mrs. Aleshire and sundry Aleshire heirs. The substitute wife, as though, once widowed, the old man had had her delivered by rail with the other supplies. He hoped she'd found some happiness.

There was a first revelation—that cool dew soaked through denim—though what was done was done, and couldn't a cold, wet ass be a gift from Gaia? He closed his eyes, tried to focus on the sense of his palms against the earth and on his breath. He imagined Elena smiling when he told her.

He was about to stand and head home for dry jeans when the shock hit. The charge passed through him, contracted every muscle, pulled his arms and legs as if to remove them. When it struck, his eyes were on his sprawled right hand and he saw through it like an x-ray.

As he returned to himself, he smelled metal, wondered whether there'd actually been a yellow flash or only some retinal excitement. He was on his back, head on the curb of a neighbouring plot. He was the nearly departed, head on mortuary block, features not yet set because, though his jaw was closed, he looked up at the early sky, face tingling, body vibrating, and waited, patiently at first, puzzled, for some power of movement. He thought the sky may have brightened.

It had been like touching metal with a ground fault, but more: a lightning strike maybe, though there'd been no flash or rumble. Ball lightning or St. Elmo's fire, though the weather was wrong and he was undeniably on land. He guessed his jacket would be wicking dew now too. He could be paralyzed, he thought, *locked in*, until he blinked and moved his toes in his boots. He wondered whether the rhythmic zapping in his palms would be audible to a passerby.

He managed to rub his hands together and thought of Elena. She came to him vividly: her plain, oval face, the thick, shiny hair, arrow straight to the shoulders then curled for the last two inches, her serious grey-blue eyes. He lay on the cemetery grass and imagined telling her in a breezy way that he'd tried her butt-on-the-ground technique but caught Gaia in a foul mood.

Her eyes were horrified and his thoughts turned urgently to leaving.

He stood up and walked carefully because his knees wobbled and, beyond the graveyard gate, guessed anyone he met would take his unsteadiness and wet clothing as signs he'd had the worst kind of night. Which made him laugh until the puzzlement returned. Maybe some ferroelectric phase transition beneath him? A piezoelectric effect? Telluric current? As he tried to remember what whistlers were, he saw Elena's horror again and understood the Earth had delivered the blow herself, and when he'd gone to her as one of her children, seeking a little comfort. Her rage made him step faster.

He would miss the graveyard: it had been a refuge for years but he wouldn't be back anytime soon. He remembered a similar sadness about his bedroom after October 1962 and the Cuban Crisis, because standing at his window expecting the firestorms had ruined that for him too. He tried to pick up his pace, reassured himself that there would be safety back at the house and that it was morning, not night, he was forty, not thirteen, he wasn't paralyzed at his window in slippers, but approaching a jog in flat-soled boots. He did his best to lead with his hips and to feel the fullness of the pain in his joints, but the same picture occupied him now as it had back then: the remains of everything and everyone in charred or radiated heaps as far as the dead horizon, no one buried or mourned.

The chill had gone deeply into him so he needed a bath, but when he opened the door, the smell of Barney Dogan hit hard. Alice was rinsing cups. She seemed pleased enough to see him but in a hurry to leave. She said something about his hair and asked whether he was all right. He gave a nod he hoped would suffice, tried not to shiver as he got out of his boots.

She said Barney had been over at half past six, saying he wanted to write a book about midwives of all things. Just before seven, Rain's partner called to say her water had broken. She said, "Would you believe he asked whether he could come?"

"I think that guy's really going through something," Theo said.

She had her jacket on, her bag over her shoulder, her key ring around a finger.

She came over to say goodbye. He put his arms around her and held her and, for a moment, didn't know what he wanted more: to get out of his wet clothes or to tell her everything.

"Your jacket's soaked," she said. "You're shivering."

Both true facts, and the warmth of her breath on his neck was another fact. He should say he'd been electrocuted. He should come clean about the maple tree and tell her that Gaia had had enough. Explain that a craft could launch small but unfold larger, and tell her about palladium cells. He could start with, Hey, Alice, remember Ford?

10

The next day, after a lunch of borscht and bread, they walked to Kafka's for lemons and a few other things. It was a gem of a late autumn day, even with the wind occasionally stealing their words, and they talked about the new *Artforum* article by Nalani's friend, Jane Carver, who would always be Annie Lennox to Theo. These days, Carver taught at a college in upstate New York and wrote about Winnipeg like it was Berlin. The *Artforum* piece surveyed the contemporary Winnipeg art scene and, along the way, called Theo a prairie maverick, wrote about his machines and assemblages, ran photos of a lamp and switch and of the lately-destroyed *Saviour Scientist*.

Nalani and Ben had brought a copy for Theo last night and stayed for a bonfire. Ben was a laugh and Theo felt calmer for the company and some wine and, after they left, he'd steeled himself and gone back to disassemble the electrolytic cell. There was less damage than he'd thought and he briefly considered rebuilding *Saviour Scientist*, though the more pressing task was keeping a tight lid on his discovery about palladium and burned tobacco, if it even was a discovery, because Christ knew humanity's knack for finding the most destructive uses for new technologies stretched back at least as far as Prometheus, when no sooner had humans thanked him for the fire than they began torching the huts of anyone they'd ever had a beef with. He put Addy's seawater jar back up on its shelf, removed the hardened Grapette metal with a chisel, cut a piece of clean plywood to cover the damaged tabletop.

It had been a good evening and reason had been in the ascendant. He'd closed the workshop door, breathed the cool autumn air and looked up at what stars were visible through the light pollution. Really, what were the chances of no doubt classified drawings finding their way up here, shredded or not, and hadn't Westfalia-Werke been making small spaces bigger for decades with their lifting camper van roofs? For all he knew, the Mūsà Brothers had made pop-up books a thousand years ago. Occam's razor, the law of parsimony, etc. Dollars to doughnuts, what had felt like electric shocks in the cemetery probably had to do with a B12 deficiency.

Two blocks from Kafka's, they stopped to talk with an old woman raking leaves. She was ninety if she was a day. She worked slowly, steadily. Theo listened as Alice passed the time of day with her, and wondered again how to tell Alice everything she needed to know. So, babe, remember my birthday? or, You know NASA, right? or, Maybe those chemists in Utah were onto something after all…

Across Powers, a child had set out to draw the longest hopscotch in history, drawn the first squares and numbers carefully in yellow and pink chalk, though, after twenty, resorted to sketching boxes and scrawling digits, but it went into the eighties. Alice told him that Gracie's youngest, Kaylin, was starting with a tutor, though the problem obviously wasn't Kaylin but that battle-axe Mrs. Lamont, who had taught Addy second grade and had to deal with Alice at parent conference time. Alice said next thing you knew, Kaylin would be *put on drugs* for the convenience of the school. Sometimes Alice's certainty was a lot.

Leaning into common sense before bed last night hadn't prevented another shitty sleep, and he'd spent most of the night in an agitated twilight state subjected to another dumb theme, like a nursing home resident trapped listening to variety shows put on by volunteers—*By the Sea, Catch Me If You Can, Autumn Leaves*. Last night's program could have been called *Date With Destiny* and the volunteers had covered a lot of ground: events of the past week of course, but also the aphorism about the two most important days of your life that people insisted on misattributing to Mark Twain, flashbacks to fifth grade and his identification as *exceptional* by Eisenhower's NDEA along with other bright and, it would be noted later, mostly white, children for the sake of taking the fight to the

Soviets by bolstering the nation's intellectual and technological horsepower. He'd sat between Verna and the Judge as the officials sold them on their plan to weaponize him to fight the Cold War, but gave no pointers on how to feel any less like a visitor from another galaxy among his cognitively average grade peers less interested in learning math than racing to the water fountains at recess, and who looked blankly at him when he spoke, as though his voice ran at 600 THz instead of 100-250 Hz. His parents had nodded and the Judge ruffled his hair like he'd finally done something good, but he was no clearer about how to handle certain teachers' antipathy toward a child unlucky enough to know more than they did. Fucking destiny. He'd tossed and turned and the volunteers sang their hearts out. It had been a long night. He'd given up on sleeping well before Alice got home from delivering Rain's baby.

They were a block from Main when he noticed that Alice was facing squarely ahead as she spoke instead of turning toward him every few words and giving tiny nods. It occurred to him that she'd been doing this for a while, which meant something must be wrong. At least he'd come up for air before she noticed he hadn't been listening.

Now she was stopping to face him, squeezing his hand, and saying this time something really was wrong: her heart had been racing for no reason, doing cartwheels when she was resting. She said she'd made an appointment with Jill.

"Okay, better safe than sorry, right?" he said because there was no point saying anything else. Her mother had had her heart attack in early November and she'd worried every year around this time, checked in with Dr. June and Dr. Bob and got back on coconut water and hibiscus, hawthorn and cat's claw, then finally caved and went to see *Jill*, aka Dr. Yashchyshyn, because, as an *allopathic physician*, she might lack all holistic understanding and confuse healing with prescription of pharmaceuticals, but she could order an EKG.

"This is not about my mom," she said. "In case you're interested, I've been short of breath." She started walking again.

"Alice, go see Jill, but trust me, you've got the heart and lungs of a cheetah."

She said she'd been *irked* when Dr. Y.'s office gave her a Thursday morning appointment when she'd just said she saw her own patients that day. She only ever said *patient* when she was talking about Dr. Y., who surely winced when she saw Alice's name on the chart outside an examining room.

On their left, a couple of doors from Main, Darwin and some of his guys sat perched like potted plants along the stone bed of the blue two-storey. They smoked and cradled their early afternoon beers, had tunes playing in the front window. Darwin had a horseshoe moustache and always wore a black helmet silk. He definitely called the shots. Last spring he'd bought a camshaft lamp and Theo'd brought it by.

"Theo," he said and gave a nod.

"Darwin."

"Ma'am," Darwin said to Alice. "Beautiful day." This was organized crime community relations.

Fifty metres on, they were on the curb waiting to cross Main. There was a stalled pickup a half block south, so the traffic was crawling. A rusty Chevette was signalling into the median lane: the woman driving it saw space in front of a new Buick, but wasn't about to risk it without eye contact. The guy in the Buick pretended not to notice and, when the Chevette lady gave the politest beep of her horn, he edged forward and adjusted his stereo. He looked to be in his early fifties. He was fair-skinned, freckled, wore sideburns and square sunglasses, and had rings on three thick fingers of the hand draped over the wheel. He looked like an asshole. He looked like he golfed. The car was one of the new, longer, heavier Rivieras designed to reverse the downsizing trend of the past few years. Polished copper over silver. The full vinyl roof.

"Are you seeing this?" Theo said as he stepped through the curb lane and in front of the Riviera as the traffic started to move. He held a palm up to the asshole and waved the Chevette in. The guy swore and leaned on the horn, took off his sunglasses. The Chevette pulled in tentatively, gave a little wave.

Now Theo tried to direct Alice across like a school patrol, but she stayed put on the curb. The shiny grille of the Riviera touched his knees now. The guy was a lizard: shirt collar over the blazer lapel, top buttons of his shirt undone, chains. Bob Guccione.

"Get the fuck off the road!" Gucc roared.

"Try cooperating, asshole!"

"Theo!" Alice shouted.

"Get away from my car!" Gucc was spitting now. Theo counted three heavy chains. Seventies hair, fists like meat mallets.

Theo waved another car in. The pickup behind the Riviera honked.

"Hey, Alice, go, okay?" he said but kept his eyes on Guccione. He knew she was going to be furious.

Gucc revved the thirsty motor and tail-braked, leaned on the horn again. Theo leaned into the bumper.

"You clown. I am warning you."

"What are you going to do, Guccione?"

"Theo, stop!" Alice shouted.

Theo flicked the Buick's hood ornament and Gucc lost his mind. Undid his seatbelt and jumped out of the car, slipped out of his blazer and laid it on the seat. He was big. He turned the rings around on his fingers. He looked like someone who loved to jam fat fingers into other guys' chests. He began to close the distance.

Theo took a long, slow breath, let his eyes hover around Gucc's shoulders.

"Theo, what the hell?" Alice was saying, nearly shrieking. A yellow car in the curb lane hit its brakes, which meant she was finally crossing. He guessed it might be too late for this to end without a fight.

The yellow car started forward. Gucc looked to his right, paused, straightened. Alice was saying, "No, no, it's all right."

So Theo looked and saw Darwin with his boys. The boys seemed to want off of their leashes.

"So how are things, Theo?" Darwin said. We heard a ruckus.

"Fine, fine," Theo said and turned back to Guccione. "Just reminding this asshole he's not the only one on the road."

"So that's how it's going to be," Gucc said.

"Idiots!" Alice screamed. She grabbed Theo's arm and dragged him to the far side.

"How about you be on your way then?" Theo heard Darwin tell Gucc. It was chilling.

"You think I wanted to stop?" Gucc said. "That jackass there…"

Alice dragged Theo onto the boulevard. Theo saw Darwin glare Gucc back into his luxury car. Alice pulled him across the northbound lanes. Once they were on the far curb, she faced him squarely.

"Forget Darwin," he said. "*That's* a frightening look." But it was no time for lightness.

"What the actual fuck?" she said.

"Well, you reach a limit."

"What limit?" she said.

Which was a good question, and he considered it. What limit? Lounge lizards in new Rivieras with too many buttons undone. Winnipeg drivers who refused to give breaks, whose unwillingness ran deeper than simple small-c conservative selfishness and had the brawn of religious conviction, as though giving someone something for free was a sin because it interfered with the recipient's salvation. Or the limit reached was this week or this awful, beautiful time of year.

They were in and out of Kafka's: this was always the goal because Kafka's was an unsettling place and the feeling rubbed off. The uniquely miserable checkers who'd been there for decades, the ugly, yellow light and lifting linoleum, the carts beat to shit, wheels seized or wobbling, an unmistakable, inexplicable odour. They'd called it Kafka's since the day they searched high and low for baking soda and couldn't find help, though they'd glimpsed staff at the far ends of aisles and heard scraps of voices like the ones in nightmares. They'd sensed people up behind the one-way glass but waving had not helped. They'd finally given up and gone for the door, then stumbled over a half-dozen boxes of Arm and Hammer by the packaged cookies.

Theo loitered up front as Alice went to get the lemons. When he saw October 27 on the *Free Press*, his stomach dropped, because this was the day in 1962 when the Soviets hit Major Tom Anderson with an anti-aircraft missile over Cuba and another U-2 had entered Soviet airspace. Kennedy had played fast and loose with every life on the planet. He got his mind off of the date by finding an update on Pasadena, Texas. Five bodies recovered before an isobutane leak stopped the search for another seventeen. McDonnell Douglas had won a $146.9-million contract extension from the U.S. Army for experiments with ground-based surveillance and tracking systems. It never ended with these people: Americans not going to war would be like crows giving up their grudges.

They left and walked west. They didn't touch or talk. They avoided Luxton, which was Darwin's street. Now each step was a chore and he could have lain down on the boulevard. He guessed it was the date, or the fire in Texas or the near-dust-up with Gucc or the refrains of *Date with Destiny* and guessing you could mistake a siren song for a calling and miss the point of your life. He'd been with Alice for twenty years and never been able to express the full horror of October 1962, how near the leaders had come to turning the world to ash and vapour. There were times he envied her Canadian naiveté.

Alice was looking at him and waiting. He listened for some echo of what she'd said. He thought maybe there'd been a quiver in her voice.

"What?" he said.

Her eyes were fierce. "You're a thousand miles away. You're off in space."

"Oh really?"

"The hostility."

"Off in space," he said. "Talk about hostile."

11

You can be minding your own business, enjoying your thirteenth birthday supper at Busch's Grove, feeling for all the world like you've made a quantum leap toward adulthood in your new suit with the pocket square, you and the Judge having left the ladies in the dining room and gone through to the Men's Bar. The Judge's friends shake your hand and you say, Why, thank you very much, sir, then stand with your glass and nod along with the things they say, or chuckle, though you don't get all the jokes, and you don't even mind when the Judge shows you off like a circus monkey. Go ahead, ask him a math question, he says. Or anything about science. But then Omar will turn on the set behind the bar, the President will announce the end of the world, and whatever purchase you have is gone, and, as you free fall, it occurs to you that things have been wobbly enough, for long enough, that you should have seen it coming, though chiding yourself is only another kind of flailing. It won't even matter that, six days later, October 28, on the Sunday, Chairman Khrushchev will tell Radio Moscow he's bringing the missiles home because, even as the world breathes its sigh, you know the ending's still as certain as night following day.

Times like that, the wheel is unmistakable. The round and round of it. The recurrence has the septic scent of eternity. Maybe, in times like those or like these ones now, you could even name it if you stopped trying to scramble clear.

How easy, for instance, to prove the idiocy of Ford's proposal?

"Request," Ford said. "It's a request."

97

Demonstrate the full impossibility.

The point is, you've seen it all before, and the repetition is awful until another side pipes up and claims that destiny or fate, or the wheel are made-up things, and that you've made them to distract from the precariousness of your little arrangement with Alice and Addy, that they let you forget that everything depended on the wings of a milkweed butterfly on an Okinawa island waving twice instead of once. Without some plan or guiding hand, the accidents stab like shivs: that you could as easily have turned left instead of right that night in Taos and never laid eyes on Alice, that if one of a hundred things had been otherwise in October 1962, creation would have ended, not to mention the immeasurable unlikelihood of that exact dust and those particular gasses coagulating when they did and where by chance alone, so this unremarkable spheroid chunk had to fall into orbit around a middling star. In other words, necessity may frighten the life out of you, but the unconditioned jumble is worse and the *what-ifs* will be the death of you.

October 28, 1989 was a Saturday, and something had to give. The house echoed, not only because Alice was gone and wouldn't be back any time soon, a woman called Beth having woken to soaked bedding and the first of her worst pains, but because of the new space between them, so her leaving had durability, and because there was no counting on Addy to drop by. Theo had woken feeling lost and Alice felt it too, though she didn't say and only pretended she was in a rush and took her tea and toast to go. Beth's travails had spared them an awkward morning. The prospect of a Saturday with the house to himself was alarming so he made a run for it. At least Moose was restless too, padding back and forth on the dining room windowsill.

He pedalled them south to start, for no reason except to be moving, then followed boulevard signs to last-of-the-season garage sales. East onto College to the first one, back south to the next, then east, north a few blocks, and west over a crumbling back lane. He followed every sign, whether done carefully in bright markers and stapled to a fresh stake or scrawled in ballpoint on a pizza box lid so the address was illegible from farther than a metre, or taped to a light pole with sagging balloons or to some unwilling tree. Just now, letting accident hold the whip hand countered the inevitability, felt something like liberation. He browsed every makeshift shelf and picnic blanket in his practiced way, flipped through magazines in crates, chatted if the sellers wanted. Moose kept his place in the buggy, snoozed or took in the sun, unworried.

There was an out-of-plumb carport, where a serious couple tried to sell scented candles and old shoes. There were car lot streamers strung back and forth over a pair of lawns on Dalton Street, small children running merrily under the red and yellow triangles, in and out of a pup tent, and two sales moms sipped mimosas and cracked one another up. When a man offered eight dollars for a Miracle Jesus action figure and a Barrel of Monkeys, they laughed through their haggling, settled on ten and high fived, refilled their glasses. Theo looked at a philosophy textbook with the Spinoza chapter cut out, a coffee table book called *Tornado Alley*, a dozen reel-to-reel spools in a shoebox and a meditation tape called *Settle Your Mind!* When he reached two pairs of edible underwear, grape-flavour and cinnamon, in their packages, one of the moms said they were open to offers and her friend couldn't speak for laughing. The preschoolers squealed under the loveliest sky. The proprietor of a sale in a cramped basement wore a turquoise pant suit, pulled hard on her cigarette, and, when he said hello, her eyes didn't leave the talking Sani-Foam sponge commercial on the TV.

By the time they reached the CP rail yard, they'd been on the move for two and a half hours. The buggy was empty but for Moose, but then buying had never been the point. He stood the Roadmaster by the curb. Moose hopped down to browse the tall grass at the base of an elm. Theo fetched the water and set out a bowl and knew his heart wasn't racing because of the pedalling, though he'd kept a pace and covered some ground, but because the dread had forced it faster as he scrambled back and forth between accident and inevitability, avoided one by seeking the other. He'd stayed on the move, leaned hard into whatever randomness there could be in the sale signs, even as the impossibility of ever really giving up control smacked his face and betting that if he plotted the morning's path on an Etch A Sketch, he'd see a weeping Jesus in the jumble.

He fetched the Saturday *Province* from a pannier pocket. Someone had weighted it to a bus bench with a piece of brick and he'd taken it because that idiot, Dogan, had put out another column. Moose strolled with essential ease. He *was the strolling*, as one of Alice's gurus had put it, so as Theo leaned against the rail yard chain link and under the three-wire corner barbed wire arms, he thought, *I am the reading of a tabloid.*

The standard sitcom episode about childbirth always ends at the hospital. *I Love Lucy* was an early example, and so was Maxwell Smart rushing 99 to the ER but getting lost because he used a KAOS map by mistake. And *All in the Family*, where Archie and Edith made it there before Gloria, who was stuck in a phone booth. Arch was still in blackface because his lodge brothers had hidden the cold cream. Even last November, Sondra had her baby on *Cosby*. Getting to the hospital is part of the formula: panicked hubby, go bag hanging over a shoulder, racing the little lady's wheelchair toward Maternity, so she can get busy with the pushing and hubby can pass out on the delivery room floor.

And since there's a hospital, there's going to be a doctor. On cue, that fellow struts to centre stage, very slightly behind the gloved hands he's holding up, to catch the little nipper and hand it to the nurse.

It's the way of the world, right? Baby decides it's time, some baffled folks careen toward the hospital, and Doc Rich steps up for his solo.

Or is it? Does it need to be?

On Thursday, I suggested the Health Minister make room for midwives in the Baby Biz. Have midwives handle some of the healthy pregnancies and normal birthing, and let Dr. Rich handle the trickier deliveries and C-sections. I pitched it as a matter of common sense.

Since then, the doctors' shorts have been in knots. From all the bluster, you'd think I'd proposed banning golf courses or the Mercedes S-Class. Since Thursday, someone's gotten worried about giving up part of the motherhood pie.

A few loyal readers have written to ask whether midwife Alice Towne cast a witchy spell and collapsed my common sense. If you read my column Thursday and said, Well Peg, old Barney's lost his marbles, you weren't alone.

Worry not, dear Reader. I still live on Reality Street and don't go out without my Q8778 Bullsh*t Detector. I still take the long way around certain gassy, gumdrop, hippie-dippie hoods, and I still don't fear hairy-legged man-haters. The Liberal-leaning CBC remains a foreign land, and I still don't think twice about taking the Beautiful People of Ottawa down a notch when they need it. I keep simple things simple, I spare you the broadsheet bull.

Baby, I've got news for you!

Yes, I clenched a little when Alice Towne said *medical-industrial complex* in a sentence, but the needle on my Q8778 did not move. I saw no reason to doubt that she'd wanted to deliver babies since she was a little girl, though, yes, when she said she'd transferred from nursing school to midwife training because nursing didn't *feed her soul*, and the Q8778 needle still didn't budge, I admit I checked the batteries. Ditto when she claimed to be content as a midwife, despite the lack of bread, other than loaves baked by grateful mothers and mothers-to-be.

I do not know the best way for a newborn to meet his mama, or the effects, better and worse, of the pharmaceuticals he ingests on the way, or of his being hauled from her insides with forceps by a guy in a mask, versus brought into the world by a kindly lady humming a lullaby. I do not know because I'm neither a lady nor a psychologist, but I'm inclined to give the nod to Mrs. Towne, since she's obviously forgotten more about birthing than most of us will ever know.

One way or another, the water always breaks, the baby falls and crowns. What's wrong with asking who the system ought to hire to help with normal deliveries?

And don't worry about TV: you leave out the parts about the hospital and the doctor and you've still got the full range of mood swings and the pickles and ice cream, and the little lady swearing like a sailor at hubby for doing this to her, squeezing his hand and breaking bones, and Dr. Rich by his phone like the Maytag repairman.

The power lines and the long, slow cracks of Selkirk Avenue converged toward their vanishing point in the west. He was up and pacing again. Thinking was perilous, so he went with *I am the seeing*, as that other touring guru had taught. Do not think of yourself as a person drinking water; rather, *be the drinking*, she'd said and jingled the bangles on her wrists. The thirsty seekers had nodded, and he'd whispered in Alice's ear, *I'm about to be the barfing*, but somehow the lesson had stuck, like the one about walking and, when he remembered, really could coax him out of his head for a while.

The long line of beige and brown bungalows across the street seemed deserted. He imagined the view from one of their front windows—the rail yard fence, the berm that didn't hide the tops of the boxcars—then told himself, I am the pointless thinking about about other people's homes, I'm the deflection of responsibility for messing things up in my own home, hurting Alice, who, way back when, should not have given me a second look.

Which was when it occurred to him that heading home and smoking a bowl might just settle the butterflies.

Time to saddle up, though Moose was stalking blackbirds twenty yards up the boulevard. He called, but Moose pounced anyway. He rarely missed. The other birds took to the air. Moose paused, jaws closed, paws holding the bird down, then stood and trotted further away, the injured blackbird in his mouth, one wing outstretched, pleading.

I am the witnessing. I'm the useless attempt to catch a cat.

He watched from his place by the chain link. Moose released the bird, batted it with a paw, body slammed it again. His ministrations involved no decision or higher calling. As *felis catus*, he was no more *called* to these rites than to ignoring the interests of his humans, and what looked like sadism was only an instinct to exhaust his prey to make the final spinal cord severing safer. You had to envy the easy patience and uncomplicated focus, the never having to fret about callings and accidents. This could take a while. He wished he'd bought a magazine at one of the sales. He wished he hadn't stopped smoking. He wished his breathing would pick a rhythm.

Asking *What if* had to be an instinct of *homo sapiens*: getting into a lather about roads not taken, as in, what if he'd sucked up his fear about the Judge and his men and couch-surfed until his exams were done, then slipped away to grad school? Would he be teaching thermodynamics to undergraduates now, or knocking together new plastics for Phillips and most of the way to paying off the split-level he'd bought with some comely Texas girl? What if he'd bumbled his way to Racine, Wisconsin and spent the past twenty years making smoked cold pack cheese instead of coming to Winnipeg to browse through people's garbage, or what if the last time he called home—the night he hit the bottom of the bottom—what if he'd followed Verna's voice like a long, long thread back to Ladue? Then where would they all be in this great interconnected Web of Being? He never would have met Alice so there'd be no Addy, and if the Kansas State Trooper had looked closer at his Ronald Lyle ID, he'd have spent two years folding laundry in Leavenworth instead of continuing north with Alice and a newborn. What if he'd paused one bloody second before he emptied his sock and underwear and T-shirt drawers into Grandma Maggie's old leather grip and asked himself whether splitting now really was righteous flight from inevitable politically motivated persecution or whether he was about to leap to a higher quantum of Theo Strahl bizarreness and disappointment?

Such questions are a protest, as in, Why, God, why? because you don't expect an answer, and the central problem with *callings*, he thought or maybe said aloud, was their unreality, because there were only accidents, interests and drives, temperament and opportunity, choices, and mistakes. Still, how lovely would it be to catch a few words on some spring breeze and know that *just one thing* had been necessary and that he could not as easily have gone over to Malmö, Sweden and met Ayla instead of Alice and had a daughter named Astrid? What you'd give for some transcendent hint to tame this dread.

You want *What ifs*, asshole? What if you hadn't slashed the Judge across the chest with a steak knife? How about that, and while we're at it, why have you never had the nuts to tell Alice? Fair questions.

He'd told her plenty, probably gone on too long about suppertime and how the Judge flashed the uglier sectors of his soul. She knew there'd been trouble at the end but he'd left the knife out and how he'd slashed broadly through the air and cut the Judge's chest and gotten away, and of course she knew nothing about his horror, three or four weeks later at the dead end of a wooded path off of a spur highway near Alvo, Nebraska, once it occurred to him suddenly that the argument might have had no more life and death import than the squabbling of any other son convinced the old man had the convictions of mashed potatoes and father who'd had it up to here with his kid questioning anyone over thirty, and that maybe the Judge never had thought about reaching for the knife, except to take custody of it since his boy had evidently lost his whole shit. Alice knew nothing of the chill that came with wondering that night near Alvo whether he'd known, even in the instant he snatched the knife off of the table, that what he was about to do was the farthest thing from self-defence and inferring *mens rea* was easy as pie, as would be showing malice aforethought.

Alice knew that he refused to set foot south of the US border, even after Carter pardoned the Vietnam draft dodgers, so-called, and invited them back home and, to her credit, she hadn't pushed. She did not know how certain he'd been ever since that, had he ever gone back to Ladue, the Judge would have found the elements for second-degree assault, if not attempted murder, and she'd had no cause to wonder how much of what kept him north of the border was fear of felony prosecution versus shame at leaving both of his parents' lives forever when his mother hadn't been the problem. For his part, he hadn't needed to insist to her that his flight from the jurisdiction and changing his appearance and his identification were reasonable responses and didn't signal consciousness of guilt, nor to deny that May 13 had been awful for two decades because it was his mother's birthday.

No, he was trying like the dickens to be the pedalling but succeeding only in being the relentless chattering about callings and how there was no such thing as a calling. Collecting Moose had taken time. He was not easily rushed, and would not consider leaving until he'd stared at Theo, snipped the bird's head off and let its body fall like the remains of a prisoner whose hangman miscalculated the drop. At last, he was the desperate pedalling, he was the attempt to outdistance his faint-heartedness. Moose was in his place again, enjoying the ride, unconcerned about the thin line of blackbird arterial spray on the white fur beneath his chin. Though he wanted to be the pedalling, he was *the noticing* that if the Judge hadn't enrolled in Grandpa August's class at Missou and never met Verna, or the sniper had got him instead of his Major, or Grandpa Strahl hadn't fallen out with Billy Sunday's people so close to Ozark and if he hadn't met Alice that night in Taos, there simply would be no Addy, and there was nothing to do in the face of such noticing but pedal harder. How could you respect a universe in which inevitability is always only backdated and the only available certainty comes with the use of the past tense? What chance did future songbirds have against all the pesticides in a universe so lacking in conviction?

He pedalled and pedalled in the hope of outrunning the scenarios and their puffs of adrenalin, then finally stopped to return what little was left of his breakfast to the ground from which it had accidentally come.

Those kids had the devil's luck, he thought as he bumped down the lane to the shop and he tasted the same envy he did in sixth grade when he longed for the simple faith of any other child in his class, to accept as self-evident the notions that God was American and things would be fine if the Commies tried some dirty sneak attack because *the Authorities* had worked everything out, and all they needed to do was to practise the drills. None of them telegraphed the slightest doubt, so, when, at recess, he corrected some factual inaccuracy in what that fool Larry Arbore had said, or pointed out a logical problem, he might as well have said it in some click-consonant Khoisan language the way they went back to whatever game and played their uncomplicated little hearts out. What he'd have given not to know the government and the grownups were lying and that there simply were no defences. Christ, but to have grown up straightforwardly.

Opening the lock on the back door should have been the easiest thing in the world, but his fingers had gone rogue.

"Breathe," Ford said once they were inside.

This time Ford came as no surprise. Nor did Moose scrambling back out the big doors.

Ford said, "You trod a funny path but, trust me, you were always on your way here."

He raced through the garden to the house as though Ford couldn't keep up, and he tried to settle once and for all on which was worse—that this moment had always been certain or only as likely as the laughing Jesus scribbled by the billionth monkey. He pulled the storm door open and some dumb part of him demanded he choose—guiding hand or accident—and another wondered what it mattered since fundamental realities weren't things you adjusted. He couldn't bear stopping, so stepped up into the kitchen with his boots on, *like an American*, Alice would say, then saw the newspapers open on the dining room table and stopped cold, unable to conceive of how they'd gotten there until he noticed the empty cup there too and how the turntable cover had been left open, and then, suddenly, missing Addy's visit was the greatest calamity of all.

He set the needle down on *All Things Must Pass*, heard the opening of "I'd Have You Anytime." There was George on the cover, on his chair in the field, the hat, the hair, the big boots. To think that this most blessed of Beatles had hidden in plain sight for a decade, then revealed himself fully in this triumphant triple record. He lit the bowl, the raunch felt good in his throat, and he held the smoke, focused on *being the toke*, did his best to ignore Ford and what sounded like tsk-tsking. He pulled hard on the pipe, guessed missing Addy's visit was the latest in a long series of missteps in a life fallen so short of its potential. He turned up the music.

"My Sweet Lord" came on and the weed deepened the twelve-string opening, dampened his thoughts and judgments. George's slide guitar and his call, *My sweet Lord*, plaintive, yearning to know God directly, longing to see and feel Him, the choir singing its Hallelujahs, the little waver in George's voice like a candle flame just glanced by the edge of a draft. The yearning, the rich, rising chant of *Hare Krishna* and the Guru Mantra, guru, remover of darkness, guide toward the path of truth, toward the inner guru. The swell sound and passion lifted him like a hundred hands, and he could almost see the woven flowers on their wrists and the tambourines, the petals moving with the zills. That great Guru, the essence of all living and nonliving things, pervading the universe. My sweet Lord, My Lord.

The track faded, then stuck, repeated *Krishn... Krishn...*, and he felt a sharp pain at the end of his thumb. *Krishn... Krishn...* How this could happen when he was so careful with his albums, and he was standing to rescue the record when he noticed the bit of the pipe hovering two centimetres from his lips and the Zippo flame over the bowl, waiting to be drawn down, burning his thumb.

"Are you nearly done?" Ford said.

He flipped the lighter closed, tended to the turntable, put on "Wah-Wah" and went back to Addy's newspapers. Jim Bakker, moving to a prison in Minnesota, while his pal Pat Robertson bought his PTL network. Three paragraphs about the clean-up in Pasadena, which were grim but no more so than the world's turtle population dropping to critical.

Then, at last, he read that National Guardsmen were hunting for the man who abducted eleven-year-old Jacob Wetterline in St. Joseph, Minnesota last Sunday. Jacob had been walking with his brother and a friend when a man with a gun jumped out of the woods. So he thought of Addy at that age, walking and laughing with Cornbread, and then some asshole with a mask and an adrenalin tsunami moved through and destroyed everything. *Blind panic*, he managed to think.

"Why is panic blind?" he thought.

"You're so stoned," Ford said.

Which was true, but hardly the point, because he felt worse than he'd ever felt in his life, and he guessed there were emergencies in the course of a person's unfolding, then thought of roadmaps unfolding and a carpet runner unrolling and emergencies like tangled yarn, so lost the point, except for the part about emergencies leaving marks, though you might not appreciate how deeply for a couple of decades. In a way, everything and all of this went back to the night he stood at his bedroom window at the pool, barely coping by wondering whether he'd see the water in it boil before the firestorm took him.

"At least drink some water," Ford said, which was reasonable.

When he woke at the kitchen table, head on his hands, he tried to think about accidents again and the decisions you take or don't but he knew perfectly well what came next.

The house was silent. The wind had subsided and a fever had broken. The water jug had come to room temperature. He drank water and felt taller, more self-assured. Ready. He was as clear as the autumn sky through the window.

Had Noah woken from an afternoon nap feeling the same inevitability settled over him like a layer of dust, the same destiny? Did he feel this resigned, and this pissed at a god whose workmanship was shitty enough His world could come to this? Of course there never was a Noah.

He poured more water.

"So what *are* you anyway?" he said. Saying *what*, and not *who*, felt good.

"You know," Ford said.

"No. I really don't think so."

"I'm nothing."

"You sound like something, and I need to see."

Ford was uncomfortable. "You don't want that," he said.

"Yeah, I do," he said with a sturdiness. "A guy's got to know what he's dealing with."

"You really don't."

"A little theophany: it's not a lot to ask. Do you have wings, or are you more of a burning bush sort of thing? You don't sound like an angel who tussles, though, if you are, I think I can take you."

"You have so much work to do."

"Look, if there's any urgency here, it's not mine. I'll wait if you need to set shit up." The right side of his mouth had curled into a snarl. He liked the feeling of it. He said, "I can wait all day," and it occurred to him the Judge would have called it *contumacy*.

The silence was profound. He'd waited so long for the wind to die.

Finally, he heard Ford sigh. He followed the sound to a spot near the back landing.

When he saw, he said, "Fuuuuuck," because the thing was as ugly as any shame. Small, bent, almost bowed, and in a partial squat. The most featureless face. Small, dark eyes that seemed to wince. A few hairs on the scalp. Its arms hung like dead things from rubbery shoulders. The skin was pale, sickly in the light, waxy in places, then blotchy pink, as though it had been scraped. Then, between bruised or dysplastic hips, the ugliest, pointy thing, too small to hang. Ford looked chilly.

Theo whistled and made his eyes flinty. He said, "Guess you weren't kidding. I could have gone my whole life without seeing this."

"All right?"

"You do not fill a room with glorious light. And what is that smell? Did you poop yourself?" He needed to be cruel more than he needed oxygen.

"Satisfied?" Ford said.

"I'm not satisfied."

12

At least it was settled, and shouldn't that be something? Wasn't equivocation the neck of the funnel, and shouldn't he be bold now? He did feel a grudging clarity and, once Ford terminated his inglorious manifestation, he pulled the back door closed behind him hard enough that it felt good, and charged through the garden and through the workshop door. Now it should be a matter of planning the work and working the plan, which sounded simple enough. He draped Grandma Maggie's blanket over his shoulders against the chill and sat waiting to take instructions for the evacuation of the tiddliest sample of humanity and its world before the rest choked or died of thirst or abruptly annihilated itself.

Ford was there all right, which meant Moose would be a mile away. The presence was plain, but without the odour, thank God.

"Okay, if we're doing this," Theo said, because the impressions were mounting an assault: little, disconnected inklings about turbulent combustion, ratios of power and weight, components shattering from pressure and speed, or bending, the importance of cooling, and others. The impressions wanted wrangling.

"Ford!" he said, because it was obviously impossible again. "How is this supposed to work?"

"*Patientia comes est sapientiae.*"

"*Patientia* the fuck."

"Just take it step by step."

"Oh, just that, huh?"

110

"You learned the science as an undergraduate. You topped your class, or you would have if you'd stayed for the exams."

"And what's your job exactly?" he said, but the asshole had left. He guessed the thing now was to get outside and look for Moose.

He drove across town to the Science and Technology Library at the University, because it was something at least when the work was vast and lacked edges, scaled over the horizon. How do you shake test a rocket thirty-stories tall, liquid fuels versus solid, unnumbered parts to build and triple-check? Maybe just list some broad areas for reading. Maybe find an account of how Apollo rolled out, but how many hundreds of engineers, chemists, welders, and you-name-it going belt and suspenders with redundancies, and a thousand programmers writing Christ knew how many lines of code, and all of it without the military-industrial complex for a leg up, and never mind the non-trivial challenge of leaving and never coming back, and bone loss over time. Compared with this, Noah's Ark was easy as shelling peas, not to mention Noah'd never had to exist beyond his myth, was no more real, in the meat and bone sense, than Hansel or Gretel.

And the crap about learning the engineering as an undergraduate? Of course he'd picked up the odd thing, despite himself, and how the Judge loved to say, You don't have to be a rocket scientist, like Theo here, but, if anything, he'd done his best not to think about Apollo, unlike all the other students and half the faculty who were high as kites on it. Back then he'd called the Space Race another Cold War front, like Berlin or Vietnam, inveighed against that reprobate Wernher von Braun and the U.S. government for smuggling him and his Nazi minions across after the war.

"Where there's a war, there's a way," he'd said, thinking himself clever and saluting certain classmates on how well they'd balanced on the epauletted shoulders of the SS Majors and Joint Chiefs Generals. He'd made no friends among those pencil heads, normal and diligent as Adolph Eichmann and who'd never heard of Hannah Arendt, much less read her, because space was in the air and of course science was awesome and, yes, the old Nazi really had hit it out of the park with Saturn V—363 feet high, two million parts, three stages, seven million pounds of thrust—but none of them could conceive of doing evil without being evil.

He made the library an hour before closing, grateful for that much time because the impressions really did need confinement to paper. He looked for an overview of building the Shuttle—orbiter, external tank, boosters—something that summarized the main areas—rocket propulsion, thermal control, etc.—if not their branches, the engines and thrusters, propellants, tankage, and never mind the branchlets for the moment, or the multitudinous twigs, any one of which could be the focus of a dozen careers.

The surprises of the hour were seeing how little progress there'd been in rocket design in twenty years, how NASA's rockets still weren't much better than fireworks you lit once and threw away, and how the national space agencies weren't quite the centre of mass they used to be. NASA's mayfly run at pimping the Shuttle to Industry as a reliable, low-cost pickup truck for space had flopped, and never before had so bloated and wheezing an organization pitched as dangerous and inefficient a widget, so maybe the new private concerns were the ones to watch.

He was back on campus Sunday and most of the next week. He watched for Addy and any of his friends but he had a cover story rehearsed. He claimed an out-of-the-way carrel, as he had back at WashU, sat for hours reading and filling page after fresh, lined yellow page and, by mid-week, if anything seemed remotely promising, it was rocketry because he remembered a bit of that. He read and sketched and practised some calculations and caught a whiff of the magic he'd felt decades ago, as when he read about a de Laval nozzle shoving the products of energetic reactions through its asymmetric hourglass, accelerating fluid to supersonic speeds and converting thermal energy into kinetic and found himself wondering all over again whether the throat could be adjustable to vary output, reshape the plume for the altitude and, that way, maybe linger in some sweet spot between under- and over-expansion. He read about hybrid fuel engines and how they seemed to avoid the downsides both of liquid fuel engines and ones that ran on solids and hypergolics, and there were moments when he thought maybe a modestly creative person with some common sense and 99.9% of an Engineering degree actually could design a better rocket.

On Thursday, as he read over derivations of the classical rocket equation—popular, impulse, acceleration—he noticed again that there was only so far you could go with designing a craft without a destination in mind. Any hint about that would have hit the spot.

Ford had been frustratingly oracular since the weekend.

"A jug fills drop by drop," was the sort of thing he said now, and when Theo suggested it wasn't so much a jug as a 10,000-gallon welded steel tank, there'd been nothing more.

"The real question is, What am I here to learn?" Ford said.

That time Theo said, "You're becoming less awesome by the minute. Maybe don't come around unless you've got something useful to contribute, like, for instance, how to tell Alice and Addy," because so far, whether he imagined saying it all at once or in a series of bite-sized pieces, telling them together or separately, at night or out strolling in daylight, Alice's eyes always went wide and her brows were arched and the right corner of Addy's mouth rose the way it did before he laughed. Theo said Ford could pitch in any time.

He'd decided to keep up his normal routine for the moment and look for openings to raise the subject, but to stay cool until the project wasn't so green. He was still up well before dawn, he poked away at a gear switch or assemblage for a show, he did his share of chores and cooking, played Scrabble with Alice and hung out with Addy when he was around. He kept up with friends. He cut out pot because it wasted time. When the others were home, he only read things he could account for plausibly, such as *Air Augmented Rocket Propulsion Concepts* between trick-or-treaters on Halloween, where he had his vacuum cleaner rocket series for cover.

He thought of prepping the sauna before Alice mentioned it this year. Winter was coming fast: the grasses had died back and the geese had gone, the garden scents hit more sharply, the late day light was urgent, and he walked with his hands in his pockets. The squirrels had their stores but shook the last acorns loose anyway or bit them off their twigs, let them ping the tin roof of Harvey Borsok's crappy garden shed like buckshot.

This time of year, the faces of neighbours and strangers seemed braced or had a poignancy, regardless of the majority expression. Everyone craved bread and jam and pies again, wore heavier, woollier clothes that smelled of naphthalene or cedar, accessorized with mixed feelings. Alice, who had gotten her annual clean bill of cardiac health, said the humidity and barometric pressure this time of year tightened her skin, subtly inflamed it, so she ate more wheat germ and brown rice for the ceramides, amaranth seed for squalene, kale and sweet potatoes for hyaluronic acid. She restarted her turmeric, avocado oil, and glycerin.

There was a normalcy to it, though he knew the time would come when the secret wouldn't hold and he'd tell her everything.

Ever since Alice heard, maybe fifteen years ago, that Saturday was the main sauna day in Finland, they'd gone with Saturdays too through the cold months. Friends knew they could bring a towel late afternoon and cook a while, eventually shower in the little stall, saunter up to the house with steam rising from their heads and shoulders, to eat something and have some wine, play some music, maybe a game.

Today, Gracie was there and, for a while, it was just the three of them. They let the heat take them, and the pine tar scent and fresh birch, the steam thick as soup.

"Glorious," Gracie said.

It was good. The sauna and the wine had slowed his thinking, which was good after so many hours in the library reading and filling pads with sketches and calculations, and wondering how much longer he'd get away with using Addy's computer before he had to buy one of his own. Ford had been no help.

Gracie couldn't believe Barney Fogan wanted to write a book about midwives.

Midwifery as civil resistance? Barney? She said he was having a midwife crisis.

"Nice one," Theo said.

She said it wouldn't be long before he got back to telling lies about her side of the legislature or goading a union or something.

"He seems sincere," Alice said.

"He's way past sincere," Theo said. "Gracie, did you hear he went to a sweat lodge?"

"Get out!"

"He got dehydrated and threw up."

Gracie was laughing when Addy and Rosemary came in. Theo put water on the stones to build the steam: it seemed like the thing to do for Rosemary's sake, though she seemed comfortable enough as she set her extra towel aside. He was glad he'd kept his own done up. Addy was wearing trunks, the way he had since he was twelve. He was as uptight in his skin as Rosemary seemed comfortable in hers.

Alice said she just didn't like the way Barney made everything into *us versus them.*

"You are joking, right?" Addy said.

"Of course not. I never called doctors fat cats who played golf all of the time. I've never thought doctors were the enemy."

"That's rich." Addy turned to Rosemary, said, "Do you know what an *allopathic doctor* is? No, you didn't, because you're a normal person. An allopath is a regular doctor, the kind you see for a check-up or strep throat. Dr. Yashchyshyn. That's our *family allopath.*"

"Okay," Rosemary said.

"It's just that there are different kinds of doctors," Alice said.

"As you've said subtly four thousand times since I was a toddler." He said, "Okay, so I'm eight years old and I've got this rager of an ear infection, so maybe get some antibiotics, right? Not so fast, soon-to-be hearing-impaired little guy, because first Alice needs to consult Dr. June, our homeopath, and our naturopath, Dr. Bob, who are nice enough people but don't do antibiotics, and she talks it all through with some herbalist pals, and before you know it I'm on the couch watching *Mr. Dressup*, ear pounding in pain, and I've got a chunk of amber in my pajamas pocket and I'm drinking the most awful tea."

"It wasn't like that," Alice said.

"Finally, she takes me to Dr. Yashchyshyn and you'd think she was doing hostage negotiations, all arms crossed and using her *assertive-not-aggressive* voice. Luckily, Dr. Y. has the patience of a saint and answers all of her questions about amoxicillin and doesn't take it personally when Alice more or less holds her responsible for her entire profession and accuses her of stifling symptoms that might be saying something important. Hello, hello, Mr. Ear Infection, what is your qi message?"

"You were so hard done by," Alice said.

"By fourteen, I was sneaking out to see Dr. Y. on my own because the qigong wasn't quite kicking the acne. But no, Alice, it's never been us versus them with the allopaths."

Gracie laughed again. Everything Addy said was endearing to Gracie.

In a while, Addy said, "Go ahead and tell them." He sounded pissed off.

"Forget it," Rosemary said. "Just enjoy the heat."

"She wants to take over this place when you go to Saturna."

"Addy...."

"Basically, she wants us to be you, which is batshit. No offence."

"None taken," Theo said.

Alice called it a wonderful idea.

Theo couldn't see it. Rosemary, sure, but not Addy, who'd more or less defined himself in opposition to them, jammed a crowbar into little differences and prised them wide. The swimming trunks, for instance: of course he'd made them out to be diehard nudists, when they'd only ever taught him a body was nothing to be ashamed of, and, until Rosemary came along, he'd have sooner broken rocks than lift a hand in the garden. How he squirmed the first time she asked to see the cold rooms. You'd have thought they kept the bodies down there. He should have grown out of it by now.

"Whatever turns your crank, Rosemary," he was saying. "Don't expect me to weed."

"Like you've ever," Alice said.

"I'll meet you back at the condo when you're done spreading the sheep shit and whatnot."

Rosemary said obviously they'd never live in a condo and the way she said it, straightforwardly but gently, she could have passed for Alice's younger sister. There were other ways too: the way she held her mouth when she listened and pitched her head when she laughed. She and Alice were starting to finish one another's sentences.

"Do you have any idea what it was like to be dragged to the Folk Festival every summer?" Addy said.

"You poor thing," Gracie said.

"Other kids went to the lake. We hung with anarchists who didn't know the 1970s were over."

"I had to go to Bible camp," Rosemary said. "I wanted to go to Folk Fest, but my dad said everyone there was high."

"They were," Addy said.

Theo smiled, but when he looked over, he accidentally saw Rosemary and it was too much: the gap between her front teeth, her body like Alice's twenty years ago—the same small, high breasts, limbs that needed growing into, her eyes wider and her face more open without her glasses, and her hair tied back.

So now he was the prude, and he checked his towel and stoked the stove. It would have felt wrong to look again, much as he needed another glimpse of her confidence and easy faith. Cool water in a hot spell.

"I'm melted," he said. He was always the first to get out. He said, "I wish there was a snowbank to jump into."

He showered and wondered whether the kids ever would take this place over, thought what a relief it would be if they did. He thought of Mrs. Podborski, who'd had the place before them: it had been too much for her for years, but she'd refused to sell to anyone who wasn't going to keep up the garden. When she moved to her apartment, she kept a metal cake pan full of soil from the triple lot under her bed, pulled it out and rested her feet in it.

He loved the crisp air after the sauna. On the path to the house, he saw the asparagus beds, dressed with mulch and ready for winter, and thought of the roots he'd transplanted on Saturna. He'd taken his time getting the drainage right, adjusted the pH with lime and sulfur. They'd moved the first few roses, taken slips of Alice's herbs, some descended from the ones she smuggled up from New Mexico in 1970. They said they'd have to ship a ton of perfect compost because it was worth its weight in gold. As he reached the back door, it startled him to notice he hadn't been thinking about Saturna, when it had been near the centre of his thoughts for years. Things were spinning so fast, and all of the work waiting. He missed Moose trailing behind, told himself it was just the dusk settling down.

Much later, the shop drew him back. Alice had fallen into bed as soon as Gracie left, Addy was at Rosemary's. He separated the seams of the Sony Betamax carton and laid the thick cardboard out over his drafting table, clear side up, brought out a T-square, pencils and sharpener, pens. He picked up a felt marker.

"Begin where you are," he heard Ford say.

"Can you lose the pseudo-profundity and just lay it out?"

"Theodore," Ford said. "Just start."

"*Just start*. What, like, write *Rocket*?"

"Fine, do that."

"I should go to bed," he said, but printed the word in the middle of the board, underlined it for emphasis, though the black felt stroke continued past the T, his hand acting but the line unmistakably leading. It drew itself several inches further, paused, and surprised him with a shift ninety degrees upward, then broke a broad counter-clockwise curve past two o'clock and around midnight, radius widening around the eight and half-past, back around nearly to four o'clock.

He felt like he was falling, so he braced against the table, drew another line from the centre to meet the spiral at ninety degrees, It formed a first right-angle triangle, then more lines until it was a curl of right angles, edge-to-edge, like a spiral staircase viewed from above. He recognized it was a square root spiral, or Pythagoras's snail, or Spiral of Theodorus, saw it was a fitting organizer for the global task, superior to any plan confined to horizontals and verticals.

It wanted headings, so he wrote them—Structure, Attitude Determination and Control, Telemetry, Tracking, Communication, Power, Thermal Control, Computer and Software, Electrical, Propulsion, Mechanical, Control, Systems Engineering. The helical plan composed itself simply and pleasingly, and in their new winding form, the areas were phases, where he'd been thinking of them as points along a line, less urgent now for their waxing and waning, the way they moved with and through one another. Time melted like muscles in a sauna, and the plan was becoming a single entity, nearly alive. He wrote Rigidity, Bus Payload, then Orbit and Attitude, Temperature Control, Rocket Motors, Electric Power, Cabin and Life Support.

It took thirty minutes to set down the plan for carrying some shard of his dying, natal world away to some better place, half an hour to salvage the life he worried he'd wasted, because now, at long last, wasn't he the one who skipped school grades like a smooth stone and strained toward chaos so fearlessly?

Ford said, "Well, Theodore, that's just fine."

13

Theo dug horseradish for St. Cecilia's Day, which fell on November 23 this year. He would have liked to keep reading, but the horseradish needed processing. The air had a bite, the leading edge of a cold system from the west. He dug a trench beside the row, loosened roots from the side and took them, thick and sturdy as baseball bats. His nose ran. A few fat snowflakes fell and he reflected on propellant load.

The helical plan had shifted things. He'd found a comfort in knowing that, through the rest of November and December and into the new decade, he'd be reading four or five books a week in his carrel at the university or in the shop, and scribbling, sketching, calculating, filling manila folders. It brought a keen new awareness of infinity. Today, Alice was with her mothers. Addy hadn't darkened the doorway for days. He would sooner have spent the solitude considering solar sails, but the horseradish wasn't going to grind itself.

They threw their first harvest feast on American Thanksgiving the year they bought the place from Mrs. Podborski. Their oldest friends remembered the early focus on draft resistance, Theo having been among the tens of thousands who'd made it across the border during those years, but they'd named the gathering after St. Cecilia, patron saint of musicians, because music was always going to be at the heart of it.

He and other Americans who'd come north used to stand around the grill with beers and talk about the wars and coups of their natal land and its unnumbered nukes, and note the tenting at the crotch of Kissinger's suit pants in photos with Pinochet. They'd noticed cracks in Canada's Boy Scout image and shaken their heads about Canadians' wide-eyed view that they were nothing like that muscle-bound bully to the south because they weren't the ones who'd blown up Vietnam and because they didn't join the latest U.S. imperialist fad or fall into step with the ideological crusade of the day 100% of the time. Even at the beginning, Theo and others who'd come north knew there hadn't been an American war that Canadians hadn't profited from through the sale of bombs or boots or C-7s, and that Canadian robber barons had thrown in with the Somozas and other dictators to build railways and dig mines through Central America to extract natural resources and turn the poverty-stricken Indigenous people into cheap and compliant labour, while politicians back home abetted them. The American war resisters knew the history of their new country, they were aware that the international honest broker had always taken sides, and that, as peace-loving and fair as it alleged itself to be, it had been stealing Indigenous children from their families for a century. They kept it in mind and pointed it out in their work as teachers and lawyers and writers but by the mid-eighties, no one passed out handbills anymore. Now the fourth Thursday in November was a day for going to Alice and Theo's place, taking an appetite and an instrument if you played one. People came and went through the day and evening, ate black bean chilli, grilled leeks, and green salads, tried a few kinds of horseradish, drank a little, and sang the night away because winter was mustering. Surely everyone knew the world was going to hell and that Cecilia had lost her head to a sword but, on the fourth Thursday in November, everyone was welcome, it was warm inside, and that could be enough. Whoever could would book the Friday off to sleep in.

In a while, he would peel and grind the roots. The fumes would drive Moose to some corner of the basement and he'd aim the fan at himself as he worked and wear Addy's snorkelling mask but the violent, isothiocyanate-filled fumes would still penetrate, his eyes would bulge and tear, his body temperature would rise and, as he cranked the cast iron grinder, he'd remove pieces of clothing until he was down to gitch, gloves, and apron. This year it would occur to him that a spacesuit would help, and that would take him back to propulsion in a relative vacuum and how that determined orientation and positioning, trajectory, any landing, and how little things had changed since the sixties when this science was still new, how the Soviets had focused on electric thrusters while the Americans insisted irrationally on chemical ones. As the stainless steel bowls filled with minced horseradish, he might think of solar sails—solar radiation pushing on mirrors like wind on the sails of a trimaran—and beam sailing, which allowed limitless thrust, though the sail sizes seemed far-fetched. He'd switch to cranking with this left arm for a while and maybe it was a given, as he prepared for St. Cecilia's again and as his eyes streamed, that thoughts of the precious early years in Canada and in this house would infiltrate like more fumes. Following, as they did, the months of wandering and despair and calling home that second time from Santa Fe and coming within a hair's breadth of going back to Ladue, but then the fluke of finding Alice in Taos, as though predestined, and Addy coming less than a year later and fleeing north in the DIVCO tire truck because the FBI were closing in, crossing the international border, coming to Winnipeg, finally stumbling over Mrs. Podborski's place.

Had it not felt glorious preparing for St. Cecilia's just last year? Hadn't it been as uncomplicated as being little and driving to Ozark for Thanksgiving, having the big back seat to himself, in his pyjamas, snug in a bed of blankets and coats, watching the tops of his parents' heads above the seat in the glow of the dashboard lights, Verna's hairdo, an earring and a smooth cheek, KMOX on low? Her perfume, the Judge's aftershave, knowing it didn't matter what time he fell asleep and that they'd carry him into Grandma Maggie's and she'd make her fuss, but quiet as a mouse just then and kissing him once he was in his bed. This year he would peel beets and grind those too for the red chrain, put a first batch of jars on the stove to sterilize, and wonder where that joy had gone. He would fill jars with horseradish mixed with mustard, some with white vinegar only, more with mayo, seal the jars and take them down.

It was St. Cecilia's Day, three p.m. and there it was again: the crushing image of Addy in the hammock eating pumpkin seeds. Eight years old, nine tops. Theo was grilling vegetables over charcoal and greeting people who came around back, catching up and trading news, waving off their solicitudes about the cold and their quips about sainthood, claiming he was fine by the grills, and near the oven and bonfire. The memory had been catching him like a needle stick all day: the boy in jeans and a red hoodie, in the hammock by the kitchen window, right ankle over left shin in a figure four, watching clouds, snacking on warm pumpkin seeds from a greasy paper bag. Theo checked the pizzas in the brick oven.

People had been arriving for three-quarters of an hour. Last year, they'd had forty-five or fifty come and go and they expected about the same today, despite the Colorado low tracking north. They'd made three cast-iron kettles of black bean chilli, a dozen apple pies and another dozen pumpkin, prepped pizza dough for rolling, toppings.

Adam Pauley brought an empty pan and took a full one back inside. Adam knew his way around a guitar and he'd come every year since the beginning. He'd come north from Kansas during the war. Other Vietnam friends still swung by for old times' sake, sometimes with a spouse, maybe kids. Theo saw Gerry Fittig a couple of times a month but most of the other friendships were past tense things, more *Remember when...?* than, *Let's do this or that*, especially after 1977, when Carter pardoned some of them, though not all, and a few went home. He'd waved them goodbye. St. Cecilia's was all too crowded for Gerry so he hadn't been in a decade. Back in the day, Russ Gamble would be one of the first to arrive and he'd stay late. He'd gotten into life insurance and was always looking for prospects, but these days his business was strong, he had his house in Richmond West plus the Winnipeg Beach place, he always had a kid to drive to hockey and of course, Ingrid had never made an effort. Ingrid was younger than any of them but her squareness made her the oldest in the room, the big hair and grand makeup, the jewellery and disapproving looks. How she'd seethed when someone said the name Jess, because that was Russ' ex, and they supposed she wanted to expunge his entire life before her, which included why and how he'd come to Canada. Russ Gamble's past was taboo, but the bonds they'd made fighting against the war were sturdy, and not even Ingrid fortified by a bump in the bathroom could break them. Ingrid did like her cocaine.

Theo had woken off balance but got the last pies in to bake and turned to the pumpkin seeds: swished them in cold water, boiled them in brine, laid them out to dry, then tossed them in coconut oil and harissa, roasted them until their edges were the precise brown and the fragrance was exact. They were always in demand and Addy used to love them too, though he'd wanted them less and less each year.

The first hit of Addy in the hammock came when he went to wake Alice and passed the open door of the vacant bedroom. Addy was always at Rosemary's these days. The memory had flattened him: he'd gotten into bed beside Alice, aching. He'd held her so she'd hold him back. Twice, she let up but he didn't, so she held him some more.

The absurd pining persisted as they made the salads, prepped vegetables, made doughs for pizza. Late morning, they got whipped cream and nutmeg onto the pumpkin pies and filled the racks in the fridge downstairs with them, put the first chilli pot on to reheat. They had all four leaves in the dining room table and they'd laid it with salads, pickles, relishes, and the horseradishes by the time people started arriving, they'd lit warmers, left space for dishes certain people brought every year, stacked plates, set out cutlery and napkins. There was a second table with the punch, bottles of wine, racks of glassware.

Theo always handled the grilling and baking. He'd lit the oven early and kept it stoked with oak. He'd be mostly on his own, given the cold, which was for the best, given how his thoughts were scurrying— Addy in his small red hoodie, the heat of Alice's cheek as she tried not to wake up, Mrs. Podborski with her feet in the pan full of soil from this garden, and others, combining, separating, recombining. He grilled carrot, parsnip, sweet potato, and beet over charcoal, with sweet onion, shallots, garlic, a bit of oil and herbs. He baked bannock circles and pizzas, felt colder each time he shuttled them through the no-man's land between the fires and the back landing.

Now he saw Alice through the kitchen window, helping Gracie's youngest spread sauce on dough. Kaylin was seven or eight. She had her long black hair tied back. Alice leaned down and whispered, and Kaylin looked up and laughed. He guessed he missed Addy like a limb that had been cut off, then gave himself hell because you should want your kid to grow up.

Untethered was a good word for wanting to burst into tears as he watched Alice help a child make a pizza, and for missing Addy when he was, at most, fifty metres away. Man up, for Christ's sake: the sky wasn't falling. Untethered from common sense, because a sky might feel cold and lonely, but that was only the human standing under it, because a sky didn't feel, and a wind could gust but not portend, a sunset did not grieve and what the hell was wrong with Addy getting out on his own? He could play his music too loud in his own place, buy his own food and wash his own clothes, maybe feel some belated gratitude for what he'd always had, and maybe if he came over for a meal, he'd show the respect of a guest.

Alice and Kaylin were in their coats and boots and coming his way, Alice carrying the little pizza and asking him whether there was any room in that oven. He fashioned a face, smiled and said, "Let's see what we can do," and slid the thing onto the peel. He asked Kaylin to help him put a log on the fire and she was delighted.

He said it would be eight minutes. They could wait by the fire or he'd take Kaylin's pizza inside.

"It's really cooled off," Alice said, then said, Brrrr! to Kaylin, and they ran back inside.

The cold really was merciless. The vegetables sizzled. He shook the grilling baskets. The chill had settled into his bones.

Nalani and Benedikt with a K arrived. Theo peeked at his watch and asked where on earth they'd been because he knew Nalani would blush. Ben laughed and asked what he could do; Theo said he could run this particular pizza inside to a girl called Kaylin.

It was relentless. Addy's baggy jeans and red hoodie, one pumpkin seed at a time, running them over his lips so he could lick the salt. Jesus. He did a run inside with vegetables and bannock.He stood on the back landing with the trays. The warmth was a miracle, and the crush of the kitchen, dining room, and front room, the talking and laughing, smell of food and wine and candle wax, a guitar somewhere. Someone arriving at the front. He had the sense he'd wandered into a stranger's party. A child squealed. When he banged ice and tree bark off of his boots, the lack of pain in his toes was alarming.

Lloyd Whitaker's nasal voice hovered like tear gas and, worse, there was Addy, shoulder against the wall just inside the dining room, cucumber-cool, cradling a bottle of beer, actually talking with the idiot, apparently engaged. He hoped the kid was high.

Thank God Elle Butler passed between Addy and Lloyd. She was saying, "You're stunned as me arse," then Kael a step behind, grinning. They were a sight for hopeless eyes.

"Here he is!" Elle called when she saw him. "The man himself." She relayed the pans to Kael and said, "'Ow's she cuttin', treasure?" Elle had lived on the prairies more than half her life, but her speech veered Newfinese when she drank. Her h's disappeared or relocated, she swapped *my* for *me*, and everyone was *b'y* or *my love* or *ducky*. Every year, she brought kelp chips and Screech. Elle had drawn Lloyd in her wake: with her there, Lloyd informing him that he must be frozen was less awful.

Elle went to grab his elbow to haul him inside, cleared a place by the fire, get him a plate.

"I've got a bit more to do," Theo said, satisfied with the cheerful sound he was making. His toes were a concern.

"Really?" Lloyd said. "There's enough to feed an army."

Theo addressed Elle and Kael when he asked, "Everyone seem okay in here?"

"Oh, we're having a time, aren't we?" Elle said. She told him to take some fortification at least and went to pour him a shot.

Addy and Lloyd resumed their tête-à-tête. Addy said, "As investments go, a Philosophy degree is a tragedy. Buy high, sell low."

"Education for its own sake," Lloyd said, but did the stupid thing with his eyes.

"Fifteen years later, you're still waiting tables and barely a dent in your student loan."

"Sure, but you're golden if some customer wants to talk Hegel."

Speaking of tragedies, Theo thought. His own son and Lloyd freaking Whitaker talking about education as if it were a commodity like copper. It really was a disappointment.

Elle handed him the shot, gave one to Kael, picked up one for herself. She said, "Long may your big jib draw."

"To your jib, Theo." That was Kael.

"Magnificent," he said, throat on fire.

"How about I come out and help?" Kael said.

Theo said not to bother, that he'd be two shakes of a lamb's tail. As he turned to go, he heard Alice start in on the health benefits of horseradish. He hoped whoever she was talking to didn't have somewhere to be because she was in an exit-only lane to Galen and Paracelsus.

Moose slipped past him as he stepped outside.

A cold gust stole his breath. He got close to the grill and the slow sizzle of vegetables. Moose had found a piece of parsnip or carrot and bore down low to eat it. The wind parted his fur. Theo slid the last pizzas into the oven and scratched the old guy's head.

Alice would be going on about the antibiotic, diuretic, appetite-stimulating, toothache relieving, anti-carcinogenic powers of horseradish with the certainty of a missionary on your doorstep. The first he'd heard of the Doctrine of Signatures was twenty years ago when she claimed shelled walnuts were good for the brain, because they bore a passing visual resemblance to it, and he thought she was joking, but she'd gone on to say tomatoes prevented heart attacks because they were red and had four chambers, and bloodroot was better than an iron supplement or hematologist, sliced mushrooms were for earaches, and of course horseradish root was a cardio-pulmonary enhancer because it could resemble an erection if your mind ranged that way, though of course she said *phallus*. She'd called it poetry, but really did seem to consider it science too, and she hadn't budged when he showed her tomatoes with three chambers or five, or when he said it was called *horseradish* and not *manradish*, and there'd never been a man with a member like a tree bough.

He heard a car door creak, turned to see Mike and Denise Borsok getting into the Datsun. Mike in his ridiculous ushanka, ear flaps down. Soviet fashion to match the bleak mood and, when he glanced across at Theo, he could have been looking over the wire at Checkpoint Charlie. God but they were grim. Either he or Alice invited them every year, and they'd never come. These days, slipping the invitation into their box was a provocation.

"Hey, neighbours!" he called, but too aggressively. He really was in a rough mood and it seemed to be getting worse.

Then, as he put wood on the bonfire, he had the most startling couplet of recognitions: first, that he enjoyed chopping wood, be it oak or birch or tamarack, for St. Cecilia's or any other time, and, second, that once they launched a craft into space, there'd never again be wood to split and there'd be no more trees.

They were simple points and they combined simply in the middle of him, converted the warmth of Elle Butler's screech into a gastrointestinal cramp. He braced against the oven, felt its heat through his glove and, of course, he had to see Addy in his hammock again, wiping his greasy fingers on the waistband of his hoodie. It occurred to him that there'd be no more pumpkin seeds either or pumpkins, no bonfires obviously, or whipped cream clouds through the workshop skylight, because there'd be no sky, and forget about pie and glaciers and bad neighbours, and, Christ Jesus, what if Alice and Addy wouldn't go? He seemed to be sweating under his watch cap. He gave Moose another piece of carrot. Moose wouldn't live to see the launch. Theo envied him for that.

The red of a coal in the bonfire caught his eye, and he recognized Ford before Moose yowled, tail and fur raised to look bigger, abandoned the carrot, backed away.

"What now?" Theo said.

"You're getting cold feet."

"You think?"

"Get it? Cold feet? You need proper boots."

"You didn't tell me any of this…"

"You can lose toes to frostbite."

"You didn't say that, when I left, there'd be no coming back."

"It went without saying."

What would he be? Major Tom in his tin can. A TV affiliate losing touch with the network. Would he exist?

"Take a breath," Ford said.

He did his best. The air kept getting colder. The snow had picked up, and the wind.

"It hits you all of a sudden," he said. "Everything feels like an ending."

"This is good," Ford said.

"It's definitely not good."

"You're getting used to smaller places."

"What the hell?" he said but knew. He remembered Alice asking whether he was disappointed with how she'd turned out. She'd been having a bad day. He'd held her and said she'd been a gift at every stage of unfolding and he couldn't be more grateful. He'd nailed it.

"Trust me," Ford said. "Best to get it out of your system."

When he came inside the last time, he wound his way through the crowd to the stairs, mixed and met on the way, reported on the wind and snow but, when someone called him a hero for doing all of this, he said, No, no, if anything, it had been too warm by the oven and bonfire, and he took care not to limp as he went up to soak his feet until the pain came back, then went back down to the kitchen and sat in front of the oven with the door open and couldn't stop shivering, even with hot food and people filling his glass, and music in the front room. "Puff," and "Susanna," before the kids went home. "Be Kind to Your Web-Footed Friends."

Only scraps registered. Meg saying, *Rosemary and Addy*, what a matchbook cover that would make, and Addy, Don't hippies think marriage is bondage? Apparently Barney Dogan had been by, looking hilarious in a bulky wool sweater, red-striped Guatemalan pants, and the slippers of a mime. He was in a midlife crisis free fall.

The music found its stride out in the front room. "Four Strong Winds," "Wimoweh," "Which Side are You On?" Guitars and a mandolin, flute and a pair of fiddles, Jake's homemade cigar box banjo, a ukulele, an accordion. He imagined them in a broad circle around the old console piano. He liked the tuning between songs, the negotiation about key. "If I Were a Carpenter," "Get Rhythm," "Amarillo by Morning."

They were singing Country Joe and "The Fish Cheer" when Gracie brought him pumpkin pie. She asked how he was doing, and he said, "Fine, Gracie, just fine." She called him a liar, said he was definitely hypothermic. She said enough was enough and next year they'd hire a caterer. In the other room, they sang their hearts out and played their instruments. Someone had a keyboard. They didn't give a damn what the fight was for, and the next stop was Vietnam. They knew the peace wasn't winnable unless you burned the whole country down.

"Who's that playing the keyboard in there?" he said. "The organ sound is just right for Country Joe."

Gracie's girl, Kaylin, came to say Daddy was taking her and her sisters home. She asked whether Gracie had seen Uncle Theo. As she asked, she seemed to be looking right through him.

"He's right here, silly," Gracie said. Theo gave a wave.

"Oh hi," Kaylin said. "Thanks for having us, Uncle Theo. Thanks for the tasty pie."

Gracie went to find coats and someone called out, *Pretty Boy Floyd*. Theo thought, Just now, much as he loved St. Cecilia's, he'd sooner be upstairs watching the storm develop. He hadn't seen Moose in a while, so went to the back door and called him. The wind forced the door wider and swallowed his voice. If anyone could handle a storm, it was Moose. He hurried back to the oven because the shivering had turned violent. He told himself he was fine, surrounded by people he loved and who loved him back. So what if he'd become invisible to small children?

Who should come by but Alice herself? Now, wasn't he really and truly fine?

"I'm buying you better boots," she said.

They heard Rosemary in the front room. She asked whether anyone knew, "Just a Closer Walk," and of course they did. She said Meg had dared her, so she had no choice, but if everyone didn't join in, she'd run right out the front door.

The room was quiet, except for a child's tiny voice somewhere, then a guitar. Rosemary began, "I am weak but thou art strong," and it sent a chill down every spine. She sang from a deep place, "Keep me from all sin and wrong," so Theo and Alice hurried through to the next room and into a space that opened up for them. She stood straight and tall beside the little piano and sang, "I am happy, Lord, as long / As I am closer Lord to Thee," as naturally as breathing, in a contralto they'd never heard but was obvious in hindsight. Her eyes lit up when the fiddle joined in and then the accordion and others. Theo almost felt warm.

She was blushing as she sang the last line of the verse, pressed her palms together begging others to sing, so the chorus swelled, "Just a closer walk with Thee…" He joined the backing vocals and noticed his breathing was better. "Grant it Jesus if you please / Only let me walk with thee / Oh let it be, dear Lord, let it be."

She began the second verse, "Draw me closer to thy side," closed her eyes, opened her voice wide. "Let me in thy love abide / 'Til my soul is satisfied / That I am closer Lord to thee," and the second chorus was bigger too. Theo and Alice stood with their fingers entwined.

Afterward, the cheering was loud and went long. Theo saw that, finally, this St. Cecilia's had turned out fine. There was Addy hugging Rosemary: two young people with beautiful souls.

"Here Comes the Sun" started. Theo saw Addy climbing the stairs and detected a lie in his smile as he stepped past people. He guessed some string had snapped after all.

The blizzard found its strength and broke things up early. Outside looked more like 1986, when thirty-five centimetres fell in a bitter wind and they couldn't see across to the Borsoks'. In 1986, people abandoned their cars in the road and went on by foot and, after a while, the only things moving were snowmobiles and military tracked carriers. Power lines snapped, roofs caved in, the airport was full of stranded passengers. When snow shovelling triggered heart attacks, graders drove ahead of ambulances. 1986 had had an apocalyptic vibe.

Gracie was the last to leave. She stayed to help. Finally, Theo started her car and brushed off the snow. They talked in the sunroom while it warmed up. Theo said he missed the old days, when Addy gave a shit. He said he hoped Gracie's girls would show more respect. He hadn't planned to say it, knew it came out harsh.

Gracie glared. "You know our kids aren't the enemy, right?"

"Obviously I didn't mean…"

"Addy is a great guy."

"He went upstairs after Rosemary's song. I saw you go after him."

"Uh huh. He would not be happy that you noticed."

"Was everything all right?"

"You know, you could talk to him sometime…"

"He and Rosemary aren't having trouble, are they? Is that it?" He saw her look of disgust. He said, "I'm warning you: *do not* say that men are clueless."

"Not all of them."

"Tell me."

She sighed. "You really are clueless."

"Gracie."

She said, "Okay, it's just that all of this is a lot for him."

"What is?"

"Everything. You and Alice. Your life. You two are pretty much forces of nature."

"Alice maybe…"

"Clueless. Anyway, he's trying to launch himself, right? Trying to be his own person, but the gravitational force is pretty strong around here. St. Cecilia's is just one example."

Her saying *gravity* and *launching* put him on edge.

"Then, after how many girlfriends, the one he really falls for turns out to love all of it. Then tonight, she sings a song and, if it's not *the* best thing anyone's ever done here, it's in the top three. Things would have been less complicated if he'd stuck with, I don't know, maybe that Goth girl who was always chewing gum."

"No, nothing was uncomplicated with Bethany."

"But at least she didn't want to spend time over here."

"Fair point."

"Anyway, that's your nickel's worth."

He made her promise to call when she got home, but knew she wouldn't.

After she left, he took the extra wine downstairs. There was wine to float a boat at the end of every St. Cecilia's, bottles to last past Easter if they drank every day. His thoughts swirled as he went up and down the stairs: Addy, apparently on some knife edge, Ford and getting used to smaller places, Rosemary's singing undoing the cold. The snow blew and he could just make out the brick oven from the window. He thought of talking to Addy. His thoughts twisted, spun, until one stopped, stared back, and packed a wallop: that Addy would be leaving very soon.

14

The utterances of this lousy oracle landed so vaguely, though whether from ineptitude, remissness, who knew, or some combination. *Something's coming,* Ford had said late yesterday morning, then fucked off back to whatever Olympus or Asgard or Hades he called home and left Theo wondering.

He put on soup for lunch and wondered what was coming: the coldest winter on record, a C.O.D. package from Eaton's? Another American war went without saying, given how pissed Bush was with Noriega for disobeying his CIA handlers after twenty years of obedience. As the soup warmed, he listened to a message from Sally Currin in Montréal, saying the May show was a go, so he wondered whether this was the thing, though, twenty minutes later, as he rinsed his dishes, he took a call from someone called Leonard Unger, of Eden Books in Burlington, Vermont, who'd read *Living out of your Back Lane* and wanted to slip it into his spring list, if Theo didn't mind a bit of editing and a shortish timeline. Theo said, Well, that sounds great, but called the man Bernard, which was awkward. Leonard took it well and said he'd FedEx the manuscript and a contract up to Canada early next week. So suddenly, two contracts coming and two deadlines, but Ford had said, Something (singular) was coming and not some things, and come to think of it, something was always coming because that's how time worked. It seemed like enigma for its own sake, the communication equivalent of a Rube Goldberg machine.

It was nearly five. He'd finished *Dynamics of Detonation and Explosion* and done some work on the model, but guessed he'd better not crack open *Thrust and Drag—Its Prediction and Verification*, because there was dinner to sort. Keeping food on the table was important: it kept Alice happy and gave a look of normalcy, like the beard, which was coming in nicely and made him look more like himself. Even sandwiches and salads would do.

At least the Electrolux rocket was taking shape. A first study in pop-up living spaces, hatches in the green exoskeleton opening under power of tiny DC motors, aluminum panels rising out and unfurling to fatten payload volume from airless to the size of a modest bungalow. When he was done, the rocket would puff out like a slow-mo corn kernel before viewers, then refold back into its hatches. He would include it in the Montréal show and building it had dulled the anxiety a little because how was he ever supposed to shift from reading and theorizing to building when Ford couldn't answer the simplest questions— about destination or paying the astonishing cost of fuel, 90% of the total mass at liftoff being propellant, only six percent engines, tanks, and fins, a mere four percent payload, where *payload* was the terrestrial refugees and their long-term living quarters and maybe a bit of soil that had never known the burn of a pesticide.

He was going for his coat when he sensed Ford in the stove or, rather, Moose did and hurled himself out through the cat door.

He'd had enough. He stabbed the coals and said, "Your choice: either say what's coming or how I'm supposed to pay for this thing. Pick one."

"The universe provides," Ford said.

"Seriously?"

Silence.

"Maybe the universe can cough up the lotto numbers…"

Ford said, "*The under part is, though stemmed, uncertain is, as sex is, as moneys are, facts to be dealt with as the sea is…*"

"What is that even? If you don't know the answer, just say."

"It's Charles Olson. 'I, Maximus of Gloucester, to You.'"

"Why is it so hard for an angel or whatever you are to talk normally? I'm pretty sure you can do better."

"It means the money part is treacherous," Ford said and flaked off again. There was no counting on him.

Theo wondered, and not for the first time, whether, as supernatural entities went, maybe Ford wasn't the pick of the litter. Maybe the things he said needed more scrutiny. As in, maybe the sick-scented bag of paper shreddings didn't actually need reassembly; maybe the point of that had been to get his attention. He swore and opened the door.

The backlit figure outside startled him. It took a moment to recognize Barney Dogan in a long dark green woollen cloak over what looked like pantaloons. He wore low winter boots, his ankles were bare. He looked cold.

Barney said he'd rung the bell at the house, but guessed Alice was running late. "Is that one of your vacuum cleaner spaceships?" he said and slipped past Theo.

"I'm just leaving. If you want to leave a message..."

"Can I wait here? Alice said to come after four-thirty... Pizza Night..."

It was a shock. How had he forgotten it was Friday? He should have lit the oven an hour ago. He grabbed tinder and kindling.

As he built a fire in the pizza oven, he wondered whether Barney would snoop. He hurried back inside.

"You seem underdressed," he said.

"Oh this," Barney said, as though he'd forgotten. "It's a *pheran*. Sort of a parka for the Kashmir Valley."

"Sure."

"It goes back to the Mughal era..."

"Right, and can you guess my next question?"

"Because a fella's got to wear something over his *kurta* and *shalwar*."

Theo smiled, then wished he hadn't.

Barney said maybe a *pheran* wasn't warm enough for December in Manitoba. He said a Kashmiri man would wear a layer of yak or goatskin under it and carry a *kangri*, which was a little fire pot in a wicker holder. It sounded like brand new knowledge.

Barney was going through something big. Alice would know what to say. She had a warm but firm way of approaching people like this.

"I brought gulab jamun," Barney said.

Theo went back out to fill the chamber. It would take an hour to get hot enough. He was adding fuel wood when two of the Whitaker girls rounded the corner. They called, "Uncle Theo, look!" and raced to be first to show him what they were holding. Last into the yard was Lauren, now twelve and too old to rush but not old enough not to want to. Alice rounded the corner next, then Lloyd, which was when Theo remembered he'd promised to make up dough. Kaylin and Brenda were shouting over one another that they'd been to the dentist and gotten parachute men for prizes. Brenda tried to untie her parachutist's strings. Kaylin held hers out to Theo. As the youngest, she expected people to do everything for her.

Lauren tried not to let on that she'd joined the race. She threw hers into the sky first. The parachute opened, the little plastic man drifted down. Whee, she said with an aggressive coolness. Brenda shouted that it wasn't fair, and threw her parachutist up, though she hadn't finished unwinding it, so it free fell to its death. Lauren's eye-rolling nudged Brenda into a rage.

Speaking of plastic men, Lloyd was heading his way, which meant as soon as he settled the girls down, he'd natter about the usual things: Lauren's hockey, Brenda's rhythmic gymnastics, repeat something cute that Kaylin had said. He'd call Gracie the ball-and-chain, then say she was too good for him, which she obviously was.

Theo checked the fire and told Lloyd he'd never guess who was waiting in the shop, as though it might be a good surprise and not Barney Dogan, who'd been taking ugly partisan potshots at Gracie for as long as she'd been an MLA. Lloyd went to see. He looked like he could use a break from the girls.

Theo helped the younger girls with their parachutists, then went to get Lloyd and Barney out of the shop and into the house.

Barney was telling Lloyd that he'd always been drawn to India, that he probably owned half of everything Bollywood had ever put on VHS. He loved the music and clothes and the colours. He didn't even mind if there were no subtitles.

Lloyd had adopted an *If-you-don't-have-anything-nice-to-say* stance. He pretended to be fascinated by the Zeta assemblage, though he'd never shown an interest in Theo's work before.

Barney said it was strange he was so comfortable in all-things-India, or Pakistan or Nepal or Bhutan when he was Danish and Irish and hadn't been outside of North America and the Caribbean. He wondered whether he'd been switched at birth with a Kashmiri baby.

"Happens a lot," Theo said.

Barney said he'd go to India in a heartbeat, but the only place Marceline would ever go was Puerto Vallarta.

"Well, at least you've got the outfit now," Lloyd said. He had his face pressed sideways to the window. Trying to see the girls.

Barney had to ask, "How about you, Theo? You and Alice doing all right?"

"What the hell? Jesus. Of course. We should go to the house."

"You two seem rock solid. With Marceline and me, it's only ever a show; behind closed doors, I'm Popeye to her Sea Hag. The tongue on that woman. Vicious. How about you and Gracie, Lloyd?"

Now Lloyd looked over, but only to make the snub explicit. He went to check on the girls.

"We should go too," Theo said but saw that Barney was tearing up, and seemed about to say something. He said the first thing to mind, namely that personal happiness was a racket, basically a Western perversion. He heard himself claim that people these days looked for meaning and soulful connection like they were shopping for a TV or F-150.

Whatever that even meant. Later, the last thing he'd remember before the Yahoos was saying, *smiling kittens shitting rainbows*, and wondering whether this would end in tears—literally end with both him and Barney crying their eyes out—though the filibuster had shown no signs of ending, and why would it when building this ark was too heavy a burden to bear and there were so many questions to answer, such as how he'd ever get what they needed up and away from the Earth when, for each kilo of payload, they'd need twenty-five kilos of rocket and propellant? Which was really going to add up, unless they cared to live their lives in quarters the size of a Cessna cockpit, which reminded him of flying all over again and the vast empty sky, which was awful, not to mention the changes in him since his WashU days, when reading was like breathing and he'd actually understood things like pitching moment, thrust-drag accounting, and relative certainty, and now he couldn't remember what the hell propagation of error was. Twenty years out of school and he was thick as a third grader. Humbling wasn't the half of it.

What he needed were clear instructions, but the tongue of the angels was so far away. These days, only mystics spoke the perfect, green language of the Divine, and certain Charismatic Christians claimed to, though, so far as he knew, speaking in tongues was performance and, likely as not, would leave the birds and the angels scratching their heads.

Somehow, he'd gotten talking about *Gulliver's Travels*, the Houyhnhnms and the horrid humanoid Yahoos endowed with just enough reason to fuck the whole world. He heard himself neigh like a wise Houyhnhnm and saw Barney looking back with quizzical but, thank Christ, dry eyes, doubtless as perplexed as he was himself about this misanthropic turn, and now a slippery slope toward Kant's crooked timber of humanity and what a gift to creation it would be if *homo sapiens* pursued voluntary self-extinction through cessation of reproduction, not that people had the self-discipline, which left nuclear or ecological Armageddon as the choices.

"Anyway...," he said. "I'd better stoke the oven or we'll never eat."

He got them out the door and locked it. The Whitaker girls stopped playing when they saw Barney. Barney said, Why, hello there, with the dingbat inflection of someone who's never known children. Kaylin looked like she might cry again, so Theo said, "Girls, it's only a *pheron*," and, "Who's ready to make a pizza?" which helped. He showed them how to tell whether the oven was ready from the colour of the inside roof and putting your hand inside and counting Mississippis until it got too hot, then yanked it out and said, "Ooch, ouch, ooch," so they'd laugh.

Inside, Lloyd was rolling pizza dough. Gracie grated cheese and seemed subdued and why not, when Barney Fucking Dogan had been assailing her in print for years. Kaylin hugged the side of her dad and stared at Barney, who had taken off his Kashmiri parka to reveal a bright, white *kurta*, creases still sharp from the package, and *shalwar*. His feet were bare. Kaylin slipped a thumb into her mouth.

Alice washed greens. Theo could tell from the lack of response when he kissed her cheek that she was pissed.

She whispered, "I thought you were making dough and sauce. I had to send Addy all the way to DeLuca's."

"I lost track of time."

"What were you even doing all day?" She still hadn't looked at him.

"Oh, I don't know, Alice: a couple of naps, worked on my tan. You're not the only one who's busy."

She slashed a purple onion. She said, "I've been up for thirty hours and delivered a baby but I'm sure you're dead on your feet. Is the oven ready at least?"

"Yeah, at least I go that right. You seriously invited Barney?"

"Can you please just…"

"You know he's lost his mind, don't you?"

Barney was telling Addy and Rosemary that the white of his *kurta* acknowledged that everybody dies. You take Muslim death shrouds, he said.

"Where do you find an outfit like that?" Addy said.

"Oh, this great Pakistani tailor on Notre Dame. Mizhir."

Theo went to check on the oven one more time. When he came back to tell them they were good to go, Barney was saying it was time he wrote another book.

"Oh yeah?" Lloyd said. "What about? How my wife eats babies?"

"Daddy!" Brenda squealed.

"Lloyd, don't," Gracie said.

Barney said he was sorry, swore he hadn't meant half of the things he'd written. It seemed to make Lloyd angrier. Barney said that if Alice changed her mind, he'd write about midwifery.

15

As he came in the back door, Rosemary was at the front, calling, "Cornbread's here." She was swaddling Addy's cassette deck in a towel. His speakers, computer, and bedside table were in the sunporch. Eight or ten cardboard boxes, wooden crates of records. Addy was coming down the stairs with his turntable. Moose lay on the sofa in a sunbeam.

"What's going on?" Theo said.

"You're kidding," Addy said. The sharpness got Moose's attention.

There was a pickup truck on the street and Cornbread was jogging up the front steps. He remembered seeing a message on the fridge—yesterday or a few days ago—that the Silverado was a go.

"You're moving?" Theo said.

"Earth to Theo," Addy said. "And thanks for all the help."

"Babe," Rosemary said.

Cornbread came inside, grinning. He said, Hey, Mr. Strahl, and banged the snow from his boots. Cornbread was always smiling or about to smile. Alice came down with a garbage bag full of pillows. Hi, Mrs. Strahl, Cornbread said.

"He's actually surprised," Addy said to her.

He actually was, though there'd been talk for weeks: how much time Addy was spending at Rosemary's, Alice pretending she couldn't wait to rent out his room. He'd forgotten or put it out of his mind and now it was a gut punch.

He said, "I thought you were going to finish school first?"

"You're in your own little world."

"Adds, go easy," Rosemary said.

The adrenalin had swept from the middle of him to his toes and fingers, his heart thundered, and there was Addy, dead-centre and up close, face at once as cold as Pluto and Mercury-hot. He sensed Alice at his nine o'clock, Rosemary and Cornbread at his one but there was only Addy in the most urgent light, flickering, saturated like old Super 8.

It was like an alarm was sounding. Like the pneumatic siren on top of Ladue City Hall that always scared you shitless because it reminded you that the drills were part of the fraud and, if the Russians really pulled the trigger, ducking under a desk or heading for a basement or some low ground amounted to pretending there was any defence. When the air-raid siren used to sound, it only underscored the hopelessness. What a thing to realize it had been wailing in some remote fold of his memory since 1959 or 1960.

It was confusing, too much at once—Addy bugging out, whatever siren wailing—at once a shock and predictable and, for some reason Verna had popped to mind, looking lonely as a ghost or a cloud, and then the Judge up in Addy's old room with a bottle, evidently having taken the vacancy for an office. Maybe things were bound to turn to shit between sons and fathers, and it didn't matter how you tried. Maybe he, of all people, should have known that.

Addy was saying, "You don't have a clue."

"Alice, did you know about this?" Theo said.

"What is wrong with you?" Addy said. "Is forty too young to get senile?"

He'd known the day would come and a kid wasn't going to stay home forever, but he'd imagined the launch would be simple and kind, he'd help out and hang pictures. It was never going to be an emergency. The kid didn't know how good he had it: it wasn't like he'd ever had to deal with a knife fight at supper time.

"I've got to say, the disrespect is disappointing." Even as he said it, he knew it wasn't what he meant. He said, "Seems like anger is the only thing you feel."

"Are you actually serious?" Addy said, eyes narrowed, shaking his head.

Theo was frozen in place. He drove his nails into the flesh of their respective palms thought, *thenar eminence* because the part wanted naming. He said, "Oh my goodness, this is *not* because I forgot your birthday…"

"What?" Addy looked baffled.

"Are you five years old?" he said and knew saying it was stupid, though he still couldn't believe he'd forgotten Addy's birthday and that, of all people, Lloyd had reminded him

"Theo, stop," he heard Alice say.

Addy was telling Cornbread to start taking boxes and the crates of records, that he'd take his computer and stereo in his car.

"And you get Corny to borrow a truck when you could use mine?" Theo said.

"Oh, it's no problem, Mr. Strahl," said Cornbread, that warrior of cheer. "It has the cap, and my uncle…"

Addy said, "Your truck is full of radiators and snow."

"Then maybe get off your ass and help me take them to the scrapyard!"

He knew he was blowing it sky high.

"Stop," Alice said, firmly, her hand on his shoulder.

"You've always been afraid to get your hands dirty," he heard himself say.

"And you've stopped making any sense at all," Addy said. Rosemary's eyes darted from Addy to Alice to Theo. Two hummingbirds looking for a place to land. She picked up a carton, then saw she didn't have shoes. Addy gestured, Go, to Cornbread.

Alice was pushing him toward the back door so he barked at her, "And whatever happened to the united front?" He hated that Rosemary was seeing this.

The whistle of the kettle brought him around. He made the tea, noticed he hadn't closed the door, got it with his foot. He willed his heart slower.

Addy had always opposed them, or no, opposed *him*, but it had been good-natured once.

"Dad, how come you don't cut your hair?"

"Because I'd lose my superhero strength."

"Dad, I know that's not even true."

"Okay, it's because you like haircuts so much. I let you have mine."

Hadn't they laughed? They'd laughed and sometimes it turned into chasing—Addy Roadrunner to his Coyote?

"Why can't we just buy things like normal people? Addy said. "Do we have to trade for everything?"

"It's barter. Anyway, I got you those jeans at an auction."

In time, the spurning got subtler. Addy's thoughtful tone made you laugh.

"I guess retirement isn't a thing when you don't have a job, huh, Theo?"

"I wonder whether, at this exact moment, somewhere on the globe, there's another sixteen-year-old listening to The Dead Kennedys and reading *Richest Man in Babylon.*"

"You and your American friends, Dad… You know Gerry Fittig makes psychedelics in his lab, right?"

They knew the rules: Theo never put Addy down and, if Addy crossed a line, he stepped right back. There was affection in the friction and it was only for the two of them. Addy's Goth girlfriend Bethany tried it with Theo, but only once. Theo had told Addy not to worry for goodness sake, and not to be too hard on her.

Alice didn't understand. She guessed it was because she'd only had a sister, and Lyle had been more of an absence than a father. She took their sparring as a fact of nature, like bluejays nipping off the marigold blossoms to treat their mites.

He paced the shop and drank tea. His mind was idling rough, wouldn't find a rhythm. Thoughts and memories, corners of memories traced through him up, down, and on the diagonal, left trails like light. He paced from his hips, could almost feel Addy on his shoulders, four or five years old, in his red-checkered jacket, as they went through a lane near Osborne, bragging that he was taller than anyone. The day they mailed his manuscript to the first publisher, it was Addy who set it on the post office counter, told the clerk his dad's book would be in the library soon and at Mary Scorer's and Prairie Sky if she wanted to have her own copy. He'd boasted to his friends at first, came home from school and asked whether the publisher had called, though that was never going to last.

Fine, so maybe this was what Ford meant when he said something was *coming*—Addy going away, severing things—but would it have killed him to give a heads-up?

He'd have to buy his own computer, and how much would that cost, with the modem and software and whatnot?

He pictured Alice inside, trying to repair things and Addy still furious but sadder now too. Rosemary nearly going out into the snow without shoes. Corny's dumb jokes falling flat, Corny pulling his tuque down over the port-wine stain by his left temple.

He could go back inside. Nothing was stopping him. He could go in and help with the loading. He wouldn't have to say a word.

The thought flared, then went out. They'd probably already driven off. God but the messed up men in this Strahl line: it was as sure as any instinct and he, of all people, should have seen this coming.

He was still pacing when Alice came out. He'd been over Abraham and Isaac, and *Streetcar* and a dozen other things, had Addy on his shoulders again declaring himself a giant, then lashed to a stone altar on some hillside, in the same red jacket, puzzled by the knife in Theo's hand. It was an ugly thought. God telling Abraham to sacrifice Isaac had to be the ugliest thing in all of human mythology: what kind of god asks for that, then changes his mind after the kid's tied down and the knife's been sharpened? Think of the awkward walk back down: Look, Isaac, I said I'm sorry, but Yahweh… Though maybe fighting with Addy amounted to sacrifice and putting him second to his own pursuits, so he was no better.

"Ford!" he called into the fire. Nothing.

What was the point without Addy? Why bother escaping if you didn't take your kin? The kid knew his computers and he could grow a dollar into five or ten. He could have piloted the thing, or he and Rosemary could have. They could have started with flying lessons at St. Andrew's.

He kicked a metal pail into the big doors. It landed with one side crumpled.

There was Addy, opening night as Stanley in *Streetcar*, Grade 12, and afterward, the hippie drama teacher coming over and throwing her arms around him, which would have been fine but for the way she claimed to love his spirit and pulled him close. Afterward, walking home, he'd said the word was Ms Everett had gone full love-in with guys at cast parties before, and he wouldn't be caught dead alone with her. Theo had been proud, doubted he'd have been half as mature at that age. The kid was better than him.

"Fuck, Ford!" he called again, stepped back, roundhouse kicked the door. It slammed closed, bounced open, slammed closed again.

"Easy," Ford said at long last.

"The thing you said was coming: was it Addy leaving?"

"A boy's got to spread his wings."

"So you're some parenting guru? You have kids of your own? Hunched, bruisy-skinned things? Boys hung like acorns?"

"Hush," Ford said.

"You hush."

"Someone's coming."

"Stop being so damned vague."

"*Someone.*"

There was a knock sure enough. Alice. He let her in with an implausible cheer. When the door was open, he heard the wind rattle a greenhouse window pane.

"Were you talking to someone?" she asked and glanced around.

"What does he think? I'll be damned if I'm going to haul his shit."

"He didn't ask you to."

"And sneaking away. If I hadn't come in…"

"What is wrong with you?"

"Of course, you're siding with him."

She uncrossed her arms. She said, "You're being an idiot. Call him. It'll be fine."

"Oh, just like that?"

"Yeah."

"What if he's *really* gone?"

Which was when he imagined Verna and the Judge after he escaped in 1968. He saw them true to life: Verna in her housecoat, exhausted, eyes bloodshot, the Judge tying his spit-polished shoes, going to work as usual because how much worse would it be staying home?

Theo said, "What if he never comes back? I can't handle him going through what I did when I left home…"

That stopped her. "Oh my god," she said.

"What?"

"Oh, now I get it," she said and actually added, "You poor thing," because she'd figured out why everything was so tangled up. Somehow he'd equated Addy moving to Rosemary's with his leaving home because his parents were awful, when the situations were completely different.

"You know I hate it when you do that," he said but listened to her say Addy was safe and secure and knew he was loved, which was the opposite of what he'd grown up with.

"Processing is for cheese," he wanted to say but another wave of dread was swelling. He focused on her mouth as she spoke. He tried to lash himself to her certainty that things would be all right again, but saw, over her left shoulder, what looked, for all the world, like a polished blade on pressed white cotton. A small part of him recognized it was only metal flashing and a folded sheet of paper, but the greater part saw Max Aberhard's roast beef knife and Addy, sixteen again, busboy in a pressed white shirt prepping for Tuesday dinner, looking for the punch to open a clamato juice can and not seeing it, picking up a walnut-handled knife instead, standing it upright, point to the tin, giving the handle a thump with his palm, then laying the knife back on the soft leather where he'd found it, innocent as a field mouse in the sights of a raven, because that sous chef, Aberhard, disposed to raging on his best day, was closing the space and taking hold, hurling him like a scrap of meat at the garbage bin. Addy had come home that evening with a bruise on his shoulder and a deep new understanding that front-of-house staff were not to lay their eyes on a chef's Damascus stainless steel knife, saying Max was an asshole but he'd had it coming.

He shifted his weight, hoping it would stop his leg trembling.

Alice continued to unsnarl his evidently confused psyche and he tried to listen but the scenarios interfered, each one uglier and more vivid. How much worse it could have been if the head chef hadn't shouted Max down. Max Aberhard with his bull neck and in steel-toed boots, miles past appreciating consequences. Addy's face uncomprehending, pure seraphic.

His vision had blurred. He knew his eyes would overflow if he blinked, so he didn't blink, and willed the air to dry them. He said, "This is terrifying. I just want him to be okay."

She stepped closer and her arms didn't seem real at first, but he returned the pressure, breathed her in, saw every hair on her head, and wished some shard of faith would break through. With faith and a bit of hope, the world might stand a chance. He held onto her like Peter afraid of sinking into the Sea of Galilee.

Now he was Scrooge, waking up to find he hadn't quite wrecked everything yet. Christmas was coming, people needed care, priorities wanted sorting. He did call Addy, prepared to talk, though he wasn't upset to get the machine. He'd said he'd been a prick but couldn't wait for Christmas and he'd have his shit together. He said with each passing day he was more grateful that the head chef got to Max Aberhard when he did, because the world could be shit and he hated that he couldn't watch over him all the time and protect him. He said he hoped he hadn't used up all of the tape and that his message wasn't too weird.

He was Scrooge, not sending some random kid to buy the Cratchits a turkey, but waiting in line at the Metropolitan store to buy wrapping paper and an ornament to give Alice with her coffee Christmas morning. A smiling clock-face Santa in frosted glass, the moustache tips making it 3:15 or 8:45, two bright blue dots for irises. People ahead had full carts, so the line moved slowly. He was overheating in his coat but the aim was suspending judgment of the collective dysfunction, ignore the woman just ahead of him with the outsized hairdo and basket full of red and green disposable plates and gold cutlery and the couple near the front with shitty plastic toys that would hold their kids' interest for thirty seconds tops. He was determined to think kind thoughts and concentrate on blessings. The generosity felt fragile.

He'd bought Addy a Bulova at Eaton's because the important thing this year seemed to be to show his love through purchase like a normal parent. This year, he would not give a fine found object or anything restored: he'd dropped in here behind enemy lines, spoken the language and observed the customs on his way though the crowded stores pumped full of oboe carols like carbon monoxide. Later, he and Alice were buying Addy and Rosemary a piece of pottery. Last night, he'd tied ribbons onto the little jars of horseradish and pickles for the gift baskets, packaged rounds of shortbread and not grumbled. He'd watched *Miracle on 34th Street* with Alice and not said a word about the Coca-Cola Santa. This year, he'd notice every moment of joy, as penance for his recent asinine moves and for not yet mentioning that he was building a spacecraft to escape the dying planet.

He felt the watch case in his coat pocket. This one wasn't all that different from the first wristwatch worn on the moon. He could tell the Apollo story once Addy opened it: 1971, the Apollo 15 crew having been issued Omegas, the crystal popping off of Dave Scott's, so he'd gone out moonwalking wearing a Bulova Chronograph instead. Back then, no one worried about the endorsements; the crew would have smoked Chesterfields and sipped Tang in the command module if smoking or sipping were possible in zero gravity.

The line hadn't moved. The heat was becoming a problem, so he shifted his coat back off of his shoulders. He slipped his pinkie finger through the ornament's string hanger, put the gift wrap under his arm, and skimmed the first pages of the *Free Press* he'd bought out front of Eaton's. Dan Quayle had sent out 30,000 Christmas cards with *beacon* spelled *beakon*, and the current Winnipeg cold spell was part of a system freezing the Prairies and US Midwest: -42°F in Scottsbluff, Nebraska, -47°F in Hardin, Montana, -60°F in Black Hills, South Dakota. There were so many ads this time of year as everyone made the most of the season, passed off consumption as a virtue, like justice, courage, and honesty, and hoped to the coming Baby Jesus the house of cards would keep standing for another year.

He didn't know how much longer he could take the heat, even with the coat off of his shoulders. The couple with all of the plastic toys needed price checks. He felt his mood sliding.

He flipped sections. Classified ads, continued from page 17.

A listing drew his eyes. Right-most column, just above the fold, the sale of an auto salvage yard. *Price Reduced! Excellent Business Opportunity! Established auto salvage near Gretna, MB. 6,000 sq ft bldgs on 9+ acres, 1000+ cars and light trucks, extensive parts inventory, all equip...*

The recognition was immediate, the meaning plain before he'd finished reading. The blood whooshed behind his ears, and he knew this was *definitely* the thing Ford had prophesied, not Addy's desertion or the other things, and now the only questions were about the money and how he'd break the news to Alice.

All equipment & tools incl. Turnkey operation! Contact...

He felt a tap on his shoulder.

"Something's coming," he heard a voice say over the rushing sound.

He spun and his eyes felt crazy.

"Why can't you f...?" he began, then registered a rough-looking old guy, caught a whiff of piss.

"Buddy," the man said, unsurprised by the reaction or managing not to show that he was. "I said, You're up," and he gestured toward a cashier.

"Sorry," Theo said and moved toward the counter. The ornament string had wound itself tightly enough his pinkie finger had purpled. He held the whole mess out to the cashier, let her coax the wrapping paper out from under his arm.

The cashier didn't offer him a bag.

He race walked out of the Met, felt the walk become a run across Portage. An auto wrecking yard: it was obvious. He rounded Garry Street, sprinted the half-block to his old truck with its box full of radiators, said aloud, "Salvage 1," remembered how Addy had loved the way the clever scrap dealer turned used car and truck parts into a spacecraft, how he'd played along for Addy's sake, but known the show would never get a second season.

He slowed to a walk when he reached the Olds 88 parked just ahead of the truck. He ears and cheeks and fingers were cold: he remembered the gloves stuffed into the left pocket of his coat, felt the pulsing of his pinkie finger, guessed he'd better free it from the string or risk losing it.

The truck engine turned over, thank God. He revved it, pushed the cigarette lighter in, tried to settle his breathing. When the lighter popped, he pulled it out and faced the bright red element squarely because he needed to have a word with Ford.

16

In December, Fourth Monday Supper was always the last Saturday before Christmas. He'd gone to bed planning to get up and make Coconut Curry Stuffed Peppers, but started awake at 4:45 from a brief deep sleep focused on the vital importance of combining sweet and spicy during a cold snap and needing urgently to make Pumpkin Pad Thai. He knew he wouldn't sleep again.

The garlic chili sauce packed a punch when it hit the hot wok. He drank coffee and made the sauce, added the noodles, cabbage, and edamame, bundled the cilantro, spring onions, peanuts, and crushed peppers separately, and a lime's worth of wedges. He left it all in the fridge, ready for reheating and assembly later at Nalani's.

Alice had left a note reminding him to get wine and beer for tonight and for Christmas. Its terseness chided because he'd left the chore so late. He wrote, Definitely, at the bottom, with an exclamation point and heart. The important thing was to keep his mask of normalcy on as straight as possible until he had the chance to tell her.

It was ninety minutes to Gretna and ninety minutes back. He'd be home around one and there'd be plenty of time to get to the liquor store and to buy a housecoat for Alice and a Secret Santa gift for Elena.

As he waited for the truck to warm up, he watched a pair of leaves stuck to their apple tree, like wet tongues frozen to a flagpole.

The cold snap had outstayed its welcome, burst pipes, cracked machinery, frozen fingers, ears, and noses. No one walked in this cold, but only clenched and endured, envied the black bears and ladybugs their deep sleep underground. To think there'd been sweat on his forehead ten weeks ago. Where had the time gone? he wondered but had the sense to set the question aside. He took 75 south for an hour, cut west, then south again, through Altona to Gretna, at the southern limit of the Pembina Valley before the US border. The pickup shook a klick over ninety and the visibility dropped after Rosenort, so he made Audrey's Café a half-hour late.

The realtor, Pete Thiessen, had waited, thank goodness, greeted him heartily, said not to worry. Theo declined coffee from the Santa-hatted server, managed thirty seconds of talk about the weather and road conditions before he said they'd best get going. The realtor said he liked the *down-to-business* approach, pressed his command start, buttoned his dress coat and picked up his fur hat. This was not a man who wore a tuque.

Thiessen's Buick smelled refreshingly of Brut. It was warm and the heated seats were a treat, but he drove it slowly. Thiessen said back in the day, they'd called Gretna *Smuggler's Point* because the tree cover made crossing the border a snap if someone was of a certain mind. He signalled and came to a full stop at the junction with the empty highway. This was an upstanding, disciplined, likeable man whose motivations were uncomplicated. He drove for the conditions and used the time to listen closely and to demonstrate the keenness of his interest in his client, not as a prospect but as a person. He used Theo's name often because he knew that if he said it just so, almost sang it, the sound could carry, by process of synaesthesia, echoes of the earlier handshake. He knew a man wanted to be known and wanted to be tops and he knew that, in sales, rapport set the table for collaboration, demonstrated commitment to the win-win and, if fine enough, could earn the right to presume and ask penetrating questions, such as, Brass tacks, what's it going to take? Rapport pushed back against the funny feeling that, if things ever went to hell in a handbasket, if the time came, he'd as soon stun you and sever the carotids and jugulars, hang you upside down from a rafter, maybe taste your warm blood as it ran out.

"These days, Theo," Thiessen said, "Gretna is Canada's national hotspot," then indicated the blowing snow and said, "I guess *hot* is one of those relative terms."

Theo caught the use of *relative*. Pete Thiessen was tidy and clean-living, devoted to mercantilism, his family, and his saviour, Jesus Christ, and there was one right and true way of doing something or of understanding it, and he took silent measure of this long-haired, scruffy-faced man, prepared himself to be appalled but not show it. Theo did not mention that, in 1970, he'd walked across from the US a stone's throw east of here, that Alice had dropped him at Neche in the wee hours and driven his old DIVCO tire van east to the Pembina crossing with the baby, that he'd followed the Pembina River north-northwest, then cut north and waited for her to find him. It had been cold that night too but the cold had had no power.

Perhaps it was Pete Thiessen's example, but Theo could see then that everything needed to be simpler and more straightforward and he resolved again to sit Alice down when he got home and tell her everything and if Ford didn't like it, tough.

Thiessen checked his mirrors, signalled right and slowed. Once on the gravel road, the wide, white words *Auto Parts* appeared in the distance on a gray Quonset set among a cluster of other buildings and outbuildings and rows of snow-covered car and truck carcasses. The Penner yard rose out of terrain as otherwise empty as the moon. Pete Thiessen drove them slowly toward it all and Theo knew for certain that this was what Ford had been drawing him toward.

Thiessen reached back for the features sheet and handed it to Theo. What was on offer was one of the granddaddy car and truck salvage concerns in the province, established a half-century ago in 1939, set on nine acres, six acres fenced. He said, You have 650 vehicles inside the wire, another 400 or out back, 6,000 square feet of buildings—office, warehouses, garage, more tools than I've personally ever seen. An older Case loader, two forklifts, four roll offs. Page four gives gross revenue and cash flow, inventory, FF&E.

They rolled into the little lot and stopped in front of a low, flat-roofed building with *Penner Auto Salvage* on the side and *Welcome* above the steel-caged window and beside the *Dog on Duty* sign where the chain link began. *Welcome* seemed like another of those relative terms.

The front reception smelled of oil and rubber and rot. The fluorescents were on but the room wanted light. The long, belly-high counter held catalogues on metal frames, open like accordions, and a camshaft, assorted wiring harnesses, a distributor cap, a plastic licence plate mount, and a worn rotary dial phone. There was a little hubcap collection on the wall, a handwritten sign with purchase terms, a calendar open to June, 1988, two metal chairs for waiting, a coffee machine and cloudy silex.

Pete Thiessen saw no gain in remarking on the light or on the way the wall panelling had separated from its studs, but focused on the positives. The baseboard heating did its job, he said as they passed under the *Staff Only* archway, and he called the parts inventory impressive and pointed to the shelves, floor to ceiling, labelled in black marker. He drew no special attention to the coveralls impaled on the broom handle or the tiny bare-bulbed bathroom with stained toilet and sink, and tub of hand degreaser, the curled linoleum, or notes of urine rising above the Pine Sol. He didn't linger in the office that had plainly doubled as the late proprietor's bedroom in the end, given the metal cot with its mattress removed, the hotplate and discoloured bar fridge. There was a TV with rabbit ears and an air conditioner stuffed around with pink fibreglass.

Theo imagined Otto Penner in a corduroy jacket at the steel desk, staring blankly out through the nervous piles of catalogues and Raid cans.

"I understand Mr. Penner wasn't himself at the end," Thiessen said finally. He said the heirs lived out west and were motivated to sell. He said the listing price took the aesthetics into account. Theo pictured the nephew arriving from Red Deer, suddenly as appalled by the condition of his inheritance as he'd been pleased to learn about it a few weeks earlier, doing just enough to make the place showable—getting the toilet working, carrying out the five-gallon pail Uncle Otto had been using, burning the mattress and clothes and garbage—before he signed the papers and headed the hell back west.

It was cooler out past the old loader and the disassembled forklift, in the wide bays. There was a blue Falcon in the first bay, a '59 Galaxie Town Sedan, partially restored, in the second, and a 1948 or 1949 F-1 pickup in the third. The benches were strewn with tools, an air hose ran to an air wrench by the Falcon. As they neared the steel swing door, Theo felt the shin-level draft of the dog door covered with strips of tire rubber and, in the grease, the short brown and black hairs of a German shepherd.

They stepped outside and he realized how he'd been missing the light. He took in the lines of wrecks, the hundreds of snow-covered car and truck bodies, hoods open, closed, or missing, snow-covered or wind buffed, row after row running out past the back chain link and line of naked poplars, running into the field toward their vanishing point, wanting to launch into the low, layered stratus clouds.

He felt the widening providence in the rows of wrecks, even as a lesser naysayer part of him wondered whether the feeling was ominousness, added that the cold could rob you of your senses and, for good measure, threw in an image of Otto Penner eating from a tin. The larger part countered with the ruination of the ozone and the oceans, the razing of rainforests, the explosion of the human population and the winnowing of other species moving toward an end as dire as firebombing or nuclear annihilation. The location of the place was perfect, a mile as the crow flies from the exact middle of nowhere, but could be a bargaining chip anyway, and the old inventory, though older cars had the best sheet metal. He wondered whether people passing regularly on the highway would see the rocket rise out of the old Penner place and guess it was a tourist attraction.

He was a half-dozen steps into the knee-deep snow. Pete Thiessen, not a man to risk a galosh-full without good reason, stayed in the doorway as he mentioned the three-ton flatbed parked in the far Quonset and the biggest tow truck he'd ever seen, every imaginable tail light, door handle, fender, bumper, and engine block, the inventory excellent, if older. He said, "You'll tell me if you want to see something, won't you, Theo? I've got all of the keys."

The forks of the second lift ran through the windows of a Datsun the same piss-yellow as Harvey Borsok's. Thiessen must have seen the smile because he seized on it and guessed Theo saw the potential.

Never mind the rattling. He pushed the pickup hard the whole way back, his guilt about driving south right to the border without telling her a word deepening the whole way, and he thought, No shit, the money part's going to be treacherous. He called on Ford over and over, demanded Ford say exactly what *the universe* was going to do about the damned money, though of course he never showed when you needed him.

It was nearly five when he burst through the back door. He'd kicked his boots off and stepped up into the kitchen when Alice called from the front room, "Theo! Perfect timing. We need cocktails, stat!" and he remembered the liquor store. He saw the fat FedEx envelope on the dining room table and Barney Dogan coming his way.

Barney had shaved his silly head. There was a Band-Aid over one ear. The guy held his hands out like a pair of trout.

"Theo," Barney said meaningfully, as though a deep need had been met.

"Barney."

"Thanks for letting me crash."

Theo looked at Alice.

"You didn't go to the L.C.?" she said.

"I'm going right now. I was only stopping."

"It closes at six. You know that, right?"

The FedEx package had to be the manuscript. It was all he needed. He freed his hand from Barney.

"Where have you even been all day?" she said, but he pretended not to hear.

He resisted actually running back to the pickup because making the liquor store, and finding something for Elena and Secret Santa, was going to be a squeaker. A bottle of Sambuca might have to do. Thank God he'd remembered Alice's housecoat as he rolled past the mall in Altona.

Barney Dogan's marriage was over and his job was evidently hanging by a thread, and Alice had invited him to stay with them for nineteen hours until it was time to go to the airport. He was flying to Toronto as a first leg of a journey through Munich and Delhi to Pune, India, where he was meeting a kundalini yoga master who'd promised to get him some face time with Bhagwan Shree Rajneesh. She also hadn't thought he should be alone tonight and invited him along to Nalani's.

Theo had said they ought to leave him behind with a plate of warm-ups and his rainforest CDs. He said their friends would never forgive them if they took him, but she'd made up her mind.

Barney insisted on driving. He said it was the least he could do. The car stank of cigarette smoke. He found parking a few houses down from Nalani's.

Theo said he needed a minute with Alice and sent him ahead with the food. Then, when it was just the two of them, he saw Alice looking and waiting for him to speak and he did his best to control his breath.

He said it plainly: that he'd stumbled over the ad for the Penner Yard and driven to Gretna to see it. He heard himself say that taking over a rural auto-wrecking yard was a logical next step in his scavenging career.

"What?" she said, and looked bewildered.

He told her Gretna was ninety minutes south, as though geography was the problem. He said, "You know, where you picked me up after I walked over the border in 1970?"

"Theo, what the fuck?"

"I get it. It's a lot," he said, suddenly aware that the scrapyard made no sense unless he told her about the spaceship, which meant saying, by the way, he did hear from Ford again after the night of his birthday, and that he'd chanced upon NASA drawings and the secret ingredient for cold fusion, but now the mood was all wrong.

"Let me get this straight: you want to *move* to Gretna?"

"Well no, it's a few miles out of Gretna on Highway…"

"If you're joking right now…"

"Southern Manitoba must need midwives."

"Theo, the next move we make is to Saturna Island!" she said.

"Okay, sure, we've thrown that around…"

"Thrown it around?" she said, some anger elbowing past the perplexity now.

"It's never been definite."

"Theo, what is wrong with you these days?" she said. "It has been very, very definite," and her voice buckled.

"Maybe we should go inside and pick this up later. We'd best not leave Barney."

"Jesus Christ, Theo."

"Just keep an open mind. We'll circle back around to it."

"No, I really don't think we will. Listen to me, okay? We're not buying a scrapyard and something has gone very wrong with you." She was trembling.

"Do you still even want to go inside?"

"Of course I don't. Obviously, but what the honest fuck, Theo?" She got out and slammed the door.

He caught up to her as Nalani opened her front door. Once inside, he went toward Gracie, Doc, Marnie, the fragrance chemist, and Wally Plouf. He went that way hoping she'd follow but she went the other way, toward Barney, Denis and Kael, and Lloyd in another of his careful casual outfits.

Gracie made a face in Barney's direction. "What the hell?" she whispered.

"His wife kicked him to the curb. Alice said he could sleep in Addy's room. Tonight only."

"Fuuuck."

"Is that the guy from *The Province*?" That was Marnie. She and Doc stood entwined, backs to Nalani's toaster-element fireplace. Doc had an arm over her shoulder and she had her cheek on his forearm. The ends of their pinkies touched. Llew had sent regrets again this month. He'd skipped last month too and word was he hadn't dated since October Monday Supper, when Marnie dumped him and got together with Doc. Now Llew's old buddy and his most recent ex were finishing one another's sentences.

"Yessir. He's off to India tomorrow to meet Rajneesh."

They kept their voices low, debated the meaning of his shift from hyper-partisan tabloid goon to new age seeker and champion of midwifery. Was it a U-turn like Saul on the road to Damascus or plain midlife crisis?

He could make out parts of what Barney was saying about going to Pune, which he called the Oxford of the East, and the biography of Rajneesh Osho he was going to write.

"The cult leader?" Kael said.

"No, I wouldn't call it that."

"Is that the one where the cult members wear red?" Denis said.

Alice had put on a brave face but Theo doubted she was listening to Barney. He wished she'd look over. He wished he could go back twenty minutes because the whole Penner auto salvage thing didn't make a lick of sense unless she knew about Ford and the rest. He'd left her thinking he wanted to buy a small business: of course it must sound crazy.

Gracie was talking about her old friend Nadja, who'd left a career in child welfare to open a mini-chain of dog grooming salons. She said that after decades of fighting, Nadja had given up. She said, "It's a sick world that cares more for dogs than children."

Lloyd came over, shoving too much food into his mouth.

Theo heard Gracie say, "She's opening a place just down from us on Main."

In the pause, Lloyd, the nitwit, said, "So, quite a year for Freedom, huh?"

He was watching Alice, wondering whether to go stand beside her or whether that would make things worse.

"The fall of the wall and everything. Poland, East Germany…," Lloyd said.

Thank God, Ben came around with wine. He said he admired Theo's work, and indicated the assemblage Nalani had put on a side table. That shut Lloyd up, but only until Ben moved on.

Lloyd said, "Communism's sounding a death rattle kind of thing."

The guy's mouth was full of spinach dip. Theo said, "You have got to stop reading *Time*."

"What is it with you and *Time*?"

"I've told you it's a terrible magazine. It dumbs things down, makes geopolitics an us-versus-them thing: Capitalism versus Communism, Freedom versus, I don't know, bondage?"

"Mmm, bondage," Doc murmured. Marnie was sipping wine and snorted.

"It gets people thinking in American: they forget there are actual people living in those other countries and they say things like, Quite a year for freedom. No offence."

Alice wasn't there anymore. He looked for her.

Denis was asking, "Sorry, who's Osho?"

Kael said, "Keep up. It's what Rajneesh has been calling himself since his followers poisoned some town's water supply and he got deported. Isn't that right, Barney?"

"There was salmonella in some salad bars but no proof that…"

"Weren't they trying to reduce election turnout to get their own guy in?"

Barney said, "Some bad apples. But there was no proof Osho had anything to do with it."

Meg was talking about *The Jetsons*. She asked whether anyone else had heard about a series pilot that was never aired. Apparently it opened with George and Jane and the kids flying away from Earth in the space wagon, and George checking the rear-view mirror just as the planet became a fireball.

"That can't be true."

"Network brass thought it was too dark."

"No, that has to be a joke."

"You read *Time* too much and you start thinking liberal democracy's an unstoppable river flowing east, and after forty years of Cold War everything's going to be fine."

Lloyd slopped more spinach dip in his mouth and said, "I don't get it: do you *like* Communism or something?"

He needed to get the hell away from Lloyd, but knew that if he didn't say something else, Lloyd would and everyone would have to look at the contents his mouth. He still couldn't find Alice.

He said, "It's just that the end of the USSR is going to be less of a collapse than a shattering because dozens of breakaway countries and enclaves are going to make their moves. Georgia leaves, and then the Abkhazians and South Ossetians want out, and the Armenians of Artsakh and Nagorno-Karabakh in Azerbaijan and Moldova with Transnistria, and guys in Crimea calling themselves freedom fighters. Pepper in some strongmen who want to get even with neighbours for wrongs under Moscow or during the Middle Ages... Imagine a dozen pressure cookers exploding in a room this size. The end of the USSR isn't going to be *Rocky IV*, Lloyd; it's going to be *The Andromeda Strain*."

"Wasn't there a plot to assassinate someone in the government?" he heard Kael say.

Barney said, "The mainstream press has never given Osho a fair shake. The mainstream media doesn't like a libertarian. I say that as a newspaperman."

Theo watched Gracie getting her smokes from her purse. He said, "I just don't think we're nearing the glorious end of history, Lloyd. That's all I'm saying."

He caught up to Gracie and invited himself along while she smoked. It got him away from Lloyd and, just now, maybe a few drags would soothe a bit of this vast tension.

Gracie smoked. Theo had her blow the smoke his way. They stood in Nalani's back porch. The wind flapped the heavy plastic stapled over the screens. The snow had drifted two-thirds of the way up the back fence.

Gracie was pissed that Alice had brought Barney.

"That guy's going through something big," Theo said. "All *Osho this* and *Osho that.*"

"He says he's done with politics, if you can believe that. He says he doubts he'll go back to *The Province.*"

"He's giving Marceline everything. He says all he needs are his books and his little drum."

Gracie couldn't talk about Barney Fogan anymore. She said Addy and Rosemary had dropped by her house earlier. Addy had used the fax machine. She called the two of them adorable.

"My adorable son flies the coop right before Christmas, loses his shit on me on his way, leaves Alice and me sipping eggnog with Barney f-ing Dogan."

"What are you talking about? They've been planning to live together for months."

"Oh, and there wasn't a message in the timing?"

"What message? It's Christmas break. He doesn't have classes."

Which sounded simple enough, though of course she'd missed the rejection in it, couldn't be expected to understand how rocky things had been between him and Addy because the kid behaved when she was around. How could she understand there'd never been the kind of flow that Addy had with Lloyd, of all people, when Lloyd was only the kid's godfather because Gracie was his godmother?

And again, because things weren't bad enough, he had to think of Addy on the floor of the restaurant kitchen and that mad dog Max Aberhard swinging his steel-toed boots.

He needed to leave. He went inside to tell Alice. He passed Nalani and Ben in the kitchen, said he wasn't feeling 100%, which wasn't a lie. He called a cab from the kitchen phone.

Alice was on the sofa with Elena and Lloyd. Louise was at the piano with Jade Trevino's daughter, playing Wham's "Last Christmas" four-handed. Barney was telling Marnie and Doc about Rudolf Steiner's spiritual exercises, saying they reconnected you with the direct spiritual perception people had before rationality came along and wrecked everything. More brand new knowledge.

Theo whispered to Alice that he was leaving.

"Okay, whatever," she said.

"Not up for a party."

He wanted her to talk him out of it.

"I'll just slip out," he said.

Lloyd was complaining that Gracie was hard to buy for. She'd unwrap his presents—clothes, books, whatever—say they were perfect and then, nine times out of ten, take them back to the store. This year he was giving her a weekend getaway in January, just down to Chicago. Stay at a nice hotel, see some jazz, get deep dish pizza. Her folks were going to stay with the girls.

Barney said human reason, for all its gifts, ran counter to certain spiritual impulses, cut us off from deeper kinds of knowing. Blah blah blah. He said Steiner's spiritual exercises were called anthroposophy.

"Anthroposophy," Marnie said. "That's like Kegel exercises, right?" Doc snorted.

The song finished and people clapped politely. Louise began "The Christmas Waltz." The Trevino girl watched Louise's hands for a few bars, then joined in.

Alice wasn't saying anything. Theo wondered how long the taxi would be.

Lloyd said he'd wrapped the plane tickets and hotel brochure in the box their new iron had come in, made his stupid joke face. Elena called him *a gem of a husband*, which he probably was.

Theo couldn't stand it.

"You could get her a pea-splitter," he said, more loudly than he'd meant to. Lloyd and Elena both turned. He said, "You know, to make split peas."

Lloyd said, "Okay. Stocking stuffer?"

Alice shut it down. "There's no such thing," she said. "He's being an idiot."

It wasn't too late to make a joke of it, but he'd need to break the death stare he had on Lloyd and that would be tricky.

At least Alice had gone over to him, though she was seething. She said, "You should wait for the cab outside. I'm going to get your coat." She said, "You're being so weird."

Which was true, he knew for sure, even as his thoughts swirled and as he glared at Lloyd. All he had to do was shift his eyes away from Lloyd, fake a smile, get the hell out. He could call Nalani in the morning and apologize for leaving. Blame it on a mood, no harm, no foul.

Louise and the Trevino girl sang about Christmas being merry and every song you hear wishing your New Year dreams come true. Every song really pulling for you. Louise had a nice voice.

Gracie was back. He saw her at the edge of his vision. She was slipping her coat off, looking his way with serious eyes.

"There you are, G.," Lloyd said. "I was *not* talking about your Christmas presents."

The guy was such a tool but, no doubt about it, a better husband and much more splendid father than he would ever be. Lloyd f-ing Whitaker. He couldn't stand it.

He knew the only thing to do was go get the hell outside, with or without his coat, but the clearest, most horrifying image of Addy was front and centre of his mind: Addy on the floor of the restaurant kitchen, looking upward, uncomprehending as Max Aberhard swung his steel-toed boots.

So he stepped to the back of the sofa, reached over and flicked Lloyd's skull with the index finger of his right hand. He made good contact. It made a hollowish sound. His finger stung.

"Ow!" Lloyd said.

"Theo!" Alice said behind him.

"Jeez, Theo," Lloyd said and rubbed the side of his head. Guessing it was a joke.

"I'd like to flick your split pea-brain through that window."

Louise and the Trevino girl had stopped playing. The room was quiet.

He knew it was unforgivable. He was ruining things for some of the best people in the world, but he went in for the second flick, and connected, if less solidly because Lloyd had moved.

He said, "What the heck, Theo?"

He went in with both hands this time—both thumbs holding back the tips of their forefingers, as if claiming falsely that everything was A-okay.

More than anything, he wanted lie down on the floor and sleep.

He feinted left and went in with his right. Lloyd managed to cover and got to his feet.

"It's about time," Theo said.

Alice was shouting, "What the hell are you doing?" She took hold of his left elbow and wrist, her grip strong enough to leave a bruise, which was fine.

They were getting into Barney's car when the cab came. Alice had marched him out Nalani's front door like a five-year-old who'd flipped the chips and dip table. She was driving him home and that was that. Theo apologized to the driver and gave him ten bucks for the trouble.

Alice sat, mittens on the wheel, waiting for the windshield to defrost.

He imagined Gracie and Elena tending to Lloyd's pea head. He thought he saw the bay window curtain move. Nalani had looked hurt as they left. He'd told her he was sorry but undermined himself by snarling in Lloyd's direction.

"God, this car stinks," he said.

She turned and studied him. She said, "*That's* what you want to say, is it? That Barney's car stinks?"

"Can we go?"

"You attacked Lloyd."

"*Attack* is a stretch."

"If I'd thought about it for a year, I'd never have dreamed this."

"Well, that's a relief, I guess."

"You *attacked* Lloyd."

"I flicked him."

"Who does that?"

163

"I connected, like, once. He mostly dodged the other shots. Can we go?"

She backed up a metre, shifted into drive, checked the mirror and shoulder-checked, signalled to the empty street. She deferred giving more shit until she'd completed the manoeuvre.

"He's one of our best friends."

"He's only a friend by marriage. We're stuck with him. I've never liked him."

"You *hit* him. Have you lost your mind?"

"Tell me he doesn't drive you crazy. Everything about him drives me bananas. Just once, can he not fill his mouth with food before he starts to speak? And the way he is with Addy. 'Oh, and Addy popped by the office to use the fax machine,' or, 'It being Thursday, Addy and Rosemary dropped by for cocktails and canapés...'"

"You're jealous of Lloyd?"

"Of course not."

"It sounds like you're jealous."

"Well, I'm really not."

"It's just that you've been so angry." She said it angrily but merged carefully onto the St. James Bridge.

He thought, *Flectere si nequeo superos, Acheronta movebo*, but didn't say it. He said, "You should get into the middle lane."

Her eyes told him what he could do with his routing suggestions. She said, "What is going on? You're starting to worry me."

Of course it was time to tell her that the Earth was nearing her last breaths because *homo sapiens* had killed her, focus on the why and how of escape, and the research he'd been doing and the NASA drawings, and the secret sauce for cold fusion being burned tobacco so maybe water would be the only fuel they'd need, but say over and over that she and Addy were more important than anything else. Ask her to join him so they could invite Addy together, and maybe Rosemary, though they were young and who knew? Tell her everything: grant it might sound batshit crazy at first, acknowledge the crazy part straight off, get it out there, and only then remind her that he'd learned a thing or two about aerospace engineering back at WashU. Show her it was a matter of survival, a journey more urgent than crossing the border twenty years ago. It would be like proposing all over again: he could kneel on the bench seat of this stinky Taurus and say nothing could make him happier...

He exhaled. Evidently, he'd taken a breath to speak, then held his breath.

"You're a million miles away," she said.

That was a hook: he'd open with the million miles, say it might sound like a lot but did she know even Mars was fifty million miles...?

"You've been pushing everyone away... One by one. It's like some kind of countdown to zero."

"What does a countdown have to do with anything?"

"Now it's a scrapyard? Suddenly you're ditching all our plans to become the auto parts king of southern Manitoba?"

He was losing the thread. They were barely halfway home and things were getting murky. He wished she'd step on it.

"Is it us?" she said.

"Of course it's not us."

"Is there someone else?" She sounded braced.

"Jesus, how could you even say that?"

"It would explain a lot. You've been so weird. Is it some kind of midlife crisis?"

"Give me a bit of credit."

"You attacked Lloyd!"

"I flicked him."

"And the way you talked to Addy..."

"I apologized for that."

"You almost picked a fist fight on Main Street."

"That guy was an asshole."

"It's like I don't know you anymore..."

"He looked like Bob Guccione."

"Well, ever since your birthday. You've been different since then." He couldn't think what to say.

"You remember your birthday, right?"

"Vaguely," he said. "Of course I do."

"I want my old Theo back. He was a better kind of crazy."

She said it lovingly, but there was a warning.

They were quiet. They summited the Arlington Street Bridge over the rail yard and rolled down into the North End.

"Ford," he said.

"Right," she said and nearly smiled. "Ford."

So here it was: his best opening yet to tell her there'd been sign after sign, and all of the miracles or whatever were down to Ford, so, yes, they'd been talking since his birthday and he wasn't just a figment of a stressed-out imagination. None of the rest made sense unless she knew about Ford, and once she did know, everything else followed.

She was going to need to open her mind a bit, that was all.

This was going to be a big discussion but who knew how to start? He had to think about it and fools rushed in, etc.

They were quiet. They glanced at one another from time to time, as though confirming the other hadn't disappeared.

He needed to be careful. He needed to think about this because telling her about Ford was important, maybe the key to everything, but it was also tricky and there would only be one first pass at it.

A couple of blocks from home, she said, "It doesn't have to be me that you talk to. It's fine if it's not. Maybe a counsellor."

"Sure, maybe."

She seemed relieved.

He felt the same mixture of providence and ominousness he'd felt looking out over the rows of wrecks that morning. A mix of threat and promise, like waiting for a jump scare in a movie, or walking through the garden in July knowing that, likely as not, Moose would be crouched between the rows of carrots, lurking under that fresh green canopy, waiting to leap out and scare the shit out of you. She could send him packing the way Marceline had with Barney, and no one would blame her. That was ominous as shit: that their future was suddenly as conditional as *unless* or *so long as* or *supposing*. He'd tell her about Ford, he thought, but plan it carefully. He could not fuck it up.

She stopped in front of the house. She said that, unless he wanted to talk now, *actually talk*, she'd go back to Nalani's.

He asked her to tell Nalani sorry again.

"You'd never do something stupid, would you?" she said.

"You'll need to narrow that down."

"You'd never hurt yourself…"

"Now, that right there is the craziest thing you've ever asked me."

17

He woke on Christmas Eve 1989 thinking about Christmas Eve 1914, when, for a while, at so many points along the Western Front, French, British, German, Belgian soldiers rose from the cold, clay-slick trenches they'd haunted like it was Judgement Day, and, for a few perfect hours, stood upright in No Man's Land, shook the hands of their enemies, sang carols and toasted with brandy, gave biscuits and damp cigarettes and haircuts as gifts, told stories, and helped gather one another's dead, and a German boy dribbled out the ball for an otherworldly kick-about, so they felt their feet again, and the concertina wire disappeared, or nearly did, because the laughter was shot through, understandably, with hysteria, but their souls did thaw a little after six months of sanctioned slaughter with efficient new guns and clever gases. They were six months into an adventure their leaders had sworn would last two months (three, tops) because it was in the nature of their filicidal leaders to lie and, as each subsequent Christmas approached, the generals would warn against further displays of life and love, say it would be treason.

The house was quiet as a ceasefire, lonely as a last blade of grass above the snow. Recollections of telling Alice about Penner Auto Salvage surprised him again and again, as did flicking Lloyd's head and seeing Nalani's face as Alice dragged him away. The only possibility was going to the shop, making a fire, opening up the bag of paper shreddings and finding out whether they really were NASA drawings of an airlock device or solar cell or thruster, or some reasonable facsimile cast in front of him that day like a wiggling Red Devil designed to catch the eye of a passing bass.

He sat at his table before a nest of thin paper strips, Grandma Maggie's blanket over his shoulders. He untangled them, laid them flat, weighed down their ends, tried not to think about the other things, though he did decide that dreaming of a Christmas Eve ceasefire was fitting since Alice and he would no doubt keep a kind of peace for as long as it took to assemble the gift baskets and decorate the tree, roll out dough for the Wellington, get rid of Barney, and fake some cheer when Addy and Rosemary came over. The dream made more sense than the bits of lines and letters on the strips, and wondering whether the boy with the ball had been the Judge himself before he was stern and saturnine, someone playful you'd call by his Christian name and whose leg still worked as he chased the ball over the frozen, anguished ground, and whose knee could bend to kick, unlike the Judge, whose leg would swing like the ghastliest croquet mallet.

Of course, the boy with the ball in No Man's Land was just a private and no American could have kicked a ball with Germans in 1914, because the Americans didn't go until 1917, not to mention 1914 wasn't even the Judge's war but Grandpa Strahl's, so not to be spoken of, because of the failure, not because the Great War, so-called, had been the war to end wars forever but because mentioning it raised the spectre of George Strahl, who'd wanted to be a chaplain but been put with the foot soldiers, though he was twenty years older, and who misplaced his hope even before the troop ship made France and he saw all of those horrors, and who came back only in body and only long enough to trouble Grandma Maggie with the second pregnancy before he wandered for good, and left nothing behind but some vague cautionary tale.

The dream insisted: somehow the boy with the ball was the Judge, cast against type as vivid, verging on glorious, the indescribable morning light on his face, otherworldly. Belgian instead of Missourian, and a playful soul, because facts are different in dreams, which measure truth differently and operate by a different logic.

Who knew anything, except that he'd been ruminating on the Judge well before Verna called that night, and that reassembling the paper strips was like nailing Jell-O to a wall. He hadn't made out the NASA logo since that first day behind the 7-Eleven, and the best he'd done today was identify four strips that seemed to belong to a series of six or eight, the letters above a line suggesting the word *cloakroom*.

As usual, if Ford knew, he wasn't saying.

Undeniable too were the facts that he'd rested his head on the table only for a moment, but fallen asleep and only woken after she knocked and started through the door, and that he could have handled it all better than whipping the blanket from his shoulders and over his head, down over the drafting table so the paper strips billowed outward and the blanket did much less to conceal the secret than amplify it. Alice stood on the threshold, jacket over her housecoat, holding a steaming mug of something, as strips of paper fluttered down like anemic ticker tape. One landed across the toe of her boot. What there'd been of a saddish smile gave way.

"Alice," he said from the top of his breath. He resisted saying, It's not what it looks like, but only watched her take in the paper shreddings, an open notebook with some careful diagram or other, the colourful helical schedule, and guessed this must be what it meant for a face to be blanched. He felt a strip of paper on his forehead.

Sometimes you have no hope of listing your regrets.

"Sorry to disturb you," she said. "I brought you Kahlúa cocoa." She set it down, went back out, pulled the door closed, and he heard her feet crunch back toward the house.

They babysat Barney and the truce held. Alice worked on the Wellington. Barney helped Theo rearrange the front room for the tree and stick the fake spruce branches into the green broomstick trunk. Barney participated mindfully—with his five main senses plus his breath, named his gratitude—as they shaped the wire and plastic branches. He named the scents in his mulled wine—managed clove and cinnamon but needed help with cardamom, tangerine, Lady apples. He held the glass up to the window and tried to count the colours. Alice rolled the pastry, laid in the filling, crimped the edges, arranged pastry holly leaves, brushed the lovely thing with aquafaba to bind it.

When Barney offered to string the lights and start the decorations, Theo said, No, with too much force, then explained that Addy liked to do the decorating. He said dollars to doughnuts Addy would get around to asking why they never got a real tree like normal people, because he asked every year, and Barney needed to belly-laugh like a Buddha. As much as Theo could have shaken him, he was glad the guy would be there a couple more hours because Alice's body language told him to steer clear of the kitchen. He tried to decide whether she looked more afraid or angry, and that question took him back to 1914.

They assembled the gift baskets: jars of their fiery-sweet hot pepper jelly and grapefruit marmalade, chestnut chocolates, miso caramels, sour cherry chocolate fudge, tiffin with ginger, cranberry, and chocolate, bottles of mulled wine. Alice wrote the tags and Barney tied them on. The thought of driving around with Alice later to deliver them was awful, so he suggested he and Barney do it now, plan a route that ended at the airport. Alice didn't look up but had to understand.

They took the pickup because it smelled like 10W-30 and not cigarettes. It was a relief to get out of the house, even if it meant time with Barney and his crisis. Their delivery route took them through the North End, then south to St. Boniface, around Fort Garry and River Heights, then ended at the airport. Theo drove and Barney said he'd probably miss the cold when he got to India, because to be human was to be ungrateful. Barney's speech was as fake as the Christmas tree: he'd been rounding the sharper edges from his consonants, drawing his words out more languidly, as though three-quarters of the way into a trance. Theo tried not to encourage it. He turned the radio up a notch, made a show of listening to the documentary about people not getting funerals when they died of AIDS, because their families disowned them or the funeral homes wouldn't handle their bodies.

Barney declared himself a pacifist, said he was *a Quaker more or less* because, after a decade of creating outrage and stoking conflict, suddenly he was going to therapy and reading up on conflict resolution and mentioning Thích Nhất Hạnh and Ursula Franklin like they were old friends. Theo imagined closing Barney's windpipe with a knife hand, then adding some small thing about Ghandi as he sat choking. He thought about down payments and mortgages, wondered how Penner's nephew would take a lowball offer.

They waited for the light at the foot of the Norwood Bridge. A new desperation had drifted over Barney, an urgency, as though, if he stopped to take a breath, they'd slip the hood over his head and pull the lever. Theo thought of the boys in No Man's Land at Christmas, the meagre joys of a plague year and how the only war to end all wars would be the next one because it would also end the world.

Theo rolled into the intersection and Barney shouted, "Whoa!" because he'd spotted the jackass running the red from the north. Theo hit the brakes in time and leaned on the horn, continued toward the Village. The CBC was talking about Barbara Bush at a children's hospice, happening upon a baby the staff couldn't settle. She'd picked him up and he'd settled, because she was a grandmother, she said. Wasn't real compassion and care *contagious?* the reporter said.

Now Barney wanted to hear Theo's feelings about *resisting* the war, wanted to know what it had really been like to come to Canada back then.

"I don't think so," Theo said. "Besides, I thought you knew all there was to know about us *draft dodgers…*"

"I'm sorry about that too, then," Barney said. "I used to do such harm." He claimed it seemed like a lifetime ago, said he was trying to regret those days intelligently, whatever that meant.

"You know it's only been a few weeks, right?" Theo said.

Barney said he'd be doing many good deeds in India. Maybe sooner, even in the airport.

The CBC official time signal followed ten seconds of silence.

The memory of flicking Lloyd made him cringe again. It had been a shitty thing to do when Lloyd was just being Lloyd. And, throwing the blanket over the paper shreddings. Alice's face, the paper strip across her boot.

He had his own amends to make. He would drop Barney at the airport, then go fix things with Lloyd. Then talk to Alice somehow.

Noriega was holed up in the Vatican Embassy. The Americans had him surrounded. Bush pretended to be surprised about the cocaine trafficking and money laundering and murders, though he'd have known all about it when he was running the CIA.

"Operation Just Cause," Theo said. "The DoD guys must dream up names like that and laugh their asses off."

Barney said Manuel Noriega grew up without a healthy father figure, that he'd been lost and desperately searching, which was why he'd been loyal to Omar Torrijos. Barney knew what it meant to grow up without active male energy. He said he used to think his mother was overbearing, when the real problem had been his dad's work addiction.

"You're comparing yourself to Manuel Noriega?"

"Just the part about fathers."

"Barney."

"Rudolf Steiner said…"

"Barney! Just stop."

He stopped.

"Look, you're going through some sort of crisis, and the sooner you snap out of it the better."

Barney looked like Lloyd after the first flick.

"Sorry, man, but someone had to say it. You should patch things up with Marceline."

"Oh no. I've changed too much for that."

"Okay, have you really?"

"I'm changing."

Theo left it to hang.

"People *do* change," Barney said.

"Yeah, but sometimes it's only a costume change… speaking of which, you are not Kashmiri."

"If people can't change, I'm screwed, because all I've ever done is try to piss people off and look clever. I've been a coward. Marceline used to egg me on."

The guy was unravelling.

"Barney, you're fine," he said. He'd go easier, get the baskets delivered, drop him on the sidewalk at Departures.

"I know people have never liked me."

"You were only a dick in your columns…"

"It was the same in school. I started trouble, then stood back and watched."

Theo checked his watch, said maybe they ought to head straight to the airport.

"People have never liked me because I've never liked myself."

"Got everything you need? Plane ticket? Wallet?"

"But you," Barney said. "People like you and admire you. Your work and your art, what you have with Alice and your boy. You might be the happiest man in the world, even with the recent turmoil."

"What turmoil is that?" he said, because the word was turning his stomach.

"You and Alice are the best."

"What turmoil?"

"Say, when I get back, can you take me scavenging?"

"I doubt it."

"I think it would be fascinating. Just think of the spiritual dimensions…"

"Poking through trash isn't church."

But Barney let fly with the spiritual dimensions: how the consumer society relied on the wheel of acquisition and disposal spinning faster and faster, even as it drained more and more meaning from lives, how Theo redeemed the leavings, raised them from the dead like Jairus's daughter. Theo was a monk praying for the soul of the world.

"You just make it up as you go along, don't you?" Theo said.

"Well, actually, that was from your manuscript, more or less."

"You've been reading that? You really have made yourself at home."

"It's inspiring: finding beauty in the disaster, the inventions, the art. I loved reading that some people set things out for you, like an offering, as though they know throwing it away is a sin. You're a garbage messiah."

Theo was grateful for the chance to laugh.

"Okay, trash prophet," Barney said.

They were on Academy, heading for the Kenaston Bridge. He checked his speed because there was always a trap.

"But you're okay, right?" Barney said, his eyes a bit damp now.

"Okay? Seriously?" he said. He still wanted to know what Barney had meant by *the recent turmoil*, but said, "What kind of idiot could be *okay*? With fifty wars around the world, kids with automatic weapons, ceaseless rape and slaughter, and millions in camps surviving on millet from the same people who made the weapons they ran from, when no one even knows how many warheads there are or how many drums of sarin, never mind the old school sulphur mustard gas or cyanogen chloride, or the anthrax. A few dozen species going extinct every day because people are stupid and the forests are on fire and the farmland's turned to desert. Trust me, Barney: notice maybe one percent of it and you are not going to be *okay*."

Tabloid Barney would have called him Chicken Little, but New Barney said it came down to care of the soul. The guy lacked a core.

"Right. Got it," Theo said. "Make yourself the hero of your story. Tell yourself you really matter and all you need to do is compost and know your neighbours and vote with your wallet. Sooner or later, though, you notice there's more than just your own little enlightenment journey—no offence—and you pull your head out of your ass and notice the whole thing's a house of cards and all it takes is a coup or someone's currency going to shit or a vial of smallpox gets out of a lab or some Marsberg, which, did you know, liquifies you from the inside so your skin sweats blood? The point is, it doesn't take much before the TV goes off the air, the governments fall, and the fighting turns to the last lake-full of drinkable water and if you survive the first few hours, the fallout thirst will unhinge you and you'll wish you hadn't."

New Barney's brow had a look of concern. He said, "That's so pessimistic…"

"I'd say realistic. You hear that? It's the sound of the Horsemen saddling up."

"Even misanthropic."

"Accurate, though; you've got to give me that."

"People are better than you think. Have faith. My therapist…"

"For Christ's sake, Barney. Faith in what?" He wished his words were knives.

"Human potential," Barney said, and didn't he pronounce the potential for creativity and love to be vast, and even dust off the old nut about people only using ten percent of their brains, which was a shame because you'd expect a journalist to check a fact. Wasn't he claiming the human spirit would change the universe, then circling back to bloody Osho and how someday people weren't going to need external controls—legal, social, religious—because they'd be pure discipline, and wasn't that *something*?

Theo knew that Barney's wide, needy eyes would be too much, so he watched the road. The affected rise and fall of Barney's voice was already too much—the extra gerunds, the quarter-exhalations meant to suggest emotional intensity or release—and such shit about the inevitability of goodness and history moving in the right direction, and mentioning George Leonard and Aldous Huxley for no good reason. He'd put his faith in the power of patience and kindness, the human drive toward metamotivation, whatever the hell that was, and if he'd gotten into a Hero pose on the passenger seat, or a Half Lord of Fishes, it could not have been more embarrassing.

There was a fragility to it, like Addy, aged ten, giving himself liberty spikes, pushing the Dippity-Do beyond its capacities, and only a heart of stone would not have broken when he came down for breakfast. But this was different: Barney was just a guy in his forties in a desperate flight from a self he'd come to loathe. Whatever he'd built plainly could not survive but, just as plainly, wasn't for Theo to step on. Theo's job was to bite his tongue and let the guy go to India.

"Air Canada?" Theo said.

"Yes, please," Barney said and seemed to be wrapping up, which was good. Apparently Osho taught that every person comes into the world with a destiny, a task to complete or a message to deliver. That we're not here accidentally, but meaningfully and the universe *intends* something through us. Barney was saying, sure, there was a lot of work to do, *a whole lot of work*, but the thing to do was be patient and prepare for a miracle.

It was all too much. He said, "Jesus Christ, Barney, and what if you're Hitler and your message is fascist and your task is mass murder, or you're Oppenheimer at Los Alamos and your task is building Little Boy?" He said, "Anyway, here you go." He put the truck in park.

"Of course people can lose their way."

"You're missing the point. You can't talk about human potential without considering the potential for selfishness and evil."

"There's that pessimism again…"

"What is the matter with you? Remember old Barney? You were an asshole. The odd time I read your column—say, in a bathroom stall when it was the only thing to hand or because you'd written some ugly thing about one of my friends—if I had any response, it would be to wonder who hurt you when you were a child or to fantasize collapsing your larynx. You know? But honestly, old Barney didn't piss me off half as much as this new one."

"I should go."

"Obviously, if you breathe a certain way long enough, you'll over-oxygenate your brain and have an interesting experience, but are you really coaxing the universe forward?"

"You're starting to sound like Marceline." There was the first flicker of anger.

"Well, maybe she's on to something—I mean, the shit you've been saying and doing and, I mean, Raj-fricking-neesh, Barney? The neo-sannyasins poisoned salad bars. Look, go to India, get it out of your system, then get your ass back here and patch things up with the paper."

"Well, fuck you, too," Barney said.

"Ah, there we go, and you, practically a Quaker." He clapped Barney's shoulder and said, "But Merry Christmas."

Barney didn't look at him. His face was extra pink as he got out and closed the door. Fetched his bag from in back.

Theo pulled away and watched him in the rearview: he was standing in front of the airport, shifting his grip on the suitcase handle, as though the thing had become a burden. He wished he could have the last five minutes back. He considered stopping but didn't, so checked his own reflection instead, said aloud to himself and anyone else who might be listening, You're such a piece of shit.

Thank God Addy and Rosemary were there with Alice. They were full of the Christmas spirit, lousy with joy, and he wanted a bit of what they had. They'd built a fire and put on music, started the cocktails, broken out the Christmas jigsaw puzzle. The tree was done, the gifts piled beneath it. They greeted him like a guest. He and Alice traded kisses as though neither of their hearts hurt.

He turned over puzzle pieces while Addy went to make him the year's Christmas cocktail. He thought maybe the night could still be perfect, even if it meant doing a jigsaw. Maybe concentrating on the puzzle would oust the memory of Barney looking half-shattered as he receded in the rearview.

They worked on the border. The puzzle was called In the Valley, and had a flock of sheep grazing in the middle ground, framed by flowers and foliage. The plumpest quail watched a fox creep toward a jackrabbit; no doubt he was relieved the fox would get the dopey rabbit first. There was a stone cottage, and distant foothills in blue and mauve. They worked on the felt puzzle mat Addy had bought as a preteen because, even then, he'd loved the Christmas puzzle and the mat allowed for safe, convenient storage at meal times. Theo had never seen the point of jigsaws, of spending hours assembling the thing, then taking it apart five minutes later, but he'd always gone along for Addy's sake.

He liked the cocktail—a sidecar strained into a cinnamon-sugar-rimmed coupe glass—and Addy's Christmas mix tape. *Fairytale of New York.* Alice had her hair down, the way he liked it best. Rosemary told a story about her grandmother as a girl at Christmas. As she spoke, she pushed her glasses up with a finger. Addy wore a new blue flannel shirt. There was a scent of cloves and the time passed slowly. If life stayed just like this forever, he'd have been content, except when the image of Barney in the rearview elbowed in, or the clop sound of his finger hitting Lloyd's head, or when the awareness of how he'd screwed things up with Alice seemed to cut, or when he wondered whether a puzzle mat could speed the reassembly of the NASA plans.

He worked on the bluebirds—one perched above the fox and a second alighting—suspended disbelief in a world where a scrawny branchlet could hold a portly bird, thought, surely, the second one would land and lower them both level with the fox's muzzle and that way spare the rabbit.

Nothing in the scene, foreground to distant purply foothills, made much sense but Addy said he'd chosen it because Alice liked sheep, which got her going on trivia: that sheep can remember fifty other sheep faces and recognize human ones, and eight percent of male sheep are gay and sheep poop is good for paper-making because of all the cellulose. She said their huge pupils allow nearly 360-degree vision and she asked who could define *wether*. No one could.

Theo said sheep intestines were good for making tennis racket strings.

"That took a dark turn," Rosemary said, and raised her glass to toast it. She'd become part of the family puzzle.

They moved from sidecars to wine and, in a while, Alice reglazed the Wellington and put it in the oven. They rolled the puzzle into its mat and set the table, dressed the salad, warmed the bread and heated the plates. Theo didn't want the day to end, because tomorrow, or Boxing Day at the latest, he'd have to come clean with Alice about the end of the world and the ark, finish explaining the Penner Yard, and tell her why he wouldn't be going to Saturna after all, wouldn't be raising sheep or making cheese. He decided to stay up as late as anyone, to sit up with the kids after Alice went to bed, drink more wine, work on the jigsaw as long as they wanted.

Alice's Wellington was a wonder—its pastry tender and flaky, fatty, golden—the layers of roasted peppers, beets and ground walnuts, feta and lentils with nutmeg, toasted hazelnuts and spiced apple. She'd made a gravy of brandy, shallots, crushed peppercorns.

After dinner, they unwrapped gifts and ate sticky toffee pear pudding. Addy gave Alice and Theo the 1990 Pirelli calendar; this year a collection of Olympic athlete women shot in black and white. The kids liked the pottery but Addy actually seemed disappointed that he hadn't made them something instead. Go figure. He gave Alice the housecoat and a gold ring he'd found at a flea market and had engraved. She hugged him but when they drew apart, she couldn't meet his eyes. He wondered whether any Christmas Eve had needed a Messiah more than this.

It was just after ten and they were playing cards when the phone rang. Addy answered.

"Dad, it's for you," he said. His saying *Dad* instead of Theo would have made it serious, even without the expression.

"Who is it?"

"Just take it."

He said, "Hello."

She said, "Theodore," and inflected upward, not quite as a question, but more beseeching, and her voice at once familiar and foreign.

His belly dropped and he said, "Mom," noticed that his eyes and Alice's were locked, though now her gaze was too much so he was the one to look away. He faced the wall and the 1989 calendar on its nail: December was a winged, dark-haired nude, looking slightly down and right, leaning forward, hugging her legs, chin on her shoulder. The light bleached her face. He wished Addy had gone to Art School and not Commerce.

"Theo, your daddy died today," she said and he could hear the extra decades.

"I'll come right away," he said.

She went so quiet that he thought they'd lost the line. "Mom?" he said.

"You will, Theo?" she said, her voice breaking.

"Of course. It's a twenty-hour drive."

"Sixteen, tops," Addy said from the front room where he was pacing.

"Sixteen. I'm leaving now."

"Oh, that's wonderful," she said.

"Do you still live on Pebble Cove?"

"Yes."

"Okay. We're up in Canada."

"Is it cold?"

"You wouldn't believe how cold," he said, like a kid calling home from a school trip.

"You'll dress warmly?"

"Of course."

Verna said, "What a lovely young man Addy is. You must be proud."

He and Addy were on the road forty-five minutes after he set the receiver back in its cradle. No one suggested they wait for morning and, obviously, no one suggested Theo fly. Addy stepped up, said he'd just changed the oil in the Alfa. Alice packed food and made a thermos of coffee, said she'd book flights in the morning.

No one needed to say it would be the first time Theo crossed back over the border since he came over nearly twenty years before. He nipped out to the workshop because he hadn't cleaned since the morning. He swept the paper strips into a pile in a corner and hung the assembly board back on the wall. He gathered up some notebooks and pens, and copies of *Astronautical Guidance Systems*, and *Apparent Position Calculation*.

18

Heading south on 75 had been fine when he knew he'd be cutting west toward the salvage yard, but going all the way to the border was another thing. He told himself that crossing over was nothing, and people did it all the time. He told himself to get a bit of courage for once and Verna's voice played through him, twenty years thinner than the last time, her announcing, Your daddy died today, entreating him to dress warmly. Remembering how she'd braced herself, as though he really might not go, made him wince.

The implications of Verna knowing his area code, much less his number, when he'd been in hiding for twenty years, had not registered, or of her having an opinion on whether Addy had grown into a fine young man or an ugly, evil one had not registered by the time the boy confessed he'd been talking to her and the Judge for months. He'd gotten the number from 314 directory assistance and cold-called them, gotten to know them over long distance from Rosemary's place. There had been letters and, lately, he'd been thinking about telling them he was going to a concert in Minneapolis but driving to Missouri and Ladue instead.

He said he'd just wanted to know *something* about his Strahl side and knew he wasn't going to get it from Theo.

"*Horror vacui*," Theo said.

"Are you mad?"

"No," he said and guessed he meant it. They'd assumed Alice's family had been enough for Addy and that he'd been satisfied with the bits they'd told him early on: that Theo had grown up in a part of St. Louis called Ladue but loved visiting his Grandma Maggie in Ozark, three hours away, and that his father hadn't been an easy man. Addy knew that things finally got bad enough at home that Theo had needed to leave but that everything worked out because he'd met Alice and then Addy had been born and life was a hundred times better than it ever could have been a thousand miles and an international border south. They'd given him enough to finish a family tree for school.

Addy drove the limit. The road was good—backtop bare, good visibility, light traffic. He said that, as a kid, he'd known Theo would never talk about the Strahls or where he'd grown up, so he'd designed questions to trick him into giving something, like, Did he ever go to a Blues game and also what was the name of his elementary school? Wasn't it weird that St. Louis called their football and baseball teams both the Cardinals and did he have any cousins on the Strahl side? Did Theo know that he and Robert Wadlow were from the same hometown and, since Saturna lay at 48 degrees, 47 minutes, wasn't Theo breaking his vow never to set foot south of the 49th when he went there?

Addy talked them past the crewcut border agent. Theo thought of Cerberus and honey cakes and did his best to seem normal. The boy brought the Alfa back up to cruising speed, but kept inside of eight over the limit on I-29, and he changed the cassette. The first hour of the drive had left Theo winded.

He took the wheel at Fargo. Addy slept and left him with his muddled thoughts. About Verna so far down the phone line and how he'd suddenly needed to close the distance, her awful relief when he said he'd drive down to stand with her, and the etiquette for mourning a bad father you renounced two decades ago. About how Addy's old Alfa really could fly, though the way the gas gauge dropped, you assumed the tank had a leak, and about how badly he'd treated Barney, how he'd trampled on something new and green, even if it was an embarrassing shade, and Barney in the rearview, making no move to get out of the alarming wind, frozen there with his luggage and his new doubts, watching Theo watch him recede in the mirror. He thought of Alice waking in a few hours and there being no Christmas ornament by her cup for the first time, having to make her own Christmas Morning coffee, and he tried to remember the floor plan of his childhood home but ended up confused because his countless dreams of it since he left seemed to have moved walls and rooms. Dawn was miles and miles away, and what he'd have given for Addy to wake up and ask to play Going on a Picnic or Would You Rather the way they used to do on road trips. It occurred to him he could turn around and take them home. He opened the driver's side window for the cold, praised Addy's funny car for its thirst because it needed stopping every 200 miles to fill up.

Addy took the first shift out of Minneapolis. The day would be a straight shot south on I-35, US-218, and I-380 until they skirted the Missouri-Illinois border. Theo slept a little and one of the times he woke it was to KMOX saying Nicolae and Elena Ceaușescu had been taken straight outside to the firing squad after swift trials for genocide and self-enrichment. He dreamed of games in No Man's Land and the Judge finally able to bend his knee again, but kept circling back to Barney and wondering why he couldn't just let the guy go to India. His bullishness about humankind would give way soon enough and there'd been no more need to say that Dick Nixon and Heinz were their truest selves planning to bomb Cambodia than to tell the guy he wouldn't get to first base with the tantric sex. Theo slept his broken sleep and ruminated on his shame: why he'd wanted to smother the guy's new faith in human goodness before he even got inside the first of the next four or six airports, wondering how cold you had to be not to turn around and render assistance.

He woke Addy after Weldon Spring, before they crossed the Missouri, because the Daniel Boone Bridge seemed like something he should see and because, if Addy was awake, he might not need to stop the car to throw up whatever was left in his stomach from Iowa City. They crossed the half-mile span and Theo said the Boone had gone up in 1935 and used cantilevered Warren through-trusses, with spans up to 500 feet, and explained that the longitudinal and cross-members formed equilateral triangles, alternately right-side-up and upside-down, which was an improvement over Neville trusses, which used isosceles triangles. Addy was a good sport, though his eyes kept wanting to close and he was no more interested in compression or live loads than he'd ever been.

"Only another half hour or so," Theo said.

"Really? How long was I asleep?"

"This is Chesterfield. That airport's the Spirit of St. Louis."

"Is that where Mom and Rosemary…?"

"No, they'll come to Lambert, which is way over that way."

"You want me to drive?"

"I'm fine. You get six winds if you keep your eyes open long enough. Each gust's a little weaker, mind, but you make do." He was a hundred times the father the Judge ever was, but he guessed he really ought to be telling the boy something worthwhile.

The scene of the crime, he thought as they turned onto Warson, guts churning, then he asked himself, And what crime's that? in a voice like Ford's. They'd rolled the windows down because the late December Missouri air was as warm as April in Winnipeg and his skin felt too sensitive, like he was coming down with the flu. They followed Pebble Creek Road, more of a long, winding lane than road, until the bungalow came into view, smaller-looking, as childhood homes are, but also squat because the willow had doubled both upward and out and the cedar topped the gutters. It was as though a giant thumb had pressed the house into the ground.

"This is it," Theo said, to convince himself as much as inform Addy. The tires hit the drive one by one, made the headlights bounce as they swept left across the flagpole and front door, settled on the garage.

Verna came straight out, which meant she'd been waiting, and she came through the side door, which meant they weren't company. It had to be Verna who stepped past the egress, her stride shorter on one side. She held her cardigan closed.

Addy's wave registered at the rightmost edge of Theo's vision and the sound as he fumbled for the handle. Theo imagined the boyish grin and delighted eyes as Addy ditched all cool and leapt out. Verna said Addy's name as he approached and they embraced as easily as Theo and his Grandma Maggie used to. Verna leaned back to take Addy in some more, and Theo heard her say, I'm so glad to meet you, Addy, before she pulled him close again.

It felt like they'd come from farther than just the next country and, where ten minutes ago, he'd been desperate to get out and stretch his legs, the implausibility kept him still now, as though this was an imitation of Verna Strahl: the exaggerated, almost stagy lines by the mouth and eyes and the farfetched ones across the forehead, the way her eyes seemed smaller or the sockets larger, the lower half of the face almost abbreviated. Was it possible the chin was slightly rotated? The hair was the most obvious costume: Verna's had always been a light brown and she'd had it set every week at Geneviève's, but this hair was short, unfussy, and white as a flag.

He killed the engine and, as he unclicked the belt, Verna's gaze tracked his way. Her head straightened from what must have been a tilt. He worried everything would be wrong close-up, then wondered what kind of maroon ever doubted his mother's genuineness. He pushed the car door open and wondered what there could possibly be to say, saw Addy was looking too and that he was delighted, so guessed that, as uncomfortable as he and Verna might be, they'd contain whatever disappointments or fears or uneasy truths there were for Addy's sake.

After that, he smiled more like a person is expected to at a reunion and hoped the embrace would be convincing enough.

The first time he woke next morning, it was still dark. The radium dots of Grandma Maggie's clock said it wasn't quite four. He took a book from his bag, stole out and down the hall, past his parents' room and his old room, where Verna had put Addy. She'd wanted Theo and Alice in Grandma Maggie's room because of the double bed. The name *Alice* had sounded strange when she said it. The house was exactly as he remembered but also nothing he'd ever seen. The kitchen was as disorienting as it had been last night but he found filters for her modern Melitta, and he wondered when she'd finally retired the tall stainless percolator she'd used for as long as he'd been forming memories, looking up to check the colour of the liquid in the glass bulb as she fried eggs or buttered toast or used the special knife on grapefruit halves. Every morning, when the Judge entered in his pressed shirt and careful tie, ready to be served, the scent of his aftershave mixed with the sharp burned coffee.

While the coffee dripped, he returned to the front room, past the arrangements people had managed to order before the florists closed for Christmas, to the photos on the long side table. Grandparents and great-grandparents, Judge and Verna at their wedding, shots of him as a toddler, at nine or ten, and at sixteen, with an equivocal expression and glasses as big and square as the grille of a car. There was a portrait of Verna and Judge on their thirtieth anniversary, and a more recent shot of the Judge on a beach in a woollen flat cap, his features softened by the light. The one of Alice, Addy, and him had been a surprise last night. Rosemary had snapped it the evening of his birthday and his smile was a hoax.

He'd missed reentry by a mile. He'd put his arms around Verna for the first time in twenty years, she'd been as small as a bird and he'd actually said, "I'm sorry for your loss," like a florist arriving with an arrangement and, when she held them both and called them her Christmas miracle, he'd been hyperaware of his body in space, wanted to crawl out of his skin and disappear into the ground, and said, unaccountably, "You don't remember how fat the stars are until you drive a whole night on the highway." What could she possibly have said? Addy had said, "Okay then."

She'd said, "You must be starving," and started for the door.

The Judge's preposterous Continental sat in dry dock on the far side of the garage, and that was a surprise, then Verna's kitchen with the same Arborite table and Naugahyde chairs as 1968, though she'd toned down the wall colours. It smelled like Christmas dinner. When she sent them to wash up, she said, "Theo, can you show Addy?" as though he'd brought a friend from school.

She'd laid out sliced chicken and stuffing, mashed potatoes, peas and carrots, Brussels sprouts, cranberry sauce. She'd set no place in front of the Judge's chair: she and Theo took their old places and Addy took Grandma Maggie's. Halfway through saying grace, she stopped and said, "Oh, my Lord, but do you even eat meat?" Addy said it was perfect, that he'd have eaten a horse, but preferred chicken.

The scent of lilies was overpowering in the front room. He went back to pour coffee.

Thank God Addy was there because Theo could find neither words nor appetite. Addy was a fine guest: he ate heartily and took the extra helpings, he listened with interest, spoke lovingly and familiarly. Verna was about to get the dessert when Addy said, "Grandma, you sit… your hip," because she'd evidently told him she needed a new one and he'd remembered. Verna used Rosemary's name without prompting, knew about Addy's courses, and that he was some kind of post-punk entrepreneur. She knew about Alice's practice, how Theo had been dragged into the art world, and she knew about the book he'd written. Who was this kid, Theo had wondered, talking about his daddy's work, mailing Christmas gifts so early—a silk scarf for Verna, a pen for the Judge?

Theo spoke when spoken to, the way he used to do, and each warm remark and joyful observation between grandson and grandmother spotlit the distance between son and mother, seemed to add to the list of things unsaid. He told himself to get a grip but could find no place to start and how could he just pick up where they'd left off twenty years ago? Verna spoke, but her voice was a mystery—the voice box shifted or the larynx thinned, the lungs gone wispy.

Last night, he'd hung on as long as he could, then announced that if he didn't go to bed, he'd be face-down in his dessert. Even this morning, he doubted he could manage the kitchen table, so he took his coffee and book back down the hall. He peered into the Judge's office on the way, noticed the spines of the Judge's poetry books on one shelf and thought it was good he'd finally stopped hiding them. Of course, no one went into the office without an invitation. Theo went back to the bed he'd been given.

The second time, it was the flash that woke him: the way it used to in this house, his heart banging its cage. He woke already sitting, staring ahead, blind as a tin cup. He remembered he'd been reading. His mouth had a coffee aftertaste. He counted his breaths and waited for the room to reassemble, wished he hadn't come back to this mad place and its dreams of that grievous light.

He caught scraps of conversation between Addy and Verna in the kitchen, and another woman, or maybe two. It was right for Addy to be the centre of things for Verna, the way he'd been the centre for Grandma Maggie. As he crept across the hall for a shower, he wondered whether, back then, the Judge was the one who felt like a spare tire.

He didn't remember Ladue water being so hard. It took forever to get the shampoo out.

"There he is," Verna said. "I'll put on fresh coffee."

"I've got it, Grandma," Addy said. "Butter wouldn't melt in his mouth."

"Both of you sit," Theo said, because he'd spotted the seating problem.

"You remember Mrs. Hagan?" Verna said.

Of course he did, and Heddi Hagan was in his seat, or what used to be his, and the only free place at the table was the Judge's so he'd sooner stand. Mrs. Hagan had also forsaken her big hair and, like Verna herself, she was recognizable but wholly different. For now, he'd lean against the counter, sip coffee, listen as Addy told them everything they didn't know, and think up ways of getting through until it was time to get Alice and Rosemary.

The visits and phone calls and deliveries picked up mid-morning and, by 11:30, things had moved from the kitchen to the lily-thick· air of the front room. A procession of visitors, middle-aged to elderly, schooled in the etiquette of mourning, brought casseroles with surnames written on the bottoms, sliced meat platters and vegetable plates, melon, pineapple and strawberry arrangements, cakes precut into squares, cookies, dainties, to crowd the kitchen table and fill the fridge and freezer and the nearest shelves in the garage. June Wolover handed off potato salad and cinnamon buns, dropped her spring coat in the big bedroom, and took over from Mrs. Hagan next to Verna on the sofa. Now Heddi Hagan took the phone, answered, "Strahl residence," jotted messages, explained cross streets, said, "Why, a visit would be just fine." The Ladies of St. Peter's Episcopal did what needed doing. They poured and sliced and reheated, gathered dishes and washed them, did everything that could be done to brace Verna up, murmured, Aren't these lovely, as they unwrapped more flowers, acknowledged Mr. and Mrs. So-and-so, or from Judge and Mrs. Thingummy so Verna could hear. The Ladies met Verna's lovely grandson and remembered Theo, Yes, of course. They directed the husbands. They stayed the right length of time.

Addy sat on Verna's right-hand side, and she marvelled at her fortune, said *Christmas miracle* enough she began apologizing for the repetition. "Our Theo at last," she said. "Down from *Canada*," and, "Dear Addy," and, "grandson," to get used to it. Addy ate it up, even literally, because the Ladies kept bringing little things for Verna and her handing them off to Addy became the joke. There was no doubt it was her when she laughed, the way she raised her chin and her eyes laughed too.

Theo could not have sat still, so he appointed himself Master of the Melitta, made pot after pot, carried them around for top-ups and kept the big pump thermos full. He saw that, as much as Addy already seemed to have put down roots, he'd stayed above it all himself, the way he had as a kid and teen: he watched the terrain from a distance, did not consider landing. He found excuses to go outside, strolled past the pool Verna said they'd closed the year after he left but never removed just in case.

The priest, Mother Patricia Wynne, took his hand warmly and without judgement, when God knew what she'd heard. She asked him to call her Patricia in a voice that seemed unlikely to boom like the old timers, back to Father Walter, whose thunder had been the only possible compensation for being useless as a blow-up dartboard. No one would have called him Walter except the Bishop and maybe his own mother. Patricia wore her collar more intelligently, and easily enough Alice might like her, though damned if seeing it didn't bring Deacon Sid to mind and reprise the last night of the world—the Saturday, five days after Kennedy announced the Cuban missiles—when he found out Sid's feet were clay too and lost that last hope. He wondered whether Sid ever abandoned his campaign for conversational Latin and whether he made it out of his closet.

Still three hours until Alice and Rosemary landed, so he insisted on fetching coffee for Mother Patricia, or tea, then resumed orbiting past his parents' old friends who claimed it was good to see him as casually as if he'd been away since September. Their faces were the indictments.

He knew how the rest of the day would go. He'd fetch Alice and Rosemary from the airport in Verna's Nissan Maxima. Alice would hold him and ask how he was doing, then ask after Addy, then say, And your mother? because the subject would need opening. On the way back to Ladue, he'd sense her anticipation and he'd do what it took to keep Rosemary talking. Then the introductions back here on Pebble Creek Road, they'd have some wine and a bite and, sure as eggs, he'd notice a new warmth in Alice's regard for Verna and, as Verna introduced the ancestors in an album or two, he'd see Alice's eyes make the shift from wary and commiserating to curious, despite her long loyalty. Photos of Granny Bogges and Grandpa Mark, Grandma Maggie at her wedding, so much lovelier than her groom, whose old hand must have weighed on her shoulder, then Maggie and her boys well after the old man took off—the Judge, serious for his age, and Eugene, whom they'd have tricked into standing still and who squinted at the camera like a wild thing in wait, then Judge and Gene in their uniforms—and the more prosperous portraits of the Cases and Verna, the Judge and Verna's wedding, then him as a baby in Verna's arms, then Judge's, but happiest in the shots with Grandma Maggie. He would watch Alice watching Verna and notice how her glances cut from puzzlement toward sickened recognition, on the lines of realizing you've misread your ticket and missed your flight to somewhere grand. After that, the tension would hang like humidity and, at least once that night, he'd look at her and she'd look away.

For now, some husband was leaving. He was gripping Theo's hand and saying what a fine young man Addy was, but calling him Hadley, but Theo was listening to Verna tell someone about finding the Judge in the garage and how it was a blessing he hadn't suffered.

"Yes, yes," Theo said as he walked the husband out, it was strange being home, being simultaneously forty years old and eighteen, then adding that maybe this was what drowning was like: the slow-mo loss of footing and being pulled down, the panic as you understand you've taken your last breath and guessing it wouldn't be as bad if you didn't fight.

Jesus, but wasn't it the weirdest damned thing he'd ever said to a stranger? He resumed his coffee duty, wondered whether the rest of the guests would ever leave or just get their mail forwarded, until Addy looked over with a beatific smile and settled things.

Mother Patricia said a prayer before she left. Theo and Verna were with her at the door. He had her coat. She said, "The Lord is close to the brokenhearted."

"And saves those who are crushed in spirit," Theo said.

Verna gave the slightest gasp and her face twisted again. She raised her hand to her face, so there was nothing for Theo or Mother Patricia to do but wrap their arms around her.

19

Theo woke early. *Astronautical Guidance Systems* wasn't going to read itself and neither, he guessed, was the Judge's obituary, clipped from yesterday's *Post-Dispatch* and laid out on the kitchen table, much as they'd have laid out the Judge himself out in an earlier time, once the attentions had been paid—the sweat of death scrubbed away and, with luck, his earthly sins, his remains dressed in Sunday best to meet the Lamb of God, pennies on his eyelids, chin tied up against yawning. The Judge looked out from his obituary photo with an ease Theo had never seen, with something approaching kindness or mercy, an effect, he guessed, of the wrinkles and folds moderating the disgust, reducing signal clarity and obscuring his intentions, like the lilac or light pink paint slapped on Fat Man or Little Boy. It was plausible if you didn't know what you were looking at, though he saw through it as easily as any glossy General Electric or Exxon ad.

Judge Bogges Strahl, 76, former Judge of the 17th Judicial Circuit of Missouri (Cass & Johnson Counties) died suddenly Christmas Eve, 1989 at his home in Ladue, Missouri. He was born in 1912 in Ozark, elder son of George and Margaret (née Bogges) Strahl. After his father's death in 1919, he helped in the family's general store and, after graduating from Ozark High School during the worst of the Depression, worked full-time in the store for several years until a generous family friend subsidized his tuition to

Southwest Missouri State Teacher's College. He suspended his plans for teaching after Pearl Harbor, and followed in the WWI footsteps of Harry S. Truman by joining the Missouri National Guard and 35th Infantry (Santa Fe), and he followed President Truman too by serving as Field Artillery Battery Commander (127th F.A. Battery B.). He enlisted as a Private and separated four years later as a Captain. He fought in France and Germany and he was seriously wounded at Villers-la-Bonne-Eau, Belgium as the 35th repelled the attacks of four German Divisions. He underwent surgery in England and returned to Ozark in late 1944 for rehabilitation. For his service, he was awarded the Bronze Star for meritorious service and six campaign stars.

After the war, he attended the University of Missouri School of Law in Columbia, earned his degree in 1948 and met the love of his life, Verna Lynn Case, daughter of his Constitutional Law professor August Case and the poet Edna Case. Judge and Verna married and made their first home in Columbia so that Verna could continue her studies, and Judge practised with the Case Dennell law firm for two years. He went to work with the Circuit Attorney for the City of St. Louis, where he advanced to First Assistant Circuit Attorney. He moved from bar to bench in 1953 and the 17th Judicial Circuit, and served there for 29 years until his retirement in 1982. Judge Strahl was a gentleman and treated others with dignity and respect, both inside and outside of his courtroom. He was highly respected within the legal community. He was one of the original committee members appointed by the Missouri Supreme Court to draft the Missouri Civil Approved Jury Instructions for use in all courts of the state, and he was appointed Special Judge to sit on the Missouri Supreme Court for a term.

Judge was a person of faith and enjoyed Christian fellowship as a member of St. Peter's Episcopal Church of Ladue, serving on Vestry and as People's and Rector's Warden. He gave freely of his time to community and national organizations, ranging from the Missouri Public Defender and Missouri Legal Aid, to the American Legion, Veterans of Foreign Wars, and organizations devoted to natural conservation, animal welfare, historic preservation, and the Midwest Region of the Lincoln

& Continental Owners Club. He was an avid fisherman, an enthusiastic if frustrated golfer, and he enjoyed driving the Continental Mark V he bought new in 1960. He was a loyal alumnus of the MU Law School, devoted Tigers fan, and a lifelong Democrat.

He leaves to mourn Verna, his wife of 41 years. He was predeceased by his parents and younger brother, Eugene. Judge's greatest sorrow was the long estrangement from his and Verna's only child, Theodore, who left the family and Missouri in 1968 and with whom he never again had direct contact. He lamented the separation, but spoke with pride about the young man Theodore had become.

A few months ago, out of the blue, Theo's own son, Adrian Towne Strahl, contacted Verna and Judge, who were overjoyed to make his acquaintance by phone and through letters. There was talk of Adrian visiting this spring. So it is with much gratitude that, in addition to being survived by Verna and many good friends, Judge is survived by his son, Theodore Truman Strahl, daughter-in-law, Alice Edith Towne, and grandson, Adrian, of Winnipeg, Canada.

Judge touched and enriched countless lives in large and small ways. He made a good job of his life. Funeral services will be held at St. Peter's Episcopal Church in Ladue on Wednesday, December 27, 1989, at 10:00 am, with interment to follow immediately at Bellefontaine Cemetery. Arrangements by Gibson Funeral Home.

He was sketching thrust vectors when Verna came into the kitchen. He resisted the impulse to hide what he was doing as she sat down.

"You read the same kinds of books," she said and asked him to tell her about astronautical guidance. It's what she'd have asked at this table twenty-two years ago.

"It's how an airplane or submarine, say, integrates the available information about wind conditions, water, temperature, and what-have-you, so the control system can keep a stable heading."

Telling her was like riding a bike. How many thousands of words had they exchanged here?

"Your father used to say you'd end up in charge of Ground Control at Cape Canaveral. And to think you turned it into art," she said. "How wonderful."

The Judge looked out from his photo and his disappointment was plain enough.

She took his hand. "In the beginning, I worried you were cold or didn't have enough to eat."

"I was fine."

"I went over and over the clues I must have missed."

"I didn't leave because of you," he said. "It just wasn't safe after that night. It had been like that for years, talking about his day at supper: people who'd come before him, making examples of them, one pronouncement after another. The racist and sexist tropes, the protesters who needed haircuts, his boy LBJ. Things changed in a hurry when I finally spoke up."

He couldn't read her. She'd stayed with him forty years; she was bound to defend him. Would she say the times had been different or that he'd just been blowing off steam? Blame the generation gap? Her hands were smooth and warm. He said, "But I shouldn't be talking like this. Not today."

She said, "By the time you were at WashU, it seemed like the only thing that interested you was your work. You'd eat, excuse yourself and get back to it. Would you believe neither of us thought you were listening? I can't imagine how silly that sounds."

"I heard every word. I never got numb to the brutality of it, the matter-of-fact way he said things. I'm sorry if this hurts you..."

"It made more sense later. We were looking for you and met some of your friends. We were glad you'd made such good friends. I was proud you'd gotten into campus politics."

"I did my protesting away from home. Facing down police or National Guardsmen wasn't half as daunting as Dad. I feel sick thinking about it..."

"The way you two argued that last night: I thought if I'd been any kind of wife and mother I'd have seen it coming or somehow been able to stop it. After you left, I didn't like him for a long, long time and he didn't much like himself much either. He drank more and wouldn't hear of stopping and, after a year or so, he managed to drive into a highway end terminal. The car ricocheted into the oncoming lane but, fortunately, the road was deserted so he didn't hurt anyone else. He got away with a broken arm and two black eyes. He didn't drink again after that, which was good. He seemed more humble.

"But how glad we were to hear from Addy!" she said. "To meet him and to hear what a good life you've made for yourself. Meeting Alice has been a joy, and Rosemary. Addy has a Strahl air about him. The way he braces up with his eyes. Judge had it. You always did."

"I've always thought he was more of a Towne."

They heard someone stirring. The bathroom door closed.

"A couple of things you should know," she said. "Your father wanted you to have the Continental."

"Why on earth? I hated that car."

She smiled. "I don't know why he liked it so much."

"Weapons-grade stubbornness?"

"He said there weren't many 1960s at the car meets."

"Because they hurt the eyes. If Addy wants it…"

Verna said the other thing was that Judge had kept Theo's bank book.

"I cleaned out the account when I left."

"He decided on an allowance and deposited it every week, and what we might have spent on birthdays and at Christmas. He said it was in case you were ever strapped for cash and thought to look there. Not long after you left, he hired some kind of detective. I don't think the fellow was much good at his job. I suspect he made things up to keep your father paying. I think the bank account was the only other thing he could think of."

The easy, kinder look of the Judge in his obituary photo seemed a bit more convincing.

Theo said, "The others are waking up. I'll start breakfast."

He went through the stack of maroon passbooks like an animation flip book. As he flipped the pages, the handwritten dates, deposits, and running totals tripped and gyrated, became rows of dot-matrix digits, and the right-most column expanded leftward, four digits to five with the cents by mid-1968, then six digits, seven and, finally, eight. The last deposit, less than a week ago, brought it to $462,778.51, or $535,000 Canadian.

There were faithful weekly deposits, Mondays or an occasional Tuesday, $10 a week for the rest of 1968, then $12 through 1969, up to $14 in 1970, plus amounts the week of his birthday and before Christmas, the amounts unrounded, as though he'd gone out and found a gift he'd have purchased had the recipient not fled and deposited that plus the tax. The birthday amount was larger in 1970, as though celebrating legal drinking age in absentia, a puzzling $5,000 deposit in January 1970 and a doubling of the allowance from there. Theo imagined the Judge in line for the teller, deposit slip and cash between the passbook pages. Mrs. Wilson, already ancient when he left in 1968, initialling the entry shakily, maybe asking whether there'd been any word. Had some teller after Mrs. Wilson ever suggested the Judge buy a bond for the extra interest?

He snapped the rubber band back around the booklets, tossed the bundle onto the guest room bureau, and tried on the suit Alice had chosen for him from the Judge's closet. Dark blue. He'd always seen the Judge as big and broad, so it was a surprise when the jacket felt tight. The old man's shoes were too small, so he'd pull the cuffs down over his boots.

He felt nearly as sorry for Addy as for Verna by the time they reached the church, and he consoled them as best he could. Verna, Alice, and Rosemary went inside, while he and Addy joined the honour guard and undertakers and the other pallbearers by the hearse. Ward Greer was there. Theo had liked Mr. Greer best of the Judge's friends. His greeting seemed cool and the handshake hurried. His eyes were hard to read behind his thick lenses. He looked unfinished without a tie.

When it was time, they hoisted the flag-draped thing onto their shoulders and carried it through the front doors and into the vestibule, stopped near the guest book and photo of the Judge, the pile of leaflets, the tray of cards people had left. They watched the man from Gibsons for their cue.

Theo had only been back to St. Peter's two or three times since the last morning of the Cuban Crisis. Those times had been Christmas Eve services and it had been enough to remind himself that the past was gone and there was only the present, and there was no need to unravel again.

This morning, he was all right until the organist began "Jerusalem, My Happy Home" and the signal came for them to move. They stepped into the nave and the morning light exploded through the vast glass panes to his left. It ignited the walls and the pews and pulpit, seemed to bleach the mourners, and thrust him most of the way back to that Sunday, October 28, 1962, when he was thirteen and there had been no detaching from the emergency or the roar of imminent annihilation.

They stepped too slowly and only just inside the nave. He squeezed Addy's shoulder. Mother Patricia and the front rail were very far away and there was no denying the force of remembering that other morning just here, leading the procession down this aisle, the terror having crushed him since Monday when Kennedy came on TV and, by the Sunday, surged so far beyond his capacity to endure. Not long after church was over that morning, the news announced that Khrushchev had blinked, so creation could go on a bit longer, he was well past hearing it and on his way to the hospital, as sick as the radiation would have made him.

In this bright light, trapped under the Judge's casket, memories of that week in 1962 flashed and raised the gastrointestinal distress simmering through the morning toward a boil. They resumed their slow walk and he stumbled and felt Addy's hand close on his shoulder. He tried to walk from the hips, but the cramping made each step more painful.

He felt Ford, so turned his head to nine o'clock and there he was, back to the baptismal partition, bare, emaciated, bruised and bristly-haired, balanced on trotterish feet, service leaflet and the Judge's portrait upside down over the awful genitals. A fig leaflet, it occurred to him, and he remembered Deacon Sid in Confirmation Class saying the baptismal marked a boundary between those reconciled to God and those not. Ford looked puzzled.

Now he skittered double-time to the hymn, resisted doubling over against the cramping, clenched harder against shitting into the fine, borrowed pants. The chill made the casket heavier, though the hand on his shoulder proved Addy's was just across the casket. He loosened his own grip so as not to leave a mark on the boy's shoulder.

Halfway down the aisle, he remembered the little door to right of the sanctuary, past the front pew where Verna, Alice, and Rosemary would be sitting, and where places would be held for Addy and for him. The casket blocked his view. There was sweat in his eyes. Time was running out. He did what he could to increase the collective pace.

The instant they set the casket down, he turned and went for the door on careful steps, knew that, if the door was locked, his rectal muscles could well give way. He imagined Mother Patricia closing her hymnbook.

He pushed through the door, took the hallway and the stairs, somehow managed the multiple impacts of descending, raced for the toilet down the dim hall, knew that, if someone, maybe one of the ladies preparing the reception, was using it, he'd need to strike a balance between knocking and speaking firmly and alarming her.

The toilet was vacant. He rushed inside, closed the door, got the pants down just in time to sit. As his insides rushed out, the image of Mother Patricia came vividly: she drew the kindest breath, began the sacred rites, said joyously, I am the resurrection and the life.

He stayed on the toilet until the pain subsided and his knees stopped bouncing. He flushed three times. The smell was awful. There'd never been an exhaust fan in here. He wanted to curl up on the greenish tiles of the floor.

"I am sorry for your loss," he heard Ford say from the chrome of the toilet paper holder. "My heart goes out…"

"You don't have a heart."

"It's a figure of speech. Anyway, just remember, I said the money part was dangerous."

It called down another wave from his insides.

Ford was back to Charles Olson. *The under part is, though stemmed, uncertain is, as sex is, as moneys are…*

"*Facts to be dealt with,*" Theo said, "*As the sea is, the demand.* Can you please leave me alone?"

"… *that they be played by, that they only can be, that they must be played by the ear! But that which matters, that which insists, that which will last.*"

They were silent until the maroon-covered bank books came to mind and he realized that there was more than enough to buy the Penner Yard outright.

Meaning that Ford had raised his unsightly vestigial fingers and plucked the thin cords that hitched the worlds together. Played them like an ugly instrument.

"You killed him," Theo whispered.

"His heart gave out."

The important thing was washing and reassembling, getting back upstairs.

"Who are you really?" he said as he flushed again.

Ford heard. He said, "We've covered that."

There was a silhouette in the hallway. He was going to recommend the person find another bathroom until he saw it was Alice.

"Are you okay?" she said.

"Just a bit off," he said, and indicated his belly.

"You're pale." She straightened his tie, pushed back some hair he'd splashed against his face. "Are you up for this?" she asked, and he said he was.

As they reached the family pew, he made a face he hoped would land as *Forget about me; think of the Judge*, then sat and did his best to watch Mother Patricia and to listen to her, and not to look at the altar server, because he knew the sight of the kid in her bright white alb could throw him back to 1962 all over again, when it had been him carrying out those duties. He focused on Mother Patricia's clear, smooth voice. He resolved to leave in the morning.

Mr. Greer felt his way up to the lectern and drew some cards from a jacket pocket. The top one read, *Pact*, in letters large enough for Theo to see, and, *Work*.

Greer said, "Some years ago, Judge and I agreed that whichever of us died first would have the other speak at his funeral. Never did I imagine that I would speak for him. I begin with such a mixture of emotions and guess that, should I make it through my remarks in one piece, it will be because I've reminded myself often enough that it is a rare thing to be with him and to speak without interruption.

"Two things need saying: first, that few men ever worked as hard as Judge Strahl and, second, that he and I once decided to hold a demonstration."

He cleared his throat and adjusted his glasses.

"Judge Strahl was the finest example of a man for our brutal, idiotic age. How we all admired his ability to press on with whatever work was at hand, unwaveringly, heroically even. He'd toiled like Sisyphus in the family store as a youngster in Ozark, after the First World War swindled him out of a father. Through the Depression, only *Great* in its wicked calamitousness, he helped his mother make their meagre sales, he lifted and lugged, did the deliveries, and helped mind Gene, who was a handful. He worked like a lodge of beavers through college, which was where we met, and then he worked his soul case out through the next World War, persisted miles and miles past exhaustion, and returned with injuries to body and soul that would have finished most, though he limped up the stone steps of Tate Hall to learn about the law, read everything, argued it, did better than most, took his call, then sweat blood to make First Assistant with the Circuit Attorney. He kept that pace through three decades on the bench and, along the way, served this church and a dozen worthwhile groups, and somehow found time to keep that ludicrous car of his on the road.

"I believe that greatness sounds different depending on the ear and on the times. Judge's formative decades amounted to a series of evil emergencies but, more than just surviving, he laboured hard and thrived, and he brought loved ones and friends, strangers and even enemies safely through with him, and there was a greatness to that. The awful heat and the pounding forged a certain frame of mind in him and a compulsion to work, so, while he had his demons, he did not complain but only did the work that needed doing and drove himself on, long after staunchness had gone out of fashion.

"Which was well and good, though in every strength there lurks an awful weakness, and this fact pressed and pressed until we were a pair of silly, blustering retirees, sipping whiskey and finally wondering what our blinders may have obscured, finally beginning to list some corollaries of our bloody-minded drivenness.

"For instance, how, when we fished from a boat or from some shore, it was an activity to be gotten through efficiently. We aimed to catch the fish, but did not linger, so failed to notice fully the joyful plunk of the lure hitting the water, or its brief skip over the surface, and we paid too little attention to the breeze. A round of golf was going to war, and whoever celebrated the scent of the mown grass in combat? Judge swung a wood with the same clarity of purpose he gave a decision or chewed out counsel, which was the same way he'd aimed a Howitzer in Europe. Not that the intensity did much for his golf, because an unbending knee will vitiate the swing as much as legal blindness will impede aim, and we could only ever hope to shoot our ages if we lived to a hundred and eighteen."

His hand went to check his tie. He remembered he wasn't wearing one, so fumbled with his collar.

"The point is that for Judge, as for me, life was labour, and life away from work, be it recreation or a Saturday, still needed scheduling like the trains did and, when we could be feeling the sun on our faces, we were lining up the next task to complete or problem to solve, then wondering where the time went.

"The worst part, we saw, was the gulf we'd opened between ourselves and those we loved, because we'd each held forth but not listened and we took others' silence as actual agreement. By commission and omission, we told our families they should be like us, then wondered why we were always apart from them.

"But listen to me lecturing," Mr. Greer said, and claimed the irony of his holding forth again was not lost but that he was keeping a promise.

"So, yes, Judge worked hard in his profession and successfully, but Carmen and I never saw him as alive as when he met Verna forty years ago, or when she said, Yes, or when Theo arrived and, when Theo went away in 1968, our reassurances were pebbles down a well compared with his self-judgement, and that only began to lift when Addy called from Canada. Judge is watching now, grinning ear to ear to see his beloved Verna with Addy, and Theo and Alice, and I doubt he'd care less what it cost to bring them here."

Mr. Greer strained to read his card, then nodded.

"Yes," he said, "the demonstration. All right, it was after a first glass of whiskey this past autumn that we got to imagining this life without the wars and disasters or, in other words, life less as habituated emergency than a kind of play that restored and enriched the soul. Which was not to suggest the troubles were done—man's inhumanity to man still makes countless thousands mourn—but only that we'd fought enough. We had much better wives than we deserved, we were well-enough-heeled but exhausted. Our wars were over, or our parts in them, and we wanted to come home.

"Which was when Judge said we ought to organize a demonstration, and we imagined collecting a dozen codgers at the courthouse with signs, you know, and some songs, and someone leading a burning of neckties since we had no bras or draft cards.

"Our demonstration would not be an assertion of will, because we've asserted more than our share. It would be less demand than acceptance and listening, so, a quiet affair given the lack of bullhorns, but celebrating the passage of time and friendship, all we love and life itself needn't be noisy.

"Still, no one needed to see a pack of geezers shuffling and it wasn't in our nature to be a nuisance, but thinking it through made us smile and, anyway, we saw well enough that sitting on some shore with a line in the water or tasting whiskey or reading something, or touching someone's hand was demonstration enough so long as we paid attention. It occurs to me now that this eulogy is a demonstration, albeit with too much of my voice.

"That day, Judge and I agreed that whichever of us spoke at the other's funeral would go without a necktie, as though it had been burned, which explains my attire. Truth be told, I feel as unclad as if I'd come without my trousers, but a promise is a promise and it's my honour indeed to see my dear friend home."

Theo was unstuck again, floating between worlds, wondering whether Ford had killed the Judge for his selfish purposes and whether the Judge had really changed or whether his friend had only made it sound that way as a balm, the leaflet saying there'd be Holy Communion after the hymn, so the altar server would set down her book after the first verse to begin the tasks he'd performed himself twenty-seven years ago. Later, he would remember singing "The Lord Is My Shepherd" but thinking about heading home the next morning and getting hold of Pete Thiessen, and there would be scraps of carrying the casket again and of walking next to Addy and of the slow convoy to the cemetery and the straps above the grave, Addy and Alice looking the worse for wear and putting his arms around them both, and the bugler but no nine-man detail or drumming or volley shots, though entitled to them by his rank, because the Judge was aware of the cutbacks. A soldier must have presented Verna with the tricorn and said the thing about the President and a grateful nation, but he wouldn't recall that, and they must have lowered the Judge and left him. He would recall the lunch laid by The Ladies back at St. Peter's, in the hall where he'd first tried an oatmeal cookie dipped in sweet, white tea. Verna introduced Addy, Alice, and Rosemary and said, You remember Theo to The Bridge Bunch and Golf Gals, architects and others she'd worked with, parishioners, lawyers and judges, some politicians. She said, "Our son," and, "Our grandson," and, "Our daughter-in-law," and held them close as buttresses.

"Ward, thank you so much," she said to Mr. Greer, who was with Carmen and one of their daughters, Leslie-Anne. The Judge used to say that, when the guy upstairs put Carmen in Ward Greer's path, he more than made up for the eyesight.

Later, Theo got Mr. Greer alone. It seemed important he be understood. He said, "Sir, I'm sorry you've lost your friend."

"Your father will be sorely missed, Theo."

"I wish I'd met the man you were talking about up there. I'm afrid he wasn't the Judge I grew up with." Theo watched the man's eyes through the thick lenses.

Mr. Greer gave a little nod and he said, "I wish you could have known your father as an adult."

"Maybe in a way I did: he made me grow up too soon. Mr. Greer, I had my reasons for leaving," he said and wondered why the man's approval mattered. He said, "If I'd stayed, things would have ended very badly."

He and Alice were walking on Woodcliffe away from St. Peter's when he told her he was leaving in the morning and if Addy wanted to stay a little longer, they could buy an extra plane ticket. He claimed he needed to get ready for the Montréal show and go through the notes from Eden Press.

"And buy that junkyard?"

"Alice," he said.

"Isn't that it?"

"I don't know. Maybe. I'm not sure."

"I think I know you a little bit less with each passing day."

"Alice," he said again because it was all he had.

"Do you want a list?"

"Not really."

"And now your mother."

"What about her?"

"Just that she's lovely."

"I never said…"

"I keep waiting for horns to show through her hair. And I was so freaked out the other night hearing that Addy had been talking to her and your father."

"You didn't know he'd been doing that?"

It shocked her. "Can you imagine me keeping that from you?"

"Okay, no, of course you wouldn't. I'm glad you like Verna."

"That's it? You're glad I like your mother?"

"Verna was never the problem."

"But you still don't talk to her for, like, twenty years?"

"She and the Judge were a box set."

Next was a pause. He knew what was coming.

"I need to know more."

"About what?"

"What did he do?"

This had always been coming. It was amazing she'd lasted this long.

"You've never really told me what happened and I've never pushed," she said.

"You've met my mother and heard a nice eulogy about the Judge, and now you don't believe me?"

"It's not about believing you. I just want to understand because now I'm putting myself in your mom's shoes and I can't imagine what it would be like if Addy ran away."

Which landed, because he'd imagined it plenty.

She said, "To think Addy still had a perfectly good grandmother and, frankly, I wouldn't have minded having a mother-in-law after my mom died. I'm sorry if that hurts you, but what did your dad do to you? Unless it's too awful to say…"

"For the thousandth time, no one molested me."

"Whatever it is can't be worse than what I've already imagined."

"I've told you what a menace he was. He had no qualms about firebombing Germany and Japan or dropping atomic bombs on Hiroshima and Nagasaki because it made the surrender unconditional and gave them a free hand, though they still had the Soviets to deal with so they hired the Führer's scientists to build bigger and bigger bombs and made Walt-effing-Disney Propagandist-in-Chief to spin the atomic age as golden, as though there'd even be a future. The Judge and his hard-charging generation would track their proxy wars in the newspaper like box scores, prop up any old dictator as long as he didn't lean left. They lived for blanketing faraway lands with bombs and napalm and round casings and they were 100% ready to punch the codes. In October 1962, the Judge would sooner we were all vaporized than risk his pretty boy Kennedy looking soft. Thank Christ Khrushchev had more sense."

"I don't want to hear about geopolitics."

He said, "You need that part to understand," but the Judge's incandescent face had moved to the centre of his awareness, his hard fist rising up, and, for a moment, for the first time in years, Theo felt the old terror and loneliness in its fullness. The same as on that last night in October 1962 standing at his bedroom window, watching the sky and waiting for Armageddon, and a few years later, standing beside the kitchen table, watching as the Judge's furious face bore down, but knowing the knife was within reach.

How to express that impeccable horror to her? They were nearly back around to the church and he needed to tell her, but he'd never had the words before and there were none to hand now. He could rattle off examples of repudiation and disowning, say the Judge never managed to conceal his disgust or bafflement, and how much sterner he became after some Scotch. He could list things until he was blue but still not name the thing that emerged beyond the sum of them.

He said, "Do you think I wanted to leave school *two weeks* before I had a degree?" because he needed to say something.

"Of course not."

"Or that I'd been dreaming of a year on the run, living in a tire truck and pretending my name was Ronald Lyle, scared to death they'd get me on a warrant, ship me back and give me the choice of Vietnam or facing felony assault charges?"

"What assault charges?"

"Because the Judge would have liked nothing better than to see me in jungle fatigues with an M16."

The Judge's stark, murderous face flashed before him again and the annihilating terror rushed through him. And there it was, the thing that overarched all of the instances: that the Judge's threats and assaults and indignities all came down to the willingness of the Judge and other old men like him to murder their young. It came down to annihilation.

"Theo, what felony?"

Of course, it was something he'd never dared to say. He took a breath, started slowly. He said, "Okay, yeah. The last night I was in Ladue. Supper time at the Strahls: the Judge three sheets to the wind, wolfing down pork chops and mashed potatoes, holding us hostage as he recounted his day, this time going on about two college kids, Steve Cortez and Ray Hale, which was the case before him, and it was plain as day he'd already made up his mind, though the trial was only half over. He didn't give a shit that the college administration had entrapped both guys or that the FBI was ass-deep in COINTELPRO and its agents had wormed their way into every student organization. I'd been listening to him for years and always held my tongue, but this one was more personal, or else I'd just reached my limit. I told him he seemed less interested in upholding the rule of law than dispatching anyone who asked uncomfortable questions about the corruption and the abuse of power, and it went from there: the Judge warning me to mind my tone, and me asking some of the same uncomfortable questions. I'm not sure I knew that I was calling bullshit in such a fundamental way—maybe I realized that later—but he was raging and I saw the murder in him and it came down to who grabbed the steak knife first."

"Jesus."

"Jesus what?"

"What happened?"

"Well obviously I got to the knife first."

"Did you use it?" she said and sounded nearly as alarmed as Verna that night.

"Of course I did. I used it and bought the time to get away. And okay, I never told you that I slashed him with that knife."

Of course, he hadn't told her, and now that he had, he saw the look on her face and saw all over again the shocked look on the Judge's face, and still couldn't say for sure whether the Judge did ever make a move for the blade.

He told her the Judge would never have let it go, that if they'd caught him he wouldn't have stood a chance and his pals would have given him ten times what Cortez and Hale got because he was Judge Strahl's kid, always a little peculiar, you know, if more so once he got mixed up in the campus radicalism, then went batshit that night, having evidently saved it up, and in poor Judge's own home! They'd have heaped it on, made it Attempted Murder, and manufactured some conspiracy so they could put his friends away too.

"Are you happy?" he said. He felt her eyes on him but couldn't meet them. "I'm not the villain," he said, though he wasn't sure.

"Theo, I never said you were."

She faced him in a way that asked for an embrace and he knew it was the best thing she could have done, and it almost seemed possible that if they held one another tightly enough and long enough, things could somehow be all right again.

20

Verna said, "I decided the problem was all the wars. They never end when the shooting stops. The scars pass down from generation to generation."

It was only her and Theo in the kitchen with coffee again. The others hadn't stirred. He was packed and ready to go as soon as Rosemary got up.

Theo said he guessed that, for the Judge, going to war was what a young man did. He said, "You didn't wait to be drafted and sure as hell didn't burn your draft card."

She said, "You don't think he wanted you to go to Vietnam, do you?"

Theo's face said it was exactly what he thought.

"Oh no, that's the last thing he wanted. Your father was good at a lot of things but a child baffled him. He said so after you left and, when you think about it, where would he have learned how to be a father when your Grandpa Strahl came back so shattered from the First War and didn't even stay around? Then Judge came back from the next war with more damage than just the leg, not that he complained. And in fairness, you weren't an easy child, the way your mind could go a mile on a thing before the rest of us set out. You'd think about a thing and chew it over for so long before you said the first thing, so the words could be jarring, sometimes for the clarity of what you'd arrived at and, other times, for how far off you'd gone. Judge could mistake directness for disrespect.

"You were a perfect storm or, I should say, there was a cold war between the two of you and the times it heated up—like the night before you left and you argued about Vietnam and the draft—I did not know what to do except try to tamp it down and tell myself it would work itself out. You were both good men and there was a level of mutual respect, you know? I was far too sanguine because what would it have taken for you to untangle the strands of horror and anger and guilt and all the other things running back through a century? And I overestimated the time we'd all have. Some people don't stand a chance."

Theo said, "How badly did I hurt him that night?" It came out in a small, clenched voice.

"What do you mean?"

"The knife."

"Oh, I think he needed some Band-Aids."

"That's all?"

"It was more shocking than anything. For both of you. You looked like you'd seen a ghost."

Theo needed to move. He got up to fill their cups. Still no sound from the others.

"How we worried about you!" she said.

"I'm sorry about that part, Mom."

"And hoped you'd come back. I'd hear a car pull into the driveway and rush to the window hoping it was you… The only time I ever felt that helpless was when you were sick. When you were twelve or thirteen…"

"Thirteen."

"When the doctors couldn't figure it out and weren't sure you'd survive."

"That was the Cuban Crisis."

"Around that time, I guess, yes."

"No, I mean, that's what caused it. Don't you remember? Kennedy announced there were missiles in Cuba the night I turned thirteen and the next week did me in. On the Saturday, I was 100% sure the missiles were in the air. It marked every cell of my body and made me as sick as the radiation would have."

"Good Lord, and to think that was about a war too."

He'd already done up his seatbelt to back out when he noticed the Judge's navy tie, still tied in its Double Windsor, between the bucket seats of Addy's car. Verna said he'd best keep it in case they stopped at one of those swanky rest stops. He'd worn it around his waist like a voyageur until a filling station in Cedar Rapids, as he sat waiting for Rosemary, and he put it around his neck and tied it in a Grantchester and then a Trinity. He'd been wearing a loose Balthus over his sweatshirt ever since.

They drove straight through. At Emerson, Rosemary stirred long enough to answer the customs officer's questions and, as they rolled back over to the Canadian side, to ask whether he wanted her to drive, it being 4:15 so he must be on his last legs. She stayed awake just long enough to hear him answer.

Four minutes later, though, he turned hard onto 243, because showing Rosemary the Penner Yard was suddenly the key to everything. He'd seen the sign for the junction and decided that if he could convince Rosemary, *get her on board*, then Addy would follow and Alice might too. So now he was driving west, spellbound by the fat snowflakes rushing the windshield, acknowledging certain risks attached to the detour but convinced that finding himself down here with her, a few dozen miles from the Penner Yard, had to be another of Ford's miracles.

She woke when they left blacktop and he considered saying they were lost.

"Are we there?" she said.

"Almost." His voice was uneven. "I just wanted to show you something. I hope you don't mind."

"What time is it?"

"Nearly five."

"Where are we?"

"Near Gretna." As he pulled them into the lot, the headlights swept over the sleeping, snow-covered field, then chain link and guard dog sign, and auto wrecks, then settled on the bleak front office. He wished the moon was more than a sliver.

"What is this place?" she said, and thank God she didn't look frightened in the dash lights.

"Okay, it's an auto salvage yard. You stay here and I'll go open up." He fetched his parka from behind his seat. He closed the door before he slipped into it. The zipper caught the Judge's tie, so he freed it as he walked through the headlights, gave a wave and mouthed, Right back. Thank God she smiled.

It was cold but there wasn't much wind. He was up and over the fence easily enough. As he landed, the knee-deep snow pushed his pant leg up and filled his boot. He banged a knee against some buried thing and swore, stepped more carefully after that. The snow melted in his boots. He wished he had a flashlight. He found the corridor Pete Thiessen had cleared, found the steel swing door, got down on hands and knees and pushed past the heavy rubber strips of the dog door. He stood and felt for a first switch, made enough light to see the row of switches on the far side. The air smelled like grease and dog. He emptied his boots and banged the snow from his jeans.

He went across and flipped the whole row of switches. The garage felt better lit up, and he could see the yard lights through the back windows. He got the switch on the office side as he went through for Rosemary.

She stood waiting by the front door, wide awake now, interested, even enthusiastic.

"Welcome to the Penner Yard," he said, then saw the grime-fronted counter, ashtrays and strewn car parts from her point of view, the saggy ceiling tiles and sheets of woodgrain panelling billowing out from the wall like shit-brown sails. He said, "Don't mind the mess."

"What is this?" she said.

"Well, I guess I'm going to buy this place."

"Really? Wow, I didn't know…"

"Come on through," he said, and took her down the hall past Otto Penner's dismal room. He said, "It comes with loads of equipment— tractors, loader, lifts." He rolled up one of the big doors, said, "And get this, nine acres of cars and light trucks, more than a thousand." The snow-covered rows looked ghostly. He wished the yard lights were brighter.

"You're getting into car parts?"

"No, not that." Now his heart raced and his breathing was wrong. He'd planned this part but suddenly wasn't sure.

"You see, I'm building something," he said. "This will sound strange at first, but, well, Rosemary, the thing is, I need this place for the metal and tools and the privacy, because I'm building a sort of ark…"

"An ark?" She was still smiling.

"It's not the right word. Nothing like Noah's ark, obviously. Metal, not gopherwood, whatever that even was, and for outer space."

Something crossed her face.

"And I've had some NASA drawings basically fall into my lap." He said it, though he'd decided not to mention the drawings.

"So, like an art installation?"

He was already far off course. He wanted to say, Yes, a giant art piece for people to visit, but he said, "No, an actual spacecraft… to go to outer space."

"Really? Can you do that?"

"Absolutely. The science is decades old…"

"No, I mean, do you need some kind of permit?"

"Well, I don't know about…"

"And I don't get why you're building a spaceship."

This one he'd prepared for. He said, "The truth is, the world's on the verge of catastrophe. *Homo sapiens* has finally killed the planet, choked her out. Everything's breaking down. The condition's terminal."

She didn't say anything. He couldn't figure out her eyes behind the lenses of her glasses.

He went on. "The air's polluted, the oceans are full of plastic, and have you ever seen a river on fire? I have. They're clearing the Amazon and no one even knows how many species go extinct every day, plus Chernobyl, you know… I know this might sound whackadoodle."

He still couldn't find the sense in her eyes.

"The thing is, the world can't survive, so it's time to make a break for it."

He waited for her to say something.

"Can we close the door?" she said. "It's pretty cold."

Which was reasonable. He rolled the big door down. As he secured the chain, he knew what needed saying.

"Look, Rosemary, straight up: a spirit's been guiding me."

It was another thing he'd planned to hold back.

"Like an angel?" she said in the loveliest way. She pushed her glasses up.

What a delight: that she'd hear about a spirit and want to know more, not reject it out of hand, but thinking of Ford as an angel made him smile. Nothing but coarse hairs where the wings should be.

"I don't think he'd qualify as that. He's about the ugliest thing I've ever seen, but he knows a thing or two. Like, for instance, that the world's not going to make it."

"But it has to," she said.

"Believe me, I take no joy in saying it, but remember that every ending is also a beginning and the goal will be finding a new home." He gestured in the general direction of the sky, said, "Out there."

Her eyes didn't follow. She said, "What does Alice think?"

"Okay, well, I haven't told her everything."

"You haven't?"

"You're the first…"

"But you two talk about everything."

"Here's the thing: basically, you're the key."

"I am?"

"Because you *get* things and, if you get on board, no pun intended, you can help me convince Addy, and then the three of us can talk to Alice, because things have gotten a little shaky between us. Nothing matters without the three of you."

He was talking too quickly.

"I'm not freaking you out, am I?" He took a considerate step back.

"You want to convince Addy to go away in a spaceship?" She didn't sound freaked out.

"This is coming out badly. Really, if someone had told me six months ago that they were going to board a starship with their loved ones, I'd have thought, Woo-woo, you know?" He tried to laugh but it came out high and weird.

The silence then was worse than being called woo-woo.

"So you'll think about it?" he said, though there seemed to be a weight settling down.

"You can really build a spaceship out of old cars...?" she said. "And take animals..?"

He was about to mention Moose but caught himself for once. He said, "There are a million details..."

"It will need to be a really big spaceship," she said.

"Right, but there's a way of folding out the living space beyond the gravity well. Think pop-up books."

He suddenly hoped she wouldn't ask where they'd keep all their gear and whatever animals until the walls popped out. *Ark* was the wrong word.

He said, "And I've stumbled over a process for cold fusion."

"Nuclear power? You, Theo?"

"Oh, you're thinking of *fission*. Fusion can be safe and it's simple once you know the secret ingredient."

There was no way he could say it. He felt Ford nearby and it buoyed him at first, because he'd lost the thread and could use backup.

She said, "You can probably do it. Knowing you."

Which was a kindness.

"Where would you go? Like, Mars? One of Jupiter's moons?"

He guessed the colour had left his face.

"And I don't get what you'll do when you get there."

Nor did he just then, and landing on Mars, say, would be tricky, because the air was too thin for parachutes, and you'd freeze your ass when you left the craft. Control systems would be the key.

She said, "I guess I'm wondering whether you've thought this all the way through."

"Oh, God, like I said, a million details, but..."

"Like, what if people wrecked the next world too? Aren't people the problem?"

So leaving would amount to spreading a deadly virus. It was a point.

"And you're terrified of flying," she said.

Now it was like falling—his stomach in his throat—as he saw astronauts on their backs in their seats, imagined the engines rumbling as the thing lifted off. His head swirled. There was nowhere to sit.

His fear of flying might be the biggest problem. The Fear of Flying program hadn't helped. He'd driven to Ladue and back, fifteen hours each way, because he wouldn't get on a plane.

He spotted Ford over Rosemary's shoulder, squatting on the hood of the Galaxie 500 like a bruised, kyphotic hood ornament.

Was he supposed to tell her to turn and look? And if she did, would she see him or only the Galaxie's grey-primed hood? What would even be worse: seeing Ford's ghastly face and cadaver body, or not seeing him and knowing she was miles and miles from anywhere?

When Ford held a crooked finger in front of the gash that stood for a mouth, it was all he could do to keep from shouting, I can tell her if I want! because if this didn't count as an emergency, nothing did. Rosemary was the key to everything.

The next thought came like a gust of wind.

He said, "Of course, I didn't see before: it was never for me at all. It's for you and Addy."

Saying it removed some of the weight. His eyes were welling.

"Me and Addy?"

"I'm forty years old and this is going to take years. Maybe it's never been for me or Alice. Maybe it's always been for the two of you."

"But I don't want to leave."

"You don't have to make up your mind."

"The world is wonderful."

"Sure, but talk to Addy…"

"The world cannot be dying. Take you and Alice: your lives are practically perfect."

"Maybe don't say that."

"What?"

"That we have perfect lives. You've said that before…"

"You know what I mean."

"You're young. You don't know that things can seem all right when we're just a minute to midnight."

"The Doomsday Clock, right."

"You know about that?"

"Well, yeah, you've gone over it…"

"Okay, right."

"Because there's just no living in this world."

Now her eyes were saucers behind her glasses. She said, "Theo, you are *not* going to kill yourself, are you?"

"Jesus, Rosemary! Of course not." He saw that Ford was laughing.

"Nothing's that bad," Rosemary was saying. "Look, let's go home. We'll keep talking."

"This isn't some euphemism for suicide," he said. "I admit I can see how you might wonder, the way this is going, but hell no."

"Okay then. That's a relief."

Ford's smile was crooked, contemptuous.

She said, "We should go, okay?"

"This has been a shock," Theo said. And leaving did make a kind of sense—getting back to the highway, regrouping—but Ford's smile was making everything spin, down to the slow, frigid light and the smell of the place. Certain things wanted clarification, including the slim possibility he'd been the butt of an elaborate joke.

"You know I'd never hurt myself," he had to say again. "Not in a thousand years."

And she said, "I'm glad."

21

When she asked whether the phone even worked, he put the grease-stained receiver to his ear and did a thumbs up, as though there were a dial tone. Again, she asked him to go with her, then relented and said she'd drive the last ninety minutes alone. He'd said all he wanted was to get a deal done, claimed it made most sense to stay put until Pete Thiessen was awake and through his scrambled eggs, than go all the way home and turn around and, no, he wouldn't think of having her wait with him in a place like this. He'd aimed for a carefree tone and didn't rush his words as he told her there must be two dozen cars to drive if, by some chance, the realtor didn't just run him to the city. Take for instance the Galaxie Town in the second bay, which only needed rubber.

In truth, the only priority was gathering his thoughts, given how her questions had dispersed them. As he walked her back to Addy's old Alfa, he commented on the fat snowflakes falling and he took comfort from the fact she didn't lock the door the instant it closed. He gave the hood two little knocks as she backed out. The tail lights receded. The cold had a bite, but he waited until she'd turned onto the highway to go back inside.

"You should have seen your face when she asked about the animals," Ford said. He'd waited on the hood of the Galaxie. "You couldn't have looked more stunned. And whether you needed a permit, which wouldn't be the first thing to most minds."

"Is this some kind of joke to you?" Theo said.

"You had to blab, did you?"

"I had to get her onside."

"How many times have I told you not to blab?"

"She's the only way to Addy."

"For a clever fellow, you're breathtakingly thick. And you really took a Fear of Flying course? How about that?"

He focused on the fly strip over the bench, nicotine-coloured, filled with the tiny carcasses of a summer, and ash near the bottom because Penner must always have had a smoke burning. There was a filthy lighter.

"And when she asked if you wanted to end it all…"

"The poor kid. I obviously don't want that."

"Sure, though it's what someone would ask if they weren't thick."

He should have gone with Rosemary. He imagined her driving, face illuminated by the dashboard, dials reflected in the lenses of her glasses. He tried not to imagine what she was thinking, though the image of her calling Addy came soon enough. Imagining Addy on the phone in Verna's kitchen, Alice at his elbow, nearly took his knees.

"Still with me?" Ford asked, still crouched two metres away on the hood of the car, naked as a jay, ugly enough you'd have to look away.

Could this really have been an elaborate practical joke? Everything since the night of his birthday, an elaborate mischief to blow him up?

"Your crowning achievement," Ford said and it seemed to change the light.

The oil company ashtray caught his eye. It sat overflowing among the wrenches and sockets, calipers, bolts, and bits of wire. He thought a cigarette would ease the dread, so he used a cloudy Bic pen to search for a butt with a drag or two left. He found one, straightened it, lit it.

"You should see yourself," Ford said.

He pulled hard and welcomed the pain in his throat. He flicked the butt at Ford, nicked a bluish shoulder. The smoke did its magic, liquified him. As he looked for another, he said, "Can't help but notice the colder it gets, the tinier that dick of yours gets. Like the tip of a pencil." He exhumed another Players Plain butt and lit it.

This time, when he flicked, he aimed for Ford's crotch. It felt good to see him flinch.

He said, "Why order me to build a spaceship? Why say the world's going up in flames?"

"Well, isn't it?"

"And the miracles? Why even bother?"

"You were dying to be called."

"Not really."

"You've always fancied yourself a saviour."

"I tried to be part of the solution. Is that so bad?" He straightened another smoke, but there was a tear.

"And then there's the wide misanthropic streak," Ford said.

He pinched the tear closed and lit it.

"So I was never going to build the thing? Is that what you're saying?" He aimed for Ford's foot. He thought of Rosemary driving away frightened. He couldn't believe what he'd done.

"Oh, you were building something, all right. You'd have made Rube Goldberg proud. You know, doing a simple thing in the most complicated possible way..."

"I know what a Rube Goldberg machine is."

"The simple version is an engine hoist, some rope, and a five-gallon pail..."

Hearing it made his heart pound. Could he really get the Galaxie running, slap on some rubber, shovel a path to the fence, make it to Gretna?

There was the faintest buzzing sound at the limit of his hearing. At the edge of his vision, a housefly raised a speck of ash with the final rise and fall of its wings. He knew no fly could survive to December but turned to see.

"Who even are you?" he asked. "What?"

"Not one of your better angels."

After driving all night, the smoke and the cold were bringing an impossible fatigue. His fingers had lost their deftness, but the worst was his feet, with only some thin socks and worn boot soles between them and the concrete. Had he really brought Rosemary to the middle of nowhere in the early hours of the coldest night, with only a waxing gibbous moon, and proposed she join some doomsday escapade? Her face played vividly—the precise moment the doubt eclipsed her trust. The scrunching of her chin as she started the car and moved her hand from ignition to shifter, eyes fixed ahead. The fear was bound to mark her. Ford was hideous, but who was the monster?

"There's a question," he heard Ford say.

He had never thought of killing himself. Not at his loneliest after he left Ladue.

"There's always that tie," Ford said. There's a certain logic.

"You think so? Then, you don't know the first thing about hanging."

"Which is?"

He emptied the ashtray onto the bench, looked for one more smokable butt. He'd read about executions as a teen and knew the importance of the executioner getting the drop right, given the realities of the human neck, the small diameter and lack of bony shielding, the association of airway, major blood vessels, and spinal cord, and acceleration being constant at 9.83 m/s2 once the trap opened. The trick was generating enough negative G-force at the bottom to fracture the condemned's upper cervical spine and transect the spinal cord, and thereby avoid death by strangulation, but not so much to decapitate, as had happened with Black Jack, Tom Ketchum.

He lit a butt he guessed had two full drags left. He pulled and held the smoke.

The Judge's tie wasn't nearly long enough, though beyond the technical realities were the facts that, never in a thousand years, was he going to prove the Judge's charge that evening in Croeve Couer Park twenty-five years ago that he had no fire in the belly and never in ten thousand years could he make things even worse for Rosemary, who would always be the last to see him alive.

He waited for the nicotine spin to slow. He guessed finding a way into town was the priority.

He saw where the snow had collapsed inside when he opened the big door and the small zig-zag of Rosemary's bootprints. It narrowed him toward a flawless rage. What possible reason had there been for Ford to draw Rosemary into the catastrophe, or Addy or Alice? He was talking about giving someone enough rope to hang himself and seemed amused. He was shifting side to side, as though the cold was sinking in.

Getting to town could wait until he'd bashed Ford's syphilitic nose into his skull, mashed his head into the concrete, ripped out whatever ugly thing beat where a heart should have been.

Ford must have felt it because he stopped still. Maybe thought he'd have to dodge another cigarette butt. Theo lunged with his arms wide like a linebacker's. Ford pivoted and was dropping down from the hood when Theo caught his cold right shoulder. It twisted his torso and sent him hard to the floor. He sprang upright and moved less steadily toward the swing door and Theo vaulted over the fender. Ford dove for the dog door: his small hands pushed through the rubber strips but the impact of landing on the concrete slowed him enough for Theo to close the distance. Ford's head and shoulders were through, then one knee and his bruised, bony backside. Theo got a hand around the trailing ankle but the skin had a slipperiness and he couldn't hold on.

Theo slid the pass door latch and stepped through on two legs, pleased he hadn't switched the yard lights off, because they showed Ford on his way to the nearest row of dead cars, struggling through snow up to his waist. Theo closed in, supposed the creature would vanish when he needed to, hoped whatever rules governed corporality would stand long enough to see how good and fucked he was.

He hadn't caught up by the time Ford reached the beige Malibu at the head of the line, hoisted his ass like the flag of a small, unsightly country, and slithered up the windshield to the roof. He stood at the gap between the Malibu and the Mazda next to it, saw Theo monkey vault onto the fender, turned and leapt across, the motion uneven or jerky under the old yard lights.

Theo scrambled up to the roof and took the gap, though his crappy boot grip destabilized both launch and landing. He balanced on the Mazda and saw Ford on a Coronet two cars down, gambol a few steps, then hop over to the silver K-Car next in line.

Ford struggled on the ground through the drifts, but moved well enough over the wrecks: small in stature, bent and twisted, limbs lacking obvious musculature, but the explosive horizontal power was impressive and he was four cars ahead. Theo landed on the next car and managed not to pitch forward into the space before a Falcon, but knew he wouldn't catch up this way. He needed a better option.

He switched from Standing Broad Jump to Triple Jump, landed squarely on the near side of the next rooftop, took a short skip step to the next edge, used his forward momentum to throw himself onward.

He landed, Boom, stepped, puh... Boom, puh... Boom, like thunder in the pre-dawn dead of winter, over a discarded Mustang and a Pinto, a Vega wreck, a Buick wagon, and a Corvair, rightfully abandoned, given the unconscionable rebound camber and dynamic instability. He saw that he was gaining, and the power of his stride felt good, despite the greater risk of the larger, irreversible moves. He was five cars behind: the air blew his coat open and the Judge's tie flew behind him like the ears of a racing beagle. The footfall sounds were crisp, and the sound of his breathing and grunting, and the sound of Ford's breath too, or wheezing. Now only three cars behind, and there was a kind of freedom in it as they moved farther out into the yard.

Ford had dropped into the space between a Fiat X 1/9 and a Trans-Am so moved slowly again through the snow. What disastrous biomechanics governed the thing's vertical, Theo wondered and supposed the problem was upward thrust from the knees.

The thing moved so slowly now, and he presented a fine target.

Theo was already in flight before he spotted the X-1/9's sunroof.

He forced his right foot onto the innermost edge of the sunroof to avoid stepping through, and did his best to balance the chaotic vectors of pronated foot and ankle bent outward, through the leg and hip operating against design and training, tried to decelerate, but the compensation took him off his course, well left of Ford. He knew he'd done serious damage even before he landed headfirst into the space ahead of the Trans-Am.

Then regretted the instinct to hold his left arm out front, because the force jammed the shoulder and drove his palm onto something sharp. He rolled onto his back. There was a gash in the thenar eminence. The swiftness of the blood beginning to run was a surprise.

Ford had reached the Trans-Am T-roof but stopped to catch his breath.

Theo wanted to get up and after the thing again but, for the moment, his right kneecap had shifted around to the side of his leg.

He screamed as he forced it back and, though returning it dulled the pain, the joint refused to bend as stubbornly as the Judge's had since the war. The coincidence perturbed him. His jeans were bloody at the knee, and more blood dripped from his palm to the snow. There were tissues in a coat pocket and he pressed them against the wound.

Ford was watching as he slid the wounded hand into a pocket to warm. He glared back as he felt beneath the snow with his good hand for anything he could throw. There was a door lock cylinder and a ball joint. He set them on the belly of his parka and, though the fingers had lost most of their feeling and his wrist throbbed from cold, he went down for more, found a starter solenoid, a tie rod end, a universal joint. He used the lid of an air filter housing as a tray and allowed his good hand some time inside a pocket.

Standing was a complicated agony and he screamed again. Once he was upright, he stowed his ammunition in his wide parka pockets, picked up the air filter cover, drew it back like a Frisbee, put his body into it as he opened the elbow and stretched the arm, concentrated on the wrist snap for the sake of spin. He watched it cut the air like the flying saucer of an old movie, saw it miss but knew Ford would have felt the air move as he climbed up onto the Volkswagen bus next in line.

Theo picked his way past a collision of AMCs—a ridiculous Javelin, shit brown Gremlin, a Pacer—moved as best he could with the right leg, left shoulder and hand on fire and useless and his feet no longer feeling the cold. His head seemed out of plumb but he had other things to throw. The shin of his good leg drove into something hard. He threw the lock cylinder, but wide of Ford atop his hippie bus.

He could not run any farther down this long line of wrecks, or manage the lines running parallel on either side of it, but moving through the deep snow seemed beyond him as well, and he needed to address the advantage Ford had from elevation. He opened the VW's driver door and climbed up with his right arm and left leg. Ford kept his place up top as Theo leaned and lifted, got his butt on top of the door. He pitched the solenoid but missed by metres.

He forced himself upright, sent the tie rod end flying like half a boomerang just as Ford leapt, caught him above the elbow as he landed on the other side.

Ford turned to look at the back of his arm.

Theo drew the universal joint from his pocket and dandled it. Ford turned toward the next box truck in a hurry.

Theo set his feet at shoulder-width and, despite the cold, his fingers understood the shape of the thing, caressed the four-inch-long caps set at ninety degrees from the steel centre. He put it at three inches across and weighing a pound. He adjusted his grip, came set, wound up, threw with the control of Bob Gibson, just as Ford launched himself over the next gap.

It was clear enough the universal joint was going to find the back of Ford's head, that it was going to strike him mid-leap, and he planned to give a warlike whoop, but the metal shifted to slow-mo, and the thud was amplified and elongated, and Ford's limbs slackened mid-air though his body continued along its mathematical arc, altered only enough for his bottom half to hit the box and make a hollow boom. His torso and head continued on, slapped forward on top of the truck, bounced back horrendously. The entirety of him hovered a moment before it dropped down and out of sight.

Ford's body landed below with a low, soft whump. Theo waited on the Volkswagen bus, prayed there'd be a groan or a curse, but there was none.

The horror was instant and he wanted the metal piece back in his hand and Ford on top of the van. What had he done? He thought of Grandma Maggie telling him he had a good heart, saying kindness was his nature.

He watched himself from up high, maybe from the surface of the moon. He needed to cross over from the Volkswagen bus to the next vehicle. He cleared the gap before he remembered he couldn't.

He felt some pain as he stumbled to the far side, but pain was not at the centre of his awareness, nor gratitude for the gift of an endocrine system that could block it for a while, nor even the undisturbed snow where Ford had been, how the snow lay as flawlessly as a prairie wind could lay it out, nor the collateral hope that, if Ford had never had substance, then he could not have killed the blue and grey bruised thing. At the centre of him was the need to drop down on his belly, push the Judge's tie aside again, peer into the dim gap, call Ford's name and somehow make things right.

But there he was on his belly in the snow, one arm under his trunk and the other laid out, the back of his head darker where the universal joint had collapsed his skull, his nakedness less repulsive. Theo called him and watched for any stirring of the laid-out hand. He wished the sky would lighten.

Get down there, he commanded. *Render assistance.* Get down and cover him with your coat, get him inside. Think of the damage you've done.

He looked for a way down. He would not jump blindly into another gap, given how Penner had let things go and there could be anything under the snow, and what use would he be if he wrecked his left leg too or his right arm?

He resolved to reach the back of this van, though the pain was back and it would take more than wishing for the knee to work again. If wishes were horses, he said aloud and hauled the pointless thing along with his good arm and good leg. If turnips were bayonets, he said, because he'd killed in anger and it didn't matter that Ford was an asshole or celestial intermediary, because flesh was creation and creation was fragile and vanished without care, and someone must have loved Ford, even ages ago, so he recalled the weight of the Judge's casket on his shoulder. He fought toward the back of the vehicle, through horror and remorse that, moments earlier, he'd felt such furious drive to destroy, then even doubted his remorse and guessed this was what the Judge had meant when he said there was no fire in his belly because, if he were any kind of man, he'd drop down now to claim his prize, hold the head up high on his good arm. The heel of his boot banged the steel of the truck top and he marvelled at the crispness and indisputability of the sound moving over the snow.

When he finally reached the back edge of the van, he looked for an opportunity for descent, given the protests of the leg and the arm, then reminded himself he was needed down below, so he aimed the good leg at a place to land, walked forward on his butt cheeks, pushed off with his good arm and braced for impact.

The Judge's tie, trailing behind, caught some protruding piece of the wreck and stopped him brutally midair, wrenched his neck violently and gave it his full, decelerating weight. The pain of the tracheal crush was unfathomable. He felt both hands flail and both legs feel for some purchase.

Which was when it occurred to him he was hanging by the neck after all, when he'd sworn that was impossible, and promised Rosemary, and if he died like this, she'd always think he'd lied to her, and someone would have to find him and what if she came back and it were her?

The searing pain and continued consciousness proved the drop had been too short to break his spine, and that seemed relevant, but so did the futility of his feet, metres or miles below him, going every direction at once and banging against unidentified surfaces, and his fingers clawing the strict, taut silk seemed relevant, as did the absence of breath.

His wholly undisciplined movement turned him around 180 degrees to facing inside the vehicle, and three things clarified themselves. First, that he would fight against this ridiculous death with all of the fire in his belly, and who was the Judge to say his belly had no fire? Second, more incidentally, that the tall, flat hull into which his eyes bulged now was none other than the DIVCO tire truck they'd brought to Canada twenty years ago, meaning it was his hammock hook that had caught the blade of the Judge's tie, and hadn't the kid who bought the old thing from him lived up the road in Plum Coulee, near the reservoir, making the Penner Yard as likely a resting place as any other one? How keen that boy had been to put the pedal to the metal through the narrow window of rebellion allowed a Mennonite teen: he'd put red shag carpet on the walls, pinned up Stampeders and Rush posters, and something with Cheech and Chong. Which raised the word *finally* to his mind randomly, but as much a fact as anoxia. He still allowed it could be a trick of the asphyxiation but the cup hooks that used to hold devil's ivy, weeping fig, and dieffenbachia really were there, and the corner cupboard and ice box minus its door.

He guessed it could be some "Owl Creek Bridge" circling back in time from his terminal, abjectly desperate loneliness, but there was no denying the joy in here as he drove north with Alice and Baby Addy cozy under heavy quilts on the narrow bed, or the awful months after he fled Missouri when the only way he had to lessen the primordial pain was to stop on the shoulder and run like the devil was chasing him.

Now the darkening at the sides of his vision was undeniable and flashes as though the yard lights were bursting or some stars were exploding, or even galaxies.

Which was when the third thing clarified: that, if he could herd his panicked feet toward one side of the doorway and set his back against the side opposite, he could press himself across the gap firmly enough to stabilize the load and he could raise himself enough to loosen the knot.

He pursued this possibility with speed, because his eyes were tending blacker and his field of vision narrowing like an old CRT set switching off, its capacitors about to discharge and the cathode ray about to emit its final electrons and close down to the final white dot at the centre. He did brace across the DIVCO doorway, and he did pull himself upward to create some slack, loosened the loop a little and then some more, and finally pulled his head through.

He gasped gasps of cold air, felt himself sliding down the doorway but didn't mind. He tried to get the good foot down, but felt himself landing on the tire truck floor, tipping sideways from the deck, and down into snow that gave way like a sigh. He lay there, learning to breathe, grateful for the tight layer of air around this poor planet speck, within the universal vacuum.

He turned enough to see under the DIVCO to the place where Ford should be. He saw nothing but the undisturbed snow.

So he looked up toward the Judge's empty tie, and above that, saw Ford crouched at the edge, elbows to knees, ugly head in ugly hands, unharmed, maybe thriving in his way.

Which was when he got the joke, appreciated the whole long walk of it.

He'd have said something if he'd been capable of speech, though there was nothing stopping him blinking it out in Morse Code. He took his time, got as far as --. --- / - --- / .... . .-.. .-.. --..-- before he needed to hold them closed to wet them. When he looked up again, Ford was gone, so he did not finish blinking, Go to hell, asshole.

Somewhere nearby, a pair of ravens quarrelled like Bickersons, though as anyone knows, for all the discord, ravens are faithful as planets. He seemed to have rolled into some bare place on the ground, half beneath the tire truck and half beyond it, some windbreak space not much larger than his body, guessed he'd dozed a little. The ground under his back felt firm, almost warm, gave the fragrance of geosmin. His fingertips touched new grass shoots. Some geothermal curiosity, he took it, because snowflakes melted when they landed on it, though a few inches past his hands or boots, the flakes joined their banks. Beyond his hand, nearer the devastated right knee, two tender crocus shoots had pushed through the soil, white-stemmed, nearly translucent, their amethyst buds indicating the sky respectfully, poised to bloom. The ravens rattled, as though saying not to worry, that life is more than meat, the body more than raiment.

That he would think again of "An Occurrence at Owl Creek Bridge" seemed unavoidable, but he dispatched it easily enough: this was no hallucination the instant before a death. The sky was lightening and the throbbing of his shoulder when he tried to reach the nearer of the buds, and the agony of the knee and hip, the mutilated palm, the sound of his breath as raunchy as a raven's through the swelling. He lay on the unaccountable, undeniable grass, as good as comfortable. His palms were open.

The sky darkened a moment as the incumbent himself descended, his wife's calls trailing. He dropped down on solid legs, two talon-lengths from Theo's compromised one and beyond the crocuses, he stood magnificently, glossy blue-purple, iridescent. The Stygian eyes took him in, for the little he was worth, and the whiff of iron and decay from long involvement with rabbits and badgers popped and flattened on pavement. The great bill, august throat feathers. They shared the improbable ground; the encounter, already holier than fear, leaned toward awe. The bewildering, living eyes accepted Theo's unworthiness and, in that way, called for a different species of faith.

So, even before the field mouse emerged, he already felt the rumblings of something that would still shake and alter him weeks and months later, and that would multiply and amplify, shift the ground of him, and none of the words he tried would approximate how fully the winter had burrowed into the raven's feathers.

The grey mouse did not pause at the tunnel exit, but flitted out from the safe snowbank into the unexpected clearing and the raven's view. It browsed the new grass, took note of the sweetest ones for later, if he managed to convince the others. It had reached the first crocus and set about excavating the corm when the raven flashed and took it firmly, stood statue-still while it paddled into its terminal shock.

If Theo had thought to pray, he'd have said some words for the raven and the mouse and their kin and for the sun's rise here as it set somewhere else, and for the second time each war must be fought and for the dreams of troubled sleep. He'd have nodded to life as inescapable and terminal and love as palliative and how there is only this chain of its survivors. He guessed the error was imagining someplace else to go. Maybe heaven was the problem.

Holy, Holy, Holy. The Raven nodded (or His head dropped as His vast wings opened) and it counted as annunciation. He rose with the sound of rustling silk. The wedge tail receded up into the dawn. The right theophany, the right meal for the hunger.

So, the Raven having flown, Theo knew Ford was gone for good, this parcel of spring being the proof, and the rough sound of his breathing in, then out. After everything, there was the embrace of the sky, structure of the generous shadows, and the Earth's simple instructions. He lay with all that glory, noticed the clatter as he breathed, supposed some further swelling could obstruct the rest of the airway but staying flat might be wise in case his back was cracked.

Finally, he guessed things were perfect enough, and set himself on sitting. He gritted and rolled onto the good shoulder, felt the quick breeze on his face as it rose above the basin wall, and he called out, "Surprise!" before he knew why and though it came out as a croaky, "Urkraa!" He'd been little, three or four, in Grandma Maggie's old steel tub, down low in the water, still as a soapy crocodile with its scalp scrubbed raw, then rocketed upward, calling, Surprise! so she jumped and said he'd be the death of her. How they laughed because he'd really got her.

It was as colour-saturated as old Super 8. He rose warmed from his practice grave and made his slow way through the eager sunlight past the wrecks in their rows. The breeze tripped over itself, tossed and twisted. He went back through the bays, fetched his mitts from the bench nearest the Galaxie, limped through Otto Penner's front door and down his steps.

His hobbling had found a rhythm by the time he cleared the lot: he held the left arm snuggly, pivoted that side, made use of the momentum to slingshot the straight right leg around, guessed he'd never felt the ground as solid under his feet. He thanked his stars for the re-entry, the luck of neither burning up nor setting down too hard on the sordid world.

The wind gusted. He pivoted, slingshotted, endured in the direction of the highway, and recalled an afternoon two or maybe three autumns before: Addy in the sunporch in pressed black trousers and bright, white shirt, key ring around a finger, off to whatever restaurant it was then, bullish about the moola he was going to make, and Alice, with her tea, saying, Well, mind the karma, whatever that meant. Addy paused, as though pondering the numberless laws and how they applied, then nodded, said, *Moola, moola, moola.* Alice said, *Karma, karma, karma.*

Chance across a memory like that and it's like finding a fifty in some pants you haven't worn in years.

He moved as he was able, and saw the RCMP cruiser on the highway, watched it slow as it approached the Penner road, then turn his way. He supposed the Mountie would have come from a distance, so he noted the kindness. He ran, though it hurt and, if he couldn't smell spring yet, he thought there might be a hint of the snow longing to melt and run and reveal the land and the cities: flowers and bones, stones the cold had raised from the soil, cigarette foils, traction sand. He ran, as he could, down the road and kraa'ed, *Moola, moola, moola! Karma, karma, karma!* and thanked the sky for waking up beautifully one more time.

ABOUT THE AUTHOR

Neal Davis Anderson is an author and clinical psychologist living in Winnipeg. His first novel, *Bettina*, came out under the name Thomas J. Childs (Signature Editions) and other writing has appeared in *Grain, Prairie Fire, Canadian Fiction Magazine, Descant, Rampike*, and *Zymergy* and in the anthology *200% Cracked Wheat* (Coteau Books). He has an MFA in Creative Writing from The University of British Columbia, where he studied fiction under Keith Maillard and Linda Svendsen and where he was executive editor of *Prism international*. He has written for national magazines and his feature about the Croatian novelist Dubravka Ugrešić in *Border Crossings* won a National Magazine Award. His short serial and feature-length drama has been produced by the CBC and he's written documentary and lifestyle pieces for many CBC programs. He's married and has three adult children.

Eco-Audit
Printing this book using Rolland Enviro100 Book
instead of virgin fibres paper saved the following resources:

Trees	Water	Air Emissions
3	1,000 L	186 kg